J

RED ICE

A John Deacon Action Adventure

Mike Boshier

Copyright © 2019 Mike Boshier
All rights reserved.
ISBN: 978-0-473-50480-9
www.mikeboshier.com

Author's Other Books

High Seas Hijack - Short Story

The Jaws of Revenge

Terror of the Innocent

Crossing a Line

The Price of Deceit

Acknowledgements

I would like to thank Sandra van Eekeren for her assistance and support in completing this book.

Eternal thanks to my wife and daughters who support me in my dreams.

If you liked reading this book, please leave feedback.

Check out the rear pages of this book for details of other releases, information and free stuff.

1

Arctic Ocean

Floating slowly with the wind and tide in the icy Arctic region at the top of the world, giant ice sheets slowly circle between landmasses. Dark for months at a time, sunlight is a rare visitor to the few animals and residents who call this region home. One resident is Arctic Drift Ice Station 736, known as ADIS 736, or Ice Station Hap to its workers. Hap, Norwegian for hope, is a small outpost of humanity comprising a Swedish non-profit environmental group of 22 men and women, made up of multi-national students, scientists, and engineers, monitoring ice melt and mapping the seabed as the ice sheet slowly moves over it. It was currently passing over the edge of the Lomonosov Ridge — a massive underwater feature jutting hundreds of miles in length beneath the Arctic Sea.

Previously unreachable to all extent for eleven months of the year; now, due to global warming and the retreating northern ice sheets, the entire area is involved in disputed territorial claims by Canada, Greenland, Norway, Russia, and the USA. Early explorations confirmed the area is rich with rare earth metals and minerals.

The closest neighbors to ADIS 736 is a Danish weather monitoring research group located just over three-hundred-fifty miles away, further north and closer towards the North Pole.

The ADIS 736 base is small but self-contained. Accommodations, workshops, offices, laundry, ablutions, and a canteen are all housed within a block of eight triple-insulated interconnected Portakabins, collectively powered by a large diesel generator with a secondary as a backup in their own temporary buildings. The entire Portakabin structure is elevated six feet off the ice base to minimize heat loss, using angled support blocks. The only other structure is a mast holding various aerials and dishes. Here you are living on the edge. The hostile environment outside would do its best to kill you, should you slip up and allow it. The average daily temperature outside during the dark winter months could be as low as -24F (-31C), which could kill an unprotected human within minutes. Even wearing the latest layered warm weather gear would limit outside exposure to thirty or forty minutes before muscles became too stiff to move.

Each person at the ice station had precisely the same sized personal cabin, eight feet by seven with an access door and non-opening triple-glazed window to the outside. Equipped with a single bed, cupboard and drawers, desk, chair, and tv monitor attached to the wall, the rooms were basic but comfortable. Toilets and showers were located in the next Portakabin. Work shifts had been designed to provide 24-hour coverage, but most people worked additional hours and retreating to their own cabin was merely for sleeping. Although the weather outside could quickly kill, you'd never realize it from within. The average temperature was set at a mild 68F requiring no more than regular office wear.

The nearest sea-edge to the flow was over a half-mile away, and the density of the ice directly under the ice station was over thirty-five feet thick. The Hap base was originally set up almost three years before by a team of engineers who moved buildings and equipment from the Norwegian icebreaker, *RV Kronprins Haakon*, with the aid of helicopters and snow tractors from the sea-edge that was then over a mile distant. Although the ice flow had 'calved' several times, scientists still expected another two years before the ice station would need to be relocated.

The ongoing mission for ADIS 736 was the continual monitoring of ice thickness, ice melt, seawater temperature, seawater salinity, ice flow speed and direction of movement, air temperature, and wind speed. With those duties in mind, the workloads had been split between the available bodies. Out of the twenty-two workers available, seven were scientists, two were mechanical engineers, one was a medic and cook, and the other twelve were students. The crew was comprised of fourteen males and 8 females, ages ranging from 18 to 73, and from countries as diverse as the USA, Great Britain, France, Lithuania, Greenland, Norway, Canada, Germany, and Switzerland. Leader of the group was a well-known Danish scientist named Professor Arnold Larsen. As would often happen whenever men and women worked together in such close confines, some sexual contact started; however, relationships were frowned upon by Larsen as any future split could cause anxiety and bad feeling between the others.

During the three winter months, the ice station would be beyond reach except in emergencies; however, during the summer months the group could expect exchanges and replacements, along with stores and provisions every four weeks. Currently, in early spring, they were waiting to celebrate the spring equinox on March 21st. This was when the sun would move back into the northern hemisphere, and the daylight would extend each day until the sun would never entirely set in June, merely lowered itself to gently kiss the horizon before climbing back into the crystal blue sky before the entire summer/winter cycle would slowly repeat itself. They had an equinox party planned for tomorrow. Additional food had been allocated along with wine, beer, and champagne. Only minimal work would be completed during that time, but the automated systems would continue monitoring and recording. It had been stormy with gales and snow falling heavily for almost a week now and everyone was hoping the weather would break soon.

To assist with the seawater tests, a hole approximately three feet across had been cut to allow a sonar seabed mapper, camera and magnetometer to be lowered one hundred feet below the ice sheet. The seabed was another four hundred feet further down, but at this depth the instruments weren't affected by the aluminum and steel buildings above. With the systems on automatic, the evening shift changed and supper had just commenced when first one, then a secondary alarm sounded. The magnetometer had detected a large metal object passing almost directly under the ice hole. Rushing to the computers, the scientists watched the live camera feed, but nothing was discernible. Switching to the recordings from minutes before, they watched in awe as the seabed mapper showed two distinctive sets of tracks on the muddy seafloor. The magnetometer tracks were superimposed on these, and it was clear to see these tracks had been made by something metal. At the head of the tracks was a moving vehicle the approximate size of a large truck. Reviewing the camera recording again, they thought the vehicle had lights on it facing forward, illuminating the seabed in the direction it was traveling. It was clear it wasn't a submarine, rather something moving on the seabed.

Suddenly one of the scientists called to say the weather outside was temporarily clearing, and looking in the distance they could see a ship far out on the horizon. Normally they were alerted to any ship approaching their location due to the effect it might have to their sensitive monitoring equipment, but not this time. Beginning to look a little concerned, Professor Larsen decided they should double-check the data, and he would then call it in over the satellite system back to the Hap's base in Trondheim, Norway.

One student, known to everybody in the group as Matis Staksas, disappeared to his cabin, quickly closing and locking the door behind him. At the back of his cupboard, taped to the underside near the rollers, was a small package. Quickly unwrapping it, he powered it up, hit a speed dial button, and made rapid conversation as soon as it was answered.

Shortly after, having double-checked their data, Professor Larsen headed into the main control room, picked up one of the six phones and pressed for connection through the Iridium satellite system. Looking slightly puzzled he thumbed the 'Call' switch a number of times before trying another phone. This too was dead. Heading over to his computer, he tried to set up a video call, but atmospherics were interfering, and the circuits were down. He spent the next few minutes typing an urgent email before sending it; however, the computer responded stating that all communication circuits were currently down, but it would resend as soon as possible.

Far to the south, an Ilyushin Il-22PP electronic warfare specialist airplane had just taken off and was still climbing to operational height as its operators pressed switches and set dials. An unseen pattern of radio frequencies was streaming from the pod underneath the main fuselage blocking all forms of radio-based communication within a four-hundred mile pattern directed north. Satellite phones, computers, smartphones -- everything trying to communicate over the air was effectively blocked.

The professor was looking slightly worried but put the breakdown in communications to either the snowstorm or interference caused by the equinox – both proven to cause interference often lasting days.

Four hours later an Ilyushin 11-76 transport aircraft flying downwind to the ice station dropped twenty-four Russian VDV Airborne Troops into the thickening snowstorm. All were wearing all-encompassing snow clothes, white helmets, and goggles. Each was armed with a white AKS-74U collapsible assault rifle, along with suppressor, as well as hand weapons. Each blended in and was invisible in the snowstorm at ten yards.

The outer doors to the Portakabins weren't locked. Why would they be? To a man, all doors were opened simultaneously, and the VDV walked in, firing. Forty seconds later, they were walking around putting secondary shots in the heads of the fallen.

Matis Staksas climbed out from under his bed after the firing had stopped. Walking out, he looked around at the dead bodies. As two of the soldiers raised their weapons towards him, he raised his hands, shouting, 'No, don't fire. I'm Yuri. I'm Russian. I'm with the FSB. I called you in.'

With weapons still raised, they waited until the leader, a captain, walked up.

Staksas tried again. 'I'm Yuri. I'm a comrade sent in to spy on them. I called you in. I work for General Yermilov.'

Raising his own weapon, the captain just smiled and shot Staksas twice through the forehead.

2

Nebraska, North America

Almost 3,000 miles away in Nebraska, Captain Hank Bissett was making the final visual inspection of his aircraft. Even though the ground crew had signed off on their maintenance, Hank always liked to complete a personal check. His aircraft, a United States Air Force RC-135, operated by the 55th Wing out of Offutt Air Force Base, Nebraska, would be flying at 46,000 feet in 500-mile-long figure of eight loops with engines set for minimum consumption high above the Lincoln Sea between Greenland and the North Pole this evening. Not an area where you could afford anything to go wrong, he thought.

The RC-135 – a military version of the Boeing C-135 transport jetliner – is a crucial component in reconnaissance work and is extensively used for signals intelligence, or SIGINT as it is commonly known. Signals intelligence is intelligence-gathering by interception of signals, whether communications between people (communications intelligence — or COMINT) or electronic signals not directly used in communication (electronic intelligence — or ELINT).

The crew of nineteen electronic warfare officers had already boarded the aircraft and were currently sitting at their consoles and testing their systems. The fourteen-hour mission today was the same as yesterday and the day before. Once on station, they would relieve the other aircraft doing an identical job and fly as slowly as possible while the crew listened and monitored the skies towards the northern shores of Russia; their sensitive equipment recording and analyzing every type of radio emission they could detect.

Last to board, Captain Bissett closed and locked the access door before climbing into the pilot seat. His co-pilot had already initiated the engine start procedure. Engines one and two were already up to temperature, three was slowly warming, and four was yet to start. Ten minutes later, with all instruments in the green, the giant aircraft released brakes and slowly rolled along the taxiway. With final clearance granted, Captain Bissett, a twenty-five-year veteran of the Air Force, and the co-pilot both pushed the engine throttles to their stops as the one-hundred-thirty-foot long aircraft accelerated along the runway before gently rising into the icy early spring air.

Five hours into their fourteen-hour shift, its entire crew of twenty-one were fully alert and working hard. Hank stretched and rolled his shoulders to flex his joints. Set on autopilot, he could relax. The figure-of-eight pattern had been entered into the flight system, and the engine controls were set at the very lowest to maintain a suitable airspeed while minimizing fuel usage. Joining from college and university, where he'd majored in aeronautical engineering, and electronic design, his first roles within the USAF had been in Iraq and Afghanistan flying F-15 Strike Eagle multirole fighters. In early 2012 he'd volunteered to transition to multi-engine tankers as flying 'heavies' as they are known allows migration into commercial airliners. In 2014 he transferred to Offutt and had been running intelligence-gathering missions up over the North Pole ever since.

Six times commercial airlines had tried to tempt him away with better hours and far better pay, but each time he'd declined. He never tired of the views looking down onto the giant ice sheets of Greenland and the Arctic, the snow and ice shining brightly even on the darkest nights, and of the myriad of stars unaffected by man-made light, shining and twinkling brightly above him against the blackest of black backdrops. Most military aircraft are built for efficiency with comfort taking a distant second place. However, the 135 was different. The banks of screens and computers filling the cabins produced heat, which could be expelled or utilized in these conditions to keep everybody comfortable. Air conditioning was available for warmer times, and the seats were wide and well-cushioned. Although a large number, the crew stayed close-knit and considered each crewmember as family. To Hank, this was the family in the air he wanted. His other family, a beautiful wife and two sons, was his family on the ground, and as far as he was concerned, life was pretty damn good.

Today there was a feeling of anticipation in the air. Six months previously, at precisely 02:30, Senior Airman Alisa Travers had monitored a brief burst of extremely high power X-ray energy being emitted. It had only lasted just a five-millionth of a second and sounded like a loud crackle in her earphones. Although short in duration, the extremely sensitive Raytheon systems built into the aircraft missed nothing. Within moments it had identified the burst as man-made (identified by the constant amplitude of the X-ray burst compared to the random strength of any naturally-generated signal), as well as its approximate source coordinates and direction of travel. This was the first unusual signal the crew of the RC-135 had intercepted for almost two months. The source was approximated to have come from the mountains of the northern Urals of Russia. The only other unusual signals detected on that mission were associated with radar and command signals being sent to a drone flying at twenty thousand feet over the far northern shores of the Russian mainland, which was subsequently destroyed by the same X-ray burst.

As was expected, news of this incident was urgently passed up the chain of command, and all recorded data was sent for further analysis. Three weeks later, command ordered them and their colleagues to pay particular attention to another, stronger energy burst that was expected. Again, Alisa Travers had monitored an X-ray burst of significantly higher energy at 02:30 on the one-month anniversary of the first. It had also downed a similar drone in flight.

Each month after that, on the anniversary date of the original, a higher energy single burst had been monitored and recorded. The crew didn't know what it was from, but a U.S. KH-11 reconnaissance satellite had been positioned over Norway to further aid with detection and plotting its exact source. The level of excitement was palpable today as the time approached 02:00. Other X-ray detection systems had been added to the aircraft, and a live data link between the aircraft and the satellite had been set up. At 02:25, everybody on board seemed to hold their breath. As the digits flicked over to 02:30, the strongest energy burst yet was received. The drones had been moved further and further away and were now flying at the height of 40,000 feet and at two-hundred-and-forty miles distance, well over international waters. This drone had exploded when hit by the X-ray burst and was lost on radar entirely. Previously, the others had merely stopped communication, their engines had died and had been able to be observed on radar as they fell from the sky.

The additional triangulation capability of the satellite communicating with Hanks aircraft helped the source of the X-ray burst to be pinpointed. The exact location appeared to be deep in the Ural mountains, at a latitude and longitude of a disused sky observatory.

The only other difference today was the addition of what appeared to be man-made signal noise being generated from northern Russia. First, Alisa Travers had thought it was being created as a masking signal, to stop them monitoring the X-ray signal, but she had decided it wasn't strong enough for that. This signal was localized to an area between Svalbard Island and the northernmost areas of Greenland. However, as with every anomaly, it would be written up and reported up the line.

Angled high above the horizon, a large silver tube was pointing at the stars. Roughly two-foot in diameter and a little over twelve feet in length, this device would produce, within a tiny fraction of a second, the same amount of energy typically used to heat and light a medium-sized house for over a year. The improved efficiency of this latest X-ray laser could be linked directly to the number of diamonds it contained and the skill of the scientists in combining the output power from multiple individual laser beams all into one coordinated beam.

A drone, currently flying almost two-hundred-and-fifty miles away and at an altitude at forty thousand feet, was at the maximum distance it could be detected by radar. Shown as a blip on the radar screen, the target operator clicked the mouse to select the target, and the computers did the computations and scaling. The red target crosshairs remained red while the entire structure the silver tube was mounted on swiveled to the left, and the angle changed as it aligned its optics with the distant target. The target crosshairs changed to green and remained that way for the next six minutes.

Once targeted, computers moved the device in micro-degrees to keep the target locked. The side opening of the old optical telescope was already gaping, and the chill night air from 4,500 feet above sea-level filled the disused optical telescope enclosure.

Colonel Dudko tapped the operator on the shoulder and gave him permission to fire when ready. The structure minutely rotated while the radar kept the drone, far too small and distant to be seen even with binoculars, exactly in the center of the target ring. With a calm voice, the operator counted down, 'Three, two, one, fire' and pressed the trigger.

Nothing seemed to happen. No sudden loud noise -- in fact, no noise at all, no smoke, nothing. But the distant small image on the radar screen disappeared. In one five-millionth of a second, the burst of power disintegrated the drone at almost two-hundred-and-fifty miles distance.

The operator looked up smiling at Colonel Dudko and said, 'Sir, mission accomplished and with eight of the ten beams working. The final two lasers will be brought online as soon as we receive the remaining diamonds, and they are shaped.'

A very happy Dudko slapped the operator on the back before heading to his quarters where a large bottle of ice-cold vodka and his slim-bodied brunette mistress were waiting. He intended to indulge heavily in both this evening.

3

For three days, scientists and engineers had been trying to reach their colleagues at Ice Station Hap after the connection was lost. Initially, this had been from the Trondheim office, but having received no response, this was escalated to the Swedish environmental group located in Oslo. Finally, having still received no information or feedback, the issue was escalated to the Institute of Oceanology at the Russian Academy of Sciences - the state-owned oceanographic Institute for Arctic and Antarctic Research Institute, based in Moscow.

It was also reported to the Russian state-owned news channel, RT, as well as to most other international channels, including BBC World News, Fox News, CNN, Sky, and Al-Jazeera, where it immediately gained worldwide interest. Russia offered to get involved and would move a Search and Rescue aircraft to their northernmost airbase at Arkhangelsk Oblasto, to inspect the area and make contact. The overflight of Ice Station Hap would occur the following day at a little after eight in the morning.

It was hoped something had happened to merely knock out communications, and experts predicted the trouble to be in the generator and standby generator, thereby resulting in no power. Worst-case scenarios were determined as a possible fire causing evacuations of the station; however, experts concluded that there were enough emergency systems available to the scientists, including tents, food, and warm clothing to fully maintain life until rescue occurred. The S&R aircraft would be carrying spare equipment, radios, batteries, etc. to enable communications. Once contact had been established, the next steps of repair or removal of personnel could be decided.

With news crews gathered outside and waiting for information at the Institute of Oceanology in Moscow, the Russian system of only slowly disseminating and delivering news seemed to take an age. What wasn't expected was the official report stating that Ice Station Hap had disappeared and no trace of buildings and or personnel had been found on land, but wreckage of the buildings appeared to be floating some miles offshore.

Multiple photos taken from all different aspects accompanied the statement, but as expected, the international public wouldn't take 'no' for an answer. To add a level of complexity to the already highly confused waters, the ice flow had continued its constant drift. The area in question, where Ice Station Hap was located, or where it was expected to be, had moved out of the contested waters of Denmark's claim and was now firmly within the uncontested waters of the Russian Federation.

Both Norway and the United States offered to send aircraft and ships to help search for survivors, but both requests were immediately turned down, along with offers from Sweden and the United Kingdom. Russia would not allow any foreign military aircraft to fly within its territory, and announced any incursion would be met by immediate and decisive force. Any S&R ship or aircraft wanting to enter Russian waters had to apply for permission and had to be non-military, unarmed, and under the local command of Russian personnel. No military ships or submarines from an enemy force would be allowed to traverse Russian territorial waters.

Finally, under growing international pressure, the Russian Government agreed to allow a 'Russia Today (RT) News' film crew to accompany the planned site visit the following day.

General Yermilov picked up the handset and dialed.
  'Captain. Is everything completed?'
  'Totally, sir,' the VDV captain answered.
  'The site?'
  'Completely empty.'
  'Wreckage?'
  'Some off the shore.'
  With that, a relieved Yermilov sat back, relaxed, and lit his thirtieth cigarette of the day.

<><><>

The local Moscow news crews were instructed to be at the Domodedovo Airport in Moscow, at 05:00 the following morning, where they were flown under guard to Nagurskoye Air Base. All cameras and recording equipment were guarded separately until they were onboard the Search and Rescue aircraft, airborne, and clear of the airbase. Only then were they instructed as to what they were permitted to film and record. The individuals had to sign paperwork stating that Russian officials would check anything they wanted to disclose, along with all film taken, before being released. Any breaking of these rules would have severe penalties.

Two hours after take-off from Nagurskoye, the pilot reduced altitude to a little over three hundred feet and approached the GPS coordinates of the current position of the ice flow. With cameras trained downward through the windows, all they could record was virgin white snow. The lead reporter asked for the aircraft to circle and approach again from seaward, which was agreed to. With nothing much to film except snow, they requested they fly fifteen minutes in either direction along and off the coast in case the co-ordinates had been wrong. This also was duly done with again no sign of any man-made life until finally something was seen floating in the distance. On approach, this was identified as part of one of the Portakabin structures. Finally, the aircraft headed back to base where the film crew spent the night while their film was scrutinized by officials.

Arriving back at Domodedovo Airport late morning the following day, their news reports made the Moscow lunchtime news before being retransmitted internationally.

Experts concluded the only viable explanation was a large calving of the ice flow where the ice station was located had occurred. The ice had probably broken up on calving, and the buildings and equipment had been lost to the depths, along with the lives of all twenty-two members of staff. Nobody could survive the freezing water temperatures for more than minutes; however, Search & Rescue would continue looking over the next week, but with all hope of rescue gone and no bodies to recover unless anything positive was found, the rescue attempt would be wound down within a few days.

Church or religious services would be held for the missing, presumed dead.

General Dmitry Yermilov picked up the handset, cleared his throat, and muttered, 'Da?' He'd been waiting for this call for more than twenty-four hours, but still wasn't looking forward to it. Any contact with Moscow was always fraught. This call particularly so.

The voice on the other end of the line was immediately identifiable as it asked, 'Is it done?'

Shifting his weight a little and sitting more upright, the General answered, 'Completely, sir. It was never there.'

'Any loose ends?'

'None, sir.'

'Absolutely sure?'

'Yes, sir.'

'I need your word on it. I can't have this come back to haunt me!'

'My word and on my life, sir.'

'You are quite astute, General, and correct. On your life it is,' the caller said before hanging up.

The line in the General's ear was held open for a few more seconds before he heard a distant click of a call being disconnected, and then dial tone returned. So a third party had been listening, he thought, as beads of sweat ran down his neck. He only wished he knew who.

The cold blue eyes of President Viktor Kalygin showed no emotion as he held the receiver. The first button press had disconnected the call to General Yermilov but held open the highly-encrypted international call on the other line. Sighing slightly, Kalygin said, 'I told you my people would cover everything. You worry over nothing. Now go and enjoy your Washington weekend and we will speak again soon,' he said, before replacing the handset.

Within seconds, the President of Russia moved on to the next item on his agenda. Not one to ponder or rethink things, as far as he was concerned this item had been completed and his agent Blackbird was safe.

By the time the other generals had entered his office, saluted, and sat down, his mind had firmly moved on.

The United Nations expressed sympathy with the families and exerted increased pressure on the Russian Federation to allow better access, so, after claiming they had nothing to hide, although that part of the ice flow was now clearly in Russian waters, the Russian Government allowed select airplanes to make the same journey. A Norwegian military C130, minus all weaponry, but filled with international reporters and news crews made the eight-hour return journey. It landed on the ice flow close to where Ice Station Hap had been located.

There was nothing new to see. The station and all traces of humans ever being there were completely gone. Nearer the edge of the ice flow, there was evidence of recent activity. This was agreed by three Glaciology experts as likely to have been a sudden and violent ice calving. They estimated the event might have taken mere minutes from start to finish – certainly no time to run or call for help. The poor people would have been immersed in the icy waters, and at those temperatures would have gone into shock almost immediately. Death would have occurred in seconds or, worst case, minutes. With the height of the ice at the water's edge being nearly thirty feet thick, any attempt to climb out would have been fruitless.

Ten days later, the Norwegian C130 returned, this time with representatives of some of the missing people. A multidenominational religious service was held, and a commemorative plaque was laid.

As with any news report, most disasters have a two- or three-day life cycle. Unless something new comes up, people lose interest quickly. Armed conflicts with ISIS in the Middle East, along with Brexit in the UK and another mass shooting at a High School in the USA, captured people's hearts and minds and the front pages by the fourth day.

4

Two weeks later – Phylax Offices, Washington DC

Deacon was on the phone, speaking with a potential new client when his cell rang. Glancing at the number, he could see it was his parents calling. Important though the call from his parents was, he let it go to voice mail while he continued selling the services of Phylax to his new client.

Deacon had been a Lieutenant Commander in the US Navy SEALs. Two major missions had come to the direct notice of the previous president and the then president-elect, Thomas Wexford. Just after Wexford had been elected, he'd accepted the offer to work directly for him via Admiral Carter, and he hadn't looked back since. Jointly he and the Admiral had decided on the best set-up and cover story. Soon after, he'd resigned from the U.S. Navy. Now holding the rank of 'Honorary Lieutenant Commander,' Deacon had set up Phylax, offering close personal protection and body guarding.

Phylax is ancient Greek and means guardian or sentinel. With an office located in Dupont Circle, close to the major embassies, business soon began to roll in. Funds to set up the company came in the form of a low-interest loan through an offshore bank in the Cayman Islands, funded by a shell company in the Bahamas with many layers of isolation between it and the U.S. Government. Phylax was registered as a fully legitimate company offering close protection services to visiting elite business people and diplomats. Private endorsements by the president guaranteed success, and Phylax had quickly expanded to provide long-term in-country protection with customers based in the Middle East. Deacon's role within Phylax was CEO with most of his time spent either in the office or traveling to market his company's services. Now the company had over two hundred regular and fifty long-term live-in protection clients. Using only staff personally vetted by him, Phylax offered the highest quality of personal service. The team included Gina Panaterri - an ex-Secret Service agent who ran the office in his absence, and Sean Martock, ex-Navy SEAL - as well as forty other employees registered on their books, all being ex-Army, Special Forces, or similar. Some had even signed up from foreign agencies such as the British SAS, the German GSG 9, and the French DGSE.

With a blue-chip client list still rapidly growing and excellent references from satisfied customers, Phylax had become a major success.

Only Gina and Sean knew that although Phylax was a legitimate company, it was also a front for services directly to the president, via Admiral Douglas Carter - Chief of Naval Operations at the Pentagon. As and when the president deemed necessary, Phylax and a couple of 'select' employees would be available for specific government-designated 'black-level' work. However, in this role, Phylax would be considered a private company and not able to call on the normal protection of the U.S. Government. If injured or captured, individuals would be held accountable to the laws and legal sentences of that country. In practice, the U.S. Government would totally disown them.

Only the president and a very few in his inner circle were aware of this arrangement with Deacon and Phylax.

Finishing his call after receiving a firm commitment from his new client, he went and got a cup of black coffee before walking back to his office, closing the door and opening his cell. He knew his parents wouldn't have left a message – they never did, merely asking him to call. They were always brief on the phone as well, so he pressed a short code and waited.

'Mom, how are you doing?'

'We're well, John, both of us. My reason for the call. Do you remember a Professor Gatskil? Richard Gatskil? He and his wife Amy are neighbors. You met them the other Christmas. Remember?'

'Yeah, vaguely. Tall guy with salt and pepper hair? Wife was quite a petite lady. Both about late fifties or early sixties. Is that them?'

'Correct, John. Amy used to work at the same accountancy firm as me. That's how I met her. She's called about this disaster with the ice station. Richard was one of the scientists on there. She's heartbroken, obviously, about what's happened. I've given our condolences. But just wondering . . .'

'That's terrible, but go on.'

'She's tried contacting the government to get more answers, but nothing. She's tried the Russian Embassy, but again they won't tell her anything beyond what is in the papers. We were wondering, with your 'contacts', can you find out anything more? I think she'd just like to know he died quickly and didn't suffer. I know what the news says, but they hype everything up to sell papers…'

Agreeing to her latter statement, he confirmed he'd try to look into it if he could, but offered no promises.

After chatting for a few more minutes and promising to go visit soon, he hung up and carried on the day's business as usual.

Later that evening, sitting in a comfortable chair in Mitchel and Helen Stringers' apartment in the Adams Morgan neighborhood of Washington, he swirled the last of the wine around in his glass and chugged it down, before going over to the side table and grabbing another. Opening it, he moved towards Helen to refill her glass.

'You always bring good wine, John.'

'You always cook an excellent meal, Helen. Fair's fair. That veal escalope was amazing... and the sauce... mmmm!'

Mitch, walked back in, grabbed his empty glass, slumped into a chair, turned to Deacon, offered his glass and said, 'That's the dishwasher on and dessert sorted. Fill me up, pal.' To which Deacon duly obliged.

Mitch and Deacon had known each other for years and treated each other as brothers. Then Helen had come onto the scene, and Mitch was smitten. They'd finally married, and to Deacon it was like having a brother and yet another sister in addition to the ones he'd grown up with.

'Mom called today.'

'They both well?'

'Yeah, pretty much so, I think. She knows or knew one of the Professors on the Hap Ice Station. His wife used to work with her. She was wondering if I could find out anything more about what happened.'

'Funny you should mention that, pal. The Admiral was only talking about it earlier. He reckons it smells bad. We looked at the photos of the floating wreckage and of the site. He said he couldn't put his finger on it, but he's unhappy the way the Ruskies have acted over it. Anyway, he has spoken to the president about it. So this isn't a presidential official request, but the Admiral said if you wanted to go for a look-see, he'd arrange it.'

'And when was the Admiral thinking of mentioning it to me?' Deacon asked.

'Well, I happened to let slip you were coming around tonight, and he thought it might be useful for me to mention it. Otherwise, he'd already told me to invite you in for a meeting tomorrow afternoon,' Mitch laughed.

'So how are we gonna do this?'

'Well, the actual site of the ice station is now in Russian territory, so you can't just go there. They did allow limited access for a while to the Press, but that has now been revoked. However, Denmark has a static weather station, Solskin Station, over three hundred miles further north but on the same ice sheet. That isn't, and won't be, in Russian waters. What the Admiral suggested, and I played with the idea, was for you to fly in undercover as an engineer or similar to the weather station, via Thule AFB. That's where they normally supply from. You'd be seen as just normal turnaround replacement staff. Admiral Carter will speak with his counterpart in Denmark, Chief Mikkelsen, and get you clearance. Then you borrow a snowmobile and go and have a look,' Mitch finished with.

Taking another mouthful of wine, Deacon smiled and said, 'No, it's a bit more complex than that. First, there needs to be two of us for safety. We'll obviously need full severe weather gear, but we'll need two snowmobiles. Big ones. Powerful. Plus, a sled each. Three hundred miles could easily take three days to get there if the weather turns, and the same back so rations and fuel for eight days for two to allow a safety margin. Two all-weather tents, comms, and weapons. Also, since we'll be behind lines, and they won't be happy to see us, everything needs to be snow camouflaged.'

'As long as you're not thinking of me as your number two?'

'Nah, Helen would never forgive me, and I enjoy her cooking too much to fall out with her. Seriously, we carried out a lot of severe weather training in conjunction with the British SAS in Norway some years back when I was still in Team Three. The Brits are pretty good in those conditions, and I learned however bad you expect it to be, double it. When you get caught in a white-out and can't see more than a foot in front of your face, all you can do is stop, keep as warm as you can, and wait it out. I'll take Sean with me. He and I did the training together. Tell the Admiral if he can arrange it, we're on.'

Three days later Deacon and Sean boarded a routine US Navy flight from Naval Station Norfolk to Thule AFB, Greenland.

5

The Arctic

The nine-hour flight to Thule was uneventful, and as the aircraft was typical US Air Force, inasmuch as very little sound or heat insulation, any conversation was difficult. Therefore, both of them wrapped sleeping bags around themselves and spent as much time sleeping as they could. Arriving at Thule, they made contact with the base commander before heading to the visiting officers' quarters.

Although clear here, the weather had closed in over Solskin, and it was another eighteen hours before it finally broke, and an expected window was scheduled to arrive for conditions to improve enough to land an aircraft.

Ninety minutes later, a Danish ski-equipped C130 took off through a blizzard and heavy crosswinds for the three-hour flight to Solskin Station. The winds made for an uncomfortable ride, but to the pilot and co-pilot, this was normal. On the second attempt, the rear skis kissed the ground, the engines were cut, and the nose ski gently landed on the compacted snow.

Twenty minutes later, unloaded and reloaded, the C130 headed off for the return journey back to Thule.

Colonel Knute Knutessen was waiting for them in the makeshift control tower.

'Gentlemen, I received word from Chief Mikkelsen that all your equipment has either arrived or is available here already. On the manifest, you two were shown as replacement engineers. I suggest you stick to yourselves today, but that's your cover story if asked. We are just under three-hundred-fifty miles from where Station Hap was located. The Russian border is a moveable object, but now it is about a hundred miles to this side of it, so you will need to proceed with caution. However, on a positive note, we are expecting low pressure, so you should get a few days of low cloud and snow. Keep you hidden. Maybe some storms and winds below Force 8––'.

'Below Force 8? You call that reasonable weather?' Sean said.

'Up here it is. Yesterday was nearer Force 11, and the temperature was twenty-five below. It's positively springlike out there today,' he replied with a smile. 'In the meantime, enjoy lunch and good luck. We may be remote here, but we do have a couple of fine cooks,' he continued.

They thanked the Colonel for his hospitality and headed to the central canteen for lunch, where they helped themselves from a well-stocked hot buffet that included New York steaks, pork chops, and a full range of vegetables. Sated and happy, they dedicated the afternoon to checking and re-checking their equipment.

At this time of year, with the sun only recently moving into the northern hemisphere, the nights were still dark and long. At 03:45, two white Arctic Cat Crossover snowmobiles with sleds attached, along with tents, sleeping bags, rifles, extended food supplies and spare fuel headed out towards distant coordinates.

For the first five hours, the journey was relatively quick and easy. The wind was low and the snow light. Visibility was a few hundred feet, and with both being accomplished riders, they managed to keep up an aggressive speed. As daylight broke that speed increased until they were keeping up an average of almost twenty-five MPH. Although extremely cold outside, one of their biggest worries wasn't hypothermia, but dehydration. The cold, dry air would literally draw the moisture out of your body, so they stopped every hour for a five-minute relief and drink break. Both snowmobiles were fitted with radios, and they had turned the power output down to 0.1 watts, giving a broadcast range of only a few hundred yards. This was enough to enable communication as they rode along but it was highly unlikely they could be monitored by external forces.

As they approached the first one hundred miles traveled, they stopped for a longer break to eat and thaw out. Fingers and toes were stiff in the cold, and they spent ten minutes flexing and bending them to force movement and life back into them. Both wore dark snow goggles against the bright white of the snowscape, as well as face protection that, by now, was covered in a layer of ice.

In one of the most inhospitable regions of the world, they checked each other for any exposed areas of skin. Unprotected flesh would quickly chill until numb. Then the danger would quickly set in. Once numb, the owner had already lost all sensation of pain and would not detect ice crystals forming under the skin as the early stages of frostbite would begin to occur. These ice crystals would quickly damage skin tissue beyond repair with the skin color darkening before turning black. By then, the skin or limb would be dead. If the skin then thawed it would begin to rot causing incredible agonizing pain. If the damaged tissue was not rapidly removed by surgery or amputation, gangrene would quickly spread, and death would be unavoidable.

The terrain was relatively smooth but just pure white as far as the eye could see in any direction. This close to the North Pole, compasses were useless, and they relied on the accuracy of GPS systems built into the snowmobiles. Big and solidly-built, these models had ample power, and even the steep hills they'd come to so far hadn't slowed them.

Keeping a sharp lookout for any signs of human life they spotted a number of arctic hares and the tracks of at least one polar bear. Both Sean and Deacon were carrying rifles and would use them to frighten off any inquisitive bear. Up here in the vast openness of the Arctic, they were the food sources and the hunted, not the hunters.

By mid-afternoon, their speed had dropped. The terrain was hilly with giant cracks in the ice. Ice boulders, each the size of a house, blocked their route, and they wasted hour after hour in trying to plot a course through them, often having to backtrack miles. Storms blew in without warning, and intense snow flurries caused whiteouts that would suddenly cause visibility to drop from hundreds of yards to mere feet. That evening, as the sun finally set for the eight-hour dark of night, they set up their tents in the lee of one of the boulders. After a re-heated meal of beef stew, they squeezed their tired and aching bodies into their sleeping bags and quickly fell asleep.

As daylight broke and the sky began to brighten from dark gray to a lighter color, they were already up, fed, and ready to go. As the day before, they wasted hours slowly progressing through the ice boulders, but eventually, the obstacles thinned out, and both could open the throttles of their machines a little more.

Once when the clouds cleared and the sun shone, Deacon could see an aircraft flying high overhead and was worried the snowmobile tracks might be visible. However, at the thirty-thousand feet or more altitude it was flying at discovery was pretty slim. Also, at that height, they couldn't identify make or model of the aircraft, so they had no idea whose nationality it was. However, as a safety measure, they kept any radio transmissions to a minimum.

By the end of the second day, they had crossed into what was now deemed as Russian Federation territory and only had another fifty miles or so to go.

Another early start, another early breakfast, because Deacon wanted to make as much headway as possible. The winds and clouds had finally departed and the morning started with a crystal blue sky. The terrain had slowed their journey, and he was keen to try to make up time. Although the snow was deep, it allowed quick progress. As they approached the crest of one particular hill they suddenly heard a rifle shot and quickly dismounted, rifles at the ready. The problem with snow, Deacon had always reckoned, was that it left obvious tracks. Even worse from a snowmobile. You might as well just tell your adversaries which way you are going.

Keeping low but climbing and slithering enough forward, they peered over the ridge down towards the valley beyond, just as another shot was fired.

Two snowmobiles were stopped about four hundred yards away, with two figures standing nearby. One was aiming his rifle at a polar bear running away in the distance. A thin red trail of blood was left in its path. This shot hit the bear again, and Deacon could hear it cry out. It stumbled but continued to run, now more stiffly, partly dragging one of its back legs.

'Fuckers,' Sean said. 'I wonder what they'd think if we did that to them?'

'Tempting, Sean. Very tempting. Let's wait until they move on.'

Both were used to killing, but neither accepted the idea of killing for sport or pleasure. Especially against defenseless animals. They lay there, hidden in the snow as they watched the other soldier aim and shoot his rifle at the injured creature.

A chunk of flesh exploded from its shoulder, and it finally collapsed. The area around it was red with blood, but still it didn't die. With what sounded like laughter, the two remounted their snowmobiles and headed over to the writhing animal.

It was lying on its side, blood spilling out onto white snow as it raised a paw and tried to claw to defend itself. Its roars were getting weaker and weaker as the two danced around it. Eventually, after they took some selfies, the first soldier cocked his assault rifle and let rip a five-second burst that almost cut the animal in two. As the echoes of gunfire faded, both soldiers clapped each other on the back, mounted their vehicles and headed off.

Moving back down away from the ridge, Deacon said, 'Makes you sick, doesn't it?'

Climbing back on their snowmobiles, they continued on their journey both deep in thought and disgust.

Two hours later, both GPS's dinged and announced they had arrived at their destination.

Their 'destination' looked precisely the same as everywhere else close by. The entire area was flat, snow-covered, and devoid of anything man-made. The shore was almost a half-mile away. Towards the shoreline was a flagpole with a United Nations flag fluttering in the breeze. Driving over, there was a plaque attached to the pole.

The inscription read, '*Here lays the last known position of Danish Arctic Drift Ice Station 736 and her 22 souls. May God look after and protect them always.*'

'Nice,' said Sean, looking at it.

'Yeah, nice. Just a shame it's in the wrong place.'

'Eh? Why do you think it's in the wrong place, John?'

'People believe what they're told. They were told the ice calved, and the site has gone. So they go to the edge and look down. Human nature. Never think to look around. But the site was never here. It was over there,' he said, pointing over a half-mile back.

'How do you know?' Sean said as they both climbed aboard their snowmobiles again.

'Check the GPS. The ice sheet is constantly moving, but the recorded coordinates of the site when first built put it over there, adjusted for the current position of the ice flow.'

'But wouldn't the rescuers have checked GPS?'

'Why would they? They were taken to a spot and told it was there,' Deacon said, arriving back at the new location. He dismounted and, pulling a shovel from his sled, started digging holes about two feet deep at various locations.

On the seventh, he motioned Sean over to see.

'Look!' he said, using the blade of the shovel to hold back some snow.

Gradually the snow began to show slight pinkish against the white.

'Blood?'

'Yup, blood. But where are the bodies and the buildings?' Deacon said.

An hour later, they had some, although not many, answers. Deacon had pulled a commercial metal detector from his sled. With the volume turned up full, he walked a grid pattern until he picked up beeps. At each beep he asked Sean to dig. Sure enough, they found odd items. A couple of steel bolts, a spanner, some wire cable. But what convinced them was finding multiple brass cartridge casings. As they expanded their search radius, they also detected numerous spent full metal jacket bullets.

Leaning against one of the snowmobiles, Sean said, 'So somebody came here, had a fight and then removed all evidence of them being here? Is that likely?'

'Don't know, pal, but that's what the evidence seems to sho--'.

At that moment, an aircraft flying at a few hundred feet came in towards them from the sea. As it got closer, they could see Russian markings.

'Wave. Just be friendly,' Deacon said, and they both raised their arms and began waving. The aircraft circled twice and was flying low enough to see the pilot looking down at them. Initially, the pilot raised a hand in response, before a second face appeared in the cockpit window. After a minute or two, it turned away and began to climb slowly as it headed away.

'That, pal, isn't good. Let's get out of here.'

It took less than another two minutes to take a couple of photos before both snowmobiles were heading back the way they'd come.

They'd been riding hard for less than two hours when trouble found them.

6

With engines running flat out they'd made good time and speed, but the large, powerful motors were thirsty, especially with the added weight of the sleds. Ninety minutes into their escape they stopped to refill the tanks and had just put the gas can back when Sean tilted his head up and listened for a few seconds before saying, 'Boss, I think we've got company.'

The faint noise of engines broke the silence, but nothing could be seen. Taking off his helmet, Sean turned his head back and forth. The engine noise seemed to be from somewhere at an angle to the way they were going.

'Shit, let's go,' and they both leaped back on their machines and roared away.

They both knew the hunters would find their tracks easily. Snowmobile tracks weren't the hardest of tracks to follow, and it was really a case of speed and distance. The Russian Norwegian artificial border was at least another forty miles away, and there was no reason why they wouldn't be chased all the way across it and back to Solskin Station.

Fifteen minutes into the chase and it was evident either the hunters had yet bigger and more powerful machines, or simply the weight of the sleds were slowing them down. The two hunters were now clearly distinguishable, dressed in Arctic gear, and carrying rifles. Three times shots had gone close overhead, and the closer the hunters got, the greater the chance of a stray bullet hitting one of them or disabling a snowmobile.

From the direction these had come from, Deacon assumed it was the two bear killers from earlier.

Speaking over the two-way radio link, Deacon said, 'Sean, as they get closer wait until they fire again and I'll slew and fall. You slow, initially, then high tail it away. Turn back three minutes later. OK?'

'What if they keep firing at you to make sure you're dead?'

'Then I'll be in the shit, pal.'

As the hunters slowly gained on them, their firing became more accurate. Three times either Sean or Deacon heard the close whine of a bullet missing them by inches and a number of times they heard and felt the impact of rounds hitting the sleds still being towed behind.

When the hunters were now only four hundred yards or so behind and firing again, Deacon said, 'Now.' into his radio, swerved a little as if he'd been hit, slewed to the right, and fell off, his rifle lying close to him. Sean slowed, looked back, before opening the throttle again.

As expected, one rider kept chasing after Sean while the other pulled up a hundred feet or so away from the prone body of Deacon laying in the snow. As he walked towards Deacon, his assault rifle was pointing sideways, so confident he'd hit his target. As he neared twenty feet, in the blink of an eye Deacon rolled sideways, grabbed his rifle, aimed and fired in one smooth motion.

The inside of the plexiglass visor of the hunter turned bright red, and he collapsed like a sack. In the distance, Sean had turned back towards the second hunter who was now caught between him and Deacon. There was a sound of multiple rounds being fired before Deacon also joined in, his rounds peppering the snow and the snowmobile around the rider. Then a lucky shot from Sean. The first hit the rider in the shoulder, but he turned and tried to carry on firing. A burst of three cut across his chest, and he went down like his colleague.

After checking there were no other pursuers, they examined the hunters for injuries, but both were clearly dead. Neither Deacon or Martock felt bad. At times it was a 'them or us' world, and this time it had been them.

The dead polar bear from that morning was less than a mile away and Deacon had a thought.

Smiling, he told Sean to bring the other dead body over to the animal carcass, as he followed with the first dead hunter lying across his sled.

Dragging both bodies and propping them up against their snowmobiles, he took a pistol from one of the dead hunters and carefully placed it in one of the paws of the dead bear.

Happy with his work, he smiled and said, 'That'll make it tough for anyone who finds them to explain,' before giving Sean a lift back to his own machine and they continued on their journey.

The wind had increased, and heavy snow was falling again. As it intensified and visibility again dropped to just feet, at least it helped hide their tracks. With nothing to stop it, the wind whisked the loose snow into a violent blizzard. It was a whiteout and impossible to keep on direction, so they hunkered down next to their machines in as much shelter as they could temporarily make. After a long four hours, the storm finally passed, and over a ten-minute-period the wind dropped, the sun reappeared, and the temperature slowly climbed back towards zero Fahrenheit. Deciding to take a slightly circular route home to reduce the possibility of being tracked, they skirted some of the ice boulder fields that had delayed them the day previously.

After a fourth night away staying in tents, and considering Deacon's tent had two bullet holes rapidly patched with sticky tape, both were beyond happy when the lights of Solskin Station finally appeared through the gloom.

It was another day before they could catch a flight back to Thule, but the connecting flight to Washington had waited for them and after a total of a little over thirteen hours after walking across the hardened snow runway at Solskin, they were walking across the blacktop at Norfolk towards Deacon's dark blue F-150 crew cab.

<><><>

At 07:30 the following morning, Deacon was waiting in reception at the Pentagon to be shown up to the Admiral's office. As a civilian, Deacon was only afforded a red 'Visitor - Escort Everywhere' badge, but he only had to wait a few minutes for his chaperon.

The Admiral was already in his office, and Mitch was just arriving. Sitting down to hot coffee and bagels, Deacon gave a point-by-point account of everything that had happened on the trip. The spent ammunition he'd brought back had been quickly identified as Russian, so it was assumed that whoever had cleared the actual Hap site did so with the authority of the Russian Government.

'Still doesn't explain why or who though, does it?' the Admiral said.

'No sir, only the how. And even that's vague. Were there any injured? Are any still alive? Where are they being held? What's happened to all the buildings and equipment? Those bits of flotsam have drifted off by now. But I guess the main question is why? Why was all this done to an innocent research site? Did something happen? Were they exposed to something? Did they see something? We looked around everywhere, but there were no clues at all, sir.'

'And then they tried to shoot you?'

'Well, par for the course, I guess. We were in their country uninvited. And we were poking around. But there was no stop and question. It was kill or be killed.'

'Well, glad you're back,' the Admiral finished. He'd been informed of the possible testing of a new Russian anti-missile weapon in the last few months, but it had happened many miles away from the Hap station, and he couldn't see any form of link between the two occurrences. As this information was of the highest classification, he couldn't disclose it to Deacon unless he needed to.

Finishing the meeting, the Admiral sat in quiet contemplation for a short while.

He wasn't happy. Douglas Eugene Carter wasn't the sort of person who accepted partial answers – his view had always been 'tell me everything'. There were too many loose ends with what had happened. To make matters worse, having initially raised the idea and concern to the president who had then asked him to look into it, how could he report back in a half-assed way to him? If the president asked him questions, as he was likely to, how could the Admiral answer without more information? No, he needed more! If it was genuine and all due to an ice calving, he wanted evidence. If there was none to be found, it hinted more towards a cover-up.

The seabed area in the Arctic where the ice flow was alleged to have shelved was still in Danish Greenland waters. The ice flow floating above it had since drifted, but obviously, not the seabed. Contacting ComSubLant (Command, Submarines, Atlantic), he ordered the USS Annapolis, a Los-Angeles-class attack submarine, normally based in Groton, Connecticut, but currently on a courtesy port visit to HMNB Clyde, commonly referred to as Faslane in Scotland in the UK, to head north to the area and examine that area of seabed.

He didn't do this lightly. The Arctic Ocean was international, but Russia liked to consider it their own. Any approach was highly likely to become hostile if discovered, but more importantly, any mission requiring progress under the massive ice sheets was particularly dangerous, and he wouldn't put any of his men in danger haphazardly. At any time, millions of tons of ice could calve and drop down, and any stranded or damaged submarine in such waters could be impossible to rescue. However, the USS Annapolis had been there nine years previously, and many of the crew and officers were still the same, including Captain Dwayne Franklin. In the hostile world of the North Atlantic and Arctic Seas, experience counted.

Faslane was almost 2,400 nautical miles away from the seabed site, and it would take the Annapolis up to seven days at an average 15 knots an hour. She could easily progress at speeds in excess of 33 knots, but this mission wasn't urgent, and staying safe and not being discovered was more important than urgency.

With new standing orders now to get underway as soon as provisioning was complete, the Admiral turned to his computer and pulled up a file on the USS Annapolis.

It read: '*Ice Exercise 2009 (ICEX) had been a two-week US naval military exercise that took place during March 2009. Its aim was to test submarine operability and war-fighting capability in Arctic conditions. Even then, the polar region has become the subject of increased attention on the part of the Arctic Circle countries because of potential competition for its natural resources. Two US Atlantic Fleet Los Angeles-class attack submarines, USS Helena and USS Annapolis, took part in the exercise. The aim was to determine how accurately submarines could track and hunt under the confines of heavy ice sheets. Both the Helena and the Annapolis played the roles of hunter and hunted gaining both crews detailed and extensive knowledge of prosecuting warfare in these extreme conditions. Limitations to existing sonar, radar, and targeting and acquisition systems were identified, and a series of modifications were demanded from suppliers.'*

It took them four days until the Annapolis arrived at the edge of the Arctic Circle. The time to finish provisioning had been speeded up, and all those ashore had been rounded up and returned to duty. The Annapolis had pulled away from her berth in Faslane just twelve hours after receiving her new orders. Captain Franklin had apologized to the crew who were expecting another sixteen hours ashore closely examining British public houses, but no one complained. The bow and stern lines were dropped and the deadly, sleek submarine slowly headed out into Faslane Bay before turning south down Gare Loch. She continued on the surface along Loch Long until reaching the mouth of the Firth of Clyde when the three-hundred-sixty-foot long, nuclear-powered, fast-attack submarine submerged.

The hull and her crew wouldn't see or feel the warmth of direct sunlight for another ten weeks when she would arrive back at her home base in Groton, Connecticut.

Leaving the Isle of Arran to starboard before turning northeast and passing the Isle of Islay, famous for its whiskey, she then proceeded north between the Isle of Skye and the Outer Hebrides passing the Faroes, Iceland, and Jan Mayen Island. During this time Captain Franklin put the crew through some of the most rigorous exercise training many had completed since Naval Academy. He forewarned them by stating they were heading into extremely dangerous waters, would possibly be hunted, and would be going under areas of the Arctic ice fields where very few people had ever managed to successfully venture before.

As the submarine headed further north, the sea ice had become thicker and more compact. Multiple times the Annapolis had to stop before slowly rising to periscope depth to try and raise her communication tower through the ice, but as the ice became denser, it became more problematic.

Taking her down to an operating depth of six hundred feet, Captain Franklin kept her within some of the deepest parts of the Arctic where depths of up to 8,000 feet were common.

Most of the Lomonosov Ridge was also at this depth, but the edges of it rose sharply to just a few hundred feet below the heavy ice floating above. The most dangerous part of operating a submarine under giant ice sheets and icebergs is that most of the ice remains underwater. Active sonar emits 'pings' which reflect back to show a picture of what it sees, but the pings can easily be picked up by other craft, giving away your position. Therefore a submarine needs to keep totally quiet so as not to be detected. The only way the crew of the Annapolis could 'see' their way through the vast columns of jagged frozen ice protruding down sometimes hundreds of feet, was using spotlights on the bow and video cameras. They also used very low power sonar for close-in work, undetectable from more than a mile away, but the captain, executive officer, and navigator spent hours looking at tv screens trying to guide their boat through the masses of dense, sunken ice formations.

These ice formations would easily rip the hull to shreds, given half a chance. Razor-sharp and as solid as reinforced concrete, even a gently glancing blow at these depths would be catastrophic. The merest pinprick through the hull would result in instantaneous implosion. As they slowly continued on, the seabed began to rise. From many thousands of feet depth, it rose sharply to mere hundreds. The concern on the officers' faces was noticeable. No submarine commander likes to be pinned into a corner. A submarine needs open ocean and plenty of depth under her keel to protect both her and her crew. Here they were slowly moving into a shallower and shallower location with cathedral columns of deadly hardened ice jutting down from the ice sheet and icebergs above. In an emergency, the Annapolis had nowhere to go. She couldn't surface and breakthrough possibly up to a hundred or more feet of ice, and she couldn't go deeper to escape. She would effectively be trapped.

At just three knots an hour, similar to a brisk walking pace, the Annapolis finally reached her chosen position. The water depth was a little under three hundred feet, and the ice sheet thickness overhead was now over ninety feet thick with sixty feet of it below sea level. The Annapolis height from the top of her mast to the keel was seventy feet, so this left very little room to maneuver.

With all lights on and cameras set to downward mode, she carefully trawled the entire area recording the surface of the seabed through the clear seawater.

Small pieces of debris littered the area. Aluminum sheets, metal eyelet bolts, but not much. Certainly not the amount from the remaining buildings meant to have fallen.

On the third run, the navigator noticed markings in the red mud of the seabed.

'What's that?' he said, pointing.

'It's tracks of some sort. Like the marks an anchor dragging would make,' the executive officer said.

'No, it's far too big for that. Look, there's a pair of them,' the navigator replied.

With all of them looking closely at the tv monitor, Captain Franklin called to sonar, 'Sonar, anything yet?'

'Sir, mechanical noise eight miles away. Rhythmic and repetitive, sir. Computer analyses it as a tracked vehicle, sir.'

'What, down here?'

'That's what the computer says, sir.'

Ordering a course change, they watched and waiting as they followed the tracks until they neared the source of the noise.

'Sonar – conn,' came the urgent call.

'Conn – go ahead,' Captain Franklin replied.

'Akula detected, six miles away, crossing in front of us, sir.'

With the threat of detection by a Russian Akula class attack submarine, Captain Franklin had only one option. 'Helm, steady at 120, depth two hundred. One pass, people, one pass. All recording equipment on and keep your eyes peeled. Helm, in thirty seconds, turn to new course 193, speed ten knots,' he ordered.

That one pass was all that was needed. A dark underwater vehicle, the width of a truck, mounted on crawler caterpillar tracks was making the tracks. Large digger-type teeth on the front were removing the top dozen feet of red mud seabed, and there was a large umbilical cable connecting this remote digging device to some other equipment in the distance off to the east.

'Sonar, anything else to report?'

'Possible surface ship. Not underway. The ice is playing havoc, sir. Can't be sure where exactly she is, but somewhere east of here.'

43

With that, the thirty seconds were up, and the helm changed course away from the ever-closing danger of the approaching Russian submarine.

7

Meeting in one of the larger conference rooms was Admiral Carter, Mitch, General Warwick Dreiberg – Director of National Intelligence, General Melvin Tarrant – Secretary of Defense, and General Ulysses Mansfield – Chairman of the Joint Chiefs of Staff.

President Thomas Wexford had joined the meeting by video conference and was speaking.

'So what the heck is this digger thing?'

'We think, sir,' Admiral Carter said, 'that Russia is strip-mining the seabed that is in Danish contested waters. As you know, there's an international treaty barring exploitation of both the Arctic and the Antarctic for drilling and minerals.'

'So can we prove it?'

'Unfortunately, not yet, sir. We don't know who is involved or where they're coming from. Perhaps that's a question Charles Ingram's department might be able to get information about,' the Admiral said, referring to the Director of the CIA.

Before General Dreiberg could speak up about using the CIA, the President launched into a diatribe about how useless they'd become in the last year or so.

'The CIA? They wouldn't know their fucking ass from their elbow. How many clandestine missions have been blown this year? Twelve? Fifteen? More? Every time I speak with that dumb bastard Ingram I wonder why my asshole predecessor appointed him to that role. Any more fuck-ups, and I'll fire him. Fuck waiting for him to retire.

Total waste of space. Get Clark at the FBI onto it. There's a guy who knows how to run a department,' he ranted. 'Look, I've gotta go. Just get it done, General,' he said before disconnecting the video link.

All breathing a slight sigh of relief the president had left, Tarrant looked at Dreiberg and raised an eyebrow.

'Something we should know, Warwick?' he asked.

Slightly embarrassed at the president's reaction, Dreiberg answered, 'As you know, the CIA reports to me, via Charles. I don't know why it is, but the president has a real downer on Charles at the moment. True, there have been a large number of failures lately at the CIA, but I'm not sure all his negativity is warranted. What's more important is if it can be proven Russia was, and still is, mining in Danish waters - that's a big international incident.'

'What sort of failures have been happening, Warwick?' Tarrant asked.

'Lots of things. Far too many just to be coincidence or bad luck. We have a leak somewhere. We had been approached by a number of potential Russian spies who have then been discovered,' Dreiberg said. 'One of them made contact through our London Embassy, one was through Rome, and the last would have been a source here in Washington in their Embassy. But within days they'd been blown and recalled to Moscow. Been executed, we understand. Some of the info we've been gathering on terrorists and ISIS has also been found wanting. We've had more failures lately than successes, but I'm not yet convinced it's all Ingram's fault. Unfortunately, the president is and blames Ingram for all of it. Says he's running a loose ship and that the CIA are a waste of time. Problem is, with the number of failures happening it's awkward to argue the point. And we all know how fixed in his thinking the president can be.'

'To make matters worse, we have a potential situation in Venezuela, but let me come to that in a minute. In the meantime I'll get Clark over at the FBI to see if they can uncover anything,' he continued.

Standing up and walking over to the side table to pour himself another black coffee, General Mansfield said, 'So what's happening in Venezuela, Warwick?'

'One of the CIA's long-term assets has gone quiet,' he replied. 'Female doctor. An American Latino Pediatrics doctor working with the church in Venezuela. She's been with us for years. Suddenly gone quiet, but not officially arrested. Or at least, no announcement of it, if they have. Last contact from her was her regular schedule three weeks back. She usually reports every fortnight or sooner if there is anything urgent. We have reason to believe the local cartel has taken her. Most of them seem convinced any outsider must be a government official or a CIA spy. They usually just torture them until they admit something, or die in the process. We're not sure if they want money for her release or the publicity of denouncing her.'

'How experienced was she?'

'Very! She's been with us for over ten years and had built a very trusted set-up. Her name is Doctor Nina de la Parra, and she reports back all the gossip she hears over regular and unscheduled drug drops back to the U.S. Her handler, Lisa Kingman, reported the loss of contact two days back.'

'Kingman? Isn't she the Operations Deputy Director over at Langley?' Tarrant asked.

'Yeah, she's fairly new in that role, just a few months back, but still keeping the doctor as one of her field sources. 'Course, the main problem with Venezuela is their love of us - or lack thereof, to be exact. Anything 'State requests is either turned down carte blanche, or so much is demanded in return it's not feasible. Hopefully, that may change now their elections are over, but everyone is waiting on the old president to hand the reins over to the newly elected one, and no one knows when or even if that will happen.'

Turning to look at Admiral Carter, Tarrant said, 'Douglas. Your man?'

Mitch handed Deacon a black coffee and joined him. Also present was the Admiral and Lisa Kingman.

'So you see, John, with the current relationship between Venezuela and the US, if any US troops were to enter unannounced, it would be considered an invasion - just what Russian President Kalygin is waiting for. He'd immediately send Russian troops to support the Venezuelan president on the pretext of us trying to overturn him or destabilize him. What with their recent elections as well. Either way, Russia is just waiting for a reason to go in and support their friend, and it's not something we will tolerate,' the Admiral said. 'Moreover, unfortunately, there is no way Venezuela would grant us permission to send in anyone to rescue the doctor. They'd insist on doing it themselves, and we'd have to admit to having one of our spies there. I also wouldn't trust them to get the job done. However, on a positive note, Lisa here says it should be an easy rescue. Miss Kingman?'

'Mrs. Kingman,' she corrected. Turning to Deacon, she said, 'Thank you, Admiral. The CIA has another local asset working at the airport at Puerto Ayacucho, on the banks of the Orinoco and close to the border with Colombia. He's not able to do anything on his own but will arrange two cars with weapons to be waiting at the airport for you. As I'm sure you know, Colombia is the biggest drug supplier to the USA, mainly cocaine and heroin. 90% of U.S. imported cocaine comes from Colombia. Most countries around that area have now gotten onto the same bandwagon growing illegal drugs, but with Colombia still by far the largest, followed by Peru, Bolivia, and Venezuela. Countries borders in that region are pretty porous so most of the drugs are moved into Colombia and then on up through Mexico. As to the crowd holding Doctor de la Parra, if they believe she is a CIA spy, they will be doing their best to break her. If she does break, it will be an enormous coup for them, and we can then expect a large ransom demand for her release. However, our intel shows only six to eight drug kidnappers holding her close to where she lived. It should be an easy, quick in-and-out for you.'

While the Admiral had been talking initially, and then Lisa Kingman, Deacon had given her a brief look over. Late forties possibly very early fifties, long brown hair, slim with good body shape, average looking, smartly dressed, but no sign of her Mrs status by means of a ring.

Looking her directly in the eye, Deacon said, 'Can I ask exactly what your role at the CIA is, Mrs. Kingman?'

'I am the new Deputy Director for Operations. Been in this role for a few months. My department organizes and supplies all the information about this little venture through Charles Ingram to you, Mr. Deacon. He then double-checks everything and approves it. We will plan and arrange vehicles, weapons, maps, everything you might need,' she said, passing high-resolution maps of the area over, along with photographs of the high-value target, Doctor de la Parra.

'Please, I'm John or just Deacon.'

Turning to the Admiral, he said, 'OK, we will do it. Luckily, Jose Canetti will be lead with me. He has a strong Mediterranean look and is fluent in Spanish. Means he can also easily pass for a Mexican or South American. I'm sorry, Mrs. Kingman, but we plan our own missions. Let me head off and work with my team. I'll run it by Mitch, and he can advise you on what we need. OK?'

'That is rather unusual,' Kingman said. 'Admiral, please be aware Charles Ingram and I cannot be held accountable for any cowboy missions not vetted and approved by our department.'

'Mrs. Kingman. Deacon is a very able former SEAL with the rank of Lieutenant Commander. I believe he is fully capable of mission planning.'

Outranked, Lisa Kingman could only agree and nod acceptance.

With the current meeting finished, Deacon left the Pentagon and called Gina from his cell.

'Gina, can you get the group together in the office asap? I'm on my way in. Be with you in thirty.'

By the time Deacon arrived, three of the team were also present. The other three were heading in and would be arriving within the hour. Although the six members of his team were standard employees, he always kept them close to be able to respond to this sort of work. He'd book them out on local close protection work, but would always use others on his books to cover the longer or more distance work requirements.

Apart from Gina and Sean who knew of the tie-up to the White House, the remaining members of the team always considered these 'special' operations private operations for wealthy business people. Deacon would explain this next planned venture as the kidnapped doctor daughter of a wealthy Californian businessman paying Deacon and Phylax to get his daughter back safely.

Using the maps and aerial photos supplied, as well as looking at the local terrain online, the plan came together quickly. Deacon always found it useful, if he could, to get the buy-in of his team to any plan versus insisting on the way it should be done. However, he always made it clear that he had the controlling vote and had no hesitation in using it if he had to.

Within an hour of the meeting finishing Gina had typed up the technical requirements list for Kingman and emailed it to her via Mitch. Everything else Deacon preferred to arrange directly.

Turning to Hank Pechnik, one of the best multirole pilots he'd ever met, he said, 'Book a G550 or similar and get flight clearance to Puerto Ayacucho in Venezuela. Down tomorrow, back the following.'

To Martock and Andy Stockwell, he said, 'Normal gear onboard for 05:00 take-off.'

To the remaining three, Bill Roberts, Jose Canetti, and Goran Maričić, he just told them to be on-site at 04:00 the following morning.

8

Venezuela

The four-hour flight down was completely uneventful. As planned, everyone had arrived on time, and it was only expected to be a two-day trip. There were storms over some of the Caribbean Islands, but at their flying height of 39,000 feet, the weather below didn't disturb them. Deacon spent the time looking over the latest satellite views and ground maps. The rest of the team was relaxed, with a number of them sleeping. An hour before touchdown they each ate a high protein meal – possibly the last meal anyone would get before flying back the following day.

Although everyone had traveled wearing casual clothing, Martock and Stockwell had loaded all of their full battle dresses, along with ceramic protective gear, helmets, bone microphone two-way comms, and night-vision-goggles (NVGs). Hank Pechnik had surpassed himself, as he often seemed to do, and had managed to charter an almost new Gulfstream G650. This was bigger, faster, and more comfortable than the older and slightly smaller G550. The other advantage was the G650 had many more hidden areas for storing small items, including all the gear Martock and Stockwell had brought.

The only items they hadn't carried were the weapons themselves. If Venezuela Customs stopped and interrogated them, most of what they were carrying could be explained, along with the forged covering documents stating they were working for the Venezuela government-mining department out of Caracas. Their role was to scope out suitable land for a possible new dam to supply water to the local villages. However, a team of Americans with automatic weapons wouldn't be believed.

Due to the hilly terrain, Hank had to drop the aircraft down quite swiftly to avoid overflying the adjacent Colombian border, but they hardly felt the wheels touch before the engines were put into reverse thrust, and they slowed rapidly.

Deacon opened the door before the aircraft had come to a complete stop, and the stairs were already unfolding by the time the brakes were finally applied for the last time.

Stepping off the bottom rung, the first thing he noticed was how hot and humid the air was. A storm had either recently passed or was brewing. He looked around for the local contact, but no one was there, however, the red and blue flashing light of an approaching official's vehicle was beginning to reflect off the shiny aircraft's fuselage.

An overweight sergeant checked everyone's passports but didn't seem interested in examining inside the aircraft. Jose explained in Spanish the role they'd assumed, but the guard didn't even ask for official paperwork. Either he was too lazy to care, or maybe he was just fed up. Or possibly the US$200 slipped into his hand as a welcoming 'thank you' had the required effect.

As the Customs officer pulled away, two Toyota Land Cruisers pulled up. One was driven by an older man, the other by someone similar-looking, but younger. Realizing it was father and son, Deacon went to speak to them, but the father just shook his hand before they both turned and left without a word spoken. Looking at the vehicles they both seemed reasonable, and the engines had sounded decent as they'd pulled up. Opening their trunks, he was pleased to see a full complement of various weapons, including assault rifles, grenades, pistols, and boxes of spare ammunition.

Quickly getting changed into their camouflage gear in the privacy of the Gulfstream, the six of them pulled away five minutes later, three to a vehicle. Hank would arrange to refuel the aircraft and remain with it for security.

The maps and details provided showed a small village approximately sixty miles upriver called La Coromata. The initial plan was to approach quietly and scout out the area.

The undergrowth for the last five miles had been dense, so when they were still just over a mile away, Deacon ordered both vehicles off the muddy track and to be hidden amongst the trees. The rain had started falling, first gently, just a light shower, but then the raindrops had quickly enlarged until each one hitting the windshield was over two inches across. Leaving the vehicles and approaching the village on foot through the trees gave them a chance to observe without being seen.

The rain now was constant and heavy. The raindrops forced the leaves and branches of smaller plants to bend under their weight. The undergrowth amongst the trees was in parts impenetrable, being a mixture of dead and decaying branches, stalks, and vibrant new growth. The entire area was also thick with fallen leaves, and the intense rain was quickly turning it into a mud bath. Many of the plants were covered in poisonous spines and those that weren't seemed to be covered instead in stinging insects, some deadly. At least the thunderous noise of the rain masked any sound they would make on their approach.

The village was small, with twenty or thirty huts varying from small to large, occupying an area of an acre or so. According to the map, there were over a dozen similarly sized villages nearby, with many more further afield.

Just visible through the torrential rain at the far edge of the village was a large hut with a red cross on the roof. The upstairs contained living accommodation for the doctor, with the medical center below. Although basic by western standards, most patients were women and children needing ordinary day-to-day medicines and inoculations. The doctor also treated broken bones and cuts. The most common injury to males working in the fields was accidents with machetes. More severe injuries were sent to the main hospital in Puerto Ayacucho.

The building looked empty. The main door was closed with an armed guard standing outside keeping close into the relative shelter near the entrance. Retreating back into the forest slightly, Deacon sent Canetti to check the building out.

Moving back around in between the trees until he was close to the rear of the medical building, Canetti sprinted towards the rear wall and opened the rear window quickly. It was dark inside and after removing the insect screen without a sound, Canetti quietly climbed in and looked around. The only sounds were the incessant drumming of rain on the roof and the quieter sounds of water dripping off his wet clothes and pooling around him. The place was empty of people, and it was a mess. Paperwork was strewn everywhere on the floor, and all the cabinets had been opened with everything pulled out and dumped. It looked as if the place had been thoroughly searched. Moving further in, he found the stairs and crept quietly up.

The scene upstairs matched that of down. Every drawer and cupboard was open with their contents strewn about. The white sheets on the bed had blood smears on them, but the amount was more in line with split lips and a nosebleed than a machete attack.

After quietly radioing back to Deacon, Canetti headed back downstairs and stood behind the closed front door. On his command, Deacon whistled to make the guard look in the direction of the trees. As he did so, Canetti quietly opened the door and raised his pistol. The first the guard knew of his visitor was feeling the cold metal ring of the barrel against his neck as a hand grabbed his jacket collar. He was dragged back into the center as he saw a group of men in camouflage gear run towards him.

Within seconds, he'd been disarmed, had a gag across his mouth, had his hands cable-tied behind his back, and his legs tied to the chair he was sitting on.

Canetti loosened his gag before putting the tip of a very sharp knife an inch away from the guard's left eyeball and said, 'Habla usted Inglés?' *Do you speak English?*

'Vete a la mierda,' *Fuck off,* the guard gasped.

Canetti moved the knife in a blur. Before the pain began to register, the tip of the guard's ear was lying on his shirt. As the blood began to flow, the pain arrived, and the guard drew breath to scream. With a hand clasped over his mouth, the scream changed to a gurgle, and before it had finished, the tip of his other ear joined the first.

The look of horror on his faced went from panic to sheer terror when Canetti sliced through the cord holding his pants up and made it apparent his testicles were next.

Suddenly the guard couldn't stop talking.

No, he didn't speak English. Yes, the Doctor had been taken. Why? Because she was a filthy American spy. Where was she?

At that stage, he became reluctant to speak again until a little more pressure was applied. Canetti moved the knife until it was over his left hand and pressed the razor-sharp blade down onto the brown skin of the knuckle joint on his pinky finger. Gently applying more pressure until the skin split, Canetti looked at the guard and just raised an eyebrow in question.

Realizing what was coming next, the guard capitulated.

He sputtered out she was being held in a barn by a farm about a mile north of a tiny enclave called Raya, four miles further up a narrow muddy track at the far end of the village.

Canetti then asked how many guards were there, and the answer wasn't so good.

The track to Raya was single width and badly potholed. Deacon didn't want to take vehicles as the risk of being detected or trapped was too high. The potholes were now filled with water, and it was almost impossible to see which were shallow or deep. Visibility was limited to mere yards due to the incessant rain. Leaving the guard securely tied and gagged, Deacon left Stockwell with the two vehicles as he, Martock, Canetti, Roberts, and Maričić set out on foot, fully armed.

The track was winding but relatively flat with parts of the forest encroaching over it. The five of them walked silently, two each side, fully alert and ready for anything, with Roberts up ahead, scouting. The heat and humidity had been making them sweat. The constant flies and bugs flying around had been annoying, but the rain had changed that. Now it was cooler and the rain provided sound cover. The bug spray they'd brought with them and covered themselves in had worked, but not well enough, and they each had dozens of bites and stings on their hands and faces. At one stage they heard an engine revving, and they ducked down into the thick undergrowth just in time before a battered old truck came up from behind them and quickly disappeared noisily in the rain on towards Raya. In the back were three bandits, heavily armed and smoking some form of drugs judging by the sweet smell given off. Their hats were drawn tightly down over their faces and shoulders in a failing attempt to keep dry.

'Raw coco leaves.'

'Huh?'

'What they were smoking … raw coco leaves. Really rough taste but gives them a high,' Maričić said. 'Also keeps the bugs away, I hear, although the rain is doing that. Or maybe after a few pulls, you give up caring,' he joked.

Coming up towards the last bend before a clearing, Roberts stopped and waved them off the road. Making the last few hundred yards through the trees and careful not to make a disturbance, they spread out and looked at the area of Raya ahead.

There were two tents and four wooden huts, three quite large and one smaller but further away. From where they were hiding it looked like two of the larger huts were for accommodation as they could see what seemed to be bunks and dirty mattresses through the open doorway. The other large one had smoke coming from a steel flue, and there was a smell of cooking food hanging in the air. The small one looked to be some form of headquarters as two guards were standing outside. The roof had several aerials protruding, and next to it was a diesel generator under a lean-to shelter.

One of the tents was a washing and shower station while the other looked to be a toilet block. The truck that earlier passed them on the track was parked near the small hut.

A rough count showed over a dozen armed men who were lazing around undercover.

Cursing as the numbers had now increased, the team moved around past this clearing and followed the thinner track on towards the farm not yet visible.

Keeping within the tree line took longer, but they still made good time as they finally approached the farm. At one stage a man was seen walking briskly towards them, head bowed to keep the worst of the rain off, and wearing a wide-brimmed jungle hat.

He was almost on Deacon before he released someone was standing still in front of him. The surprise on his face was legendary as he suddenly saw a pair of boots connected to legs blocking his path. As he looked up and began to draw breath to shout, Deacon reacted and drove the tip of the ten-inch blade of his K-Bar knife up into the chest cavity. As the kidnapper's lungs collapsed and his shout turned into a feeble gasp, Deacon twisted the blade and re-thrust it deeper, this time slicing his pumping heart in two. With an astonished look in his eyes, his body slowly collapsed, and as Deacon pulled his knife back out, the rain began washing away the blood pumping out of his chest and down his shirtfront.

Leaving the dead guard stashed under cover against a tree, Deacon and the team crept on. As they neared the edge of the tree line, to the left was a small barn with an open door. From where they were, it looked empty of people, but they could see sacks of something unknown stacked inside. To the right was a second, larger barn with double doors, currently closed. This one had two armed guards standing outside, sheltering from the rain and smoking a cigarette. Further in the distance about three hundred yards away was what appeared to be a wooden and stone-built building. This was the farmhouse itself.

The heavy rain clouds had already darkened the early evening sky, and full nighttime darkness would soon be on them. That actually provided an advantage Deacon thought as he and the team had night-vision-goggles. Coupled with the noise and opaqueness of the rain, as well as human nature to try and remain dry whenever possible, it would help in getting close to the building unseen.

As the final rays of daylight faded, Deacon sent Canetti closer to the rear of the barn to see what was inside, while he sent Roberts to reconnoiter the farm building.

Twenty minutes later, just as the last faint images of the clouds disappeared, both Canetti and Roberts returned. Looking through the cracks in the walls of the building, Canetti had seen a woman tied by her wrists to a beam. She was naked and had dried blood on her face and body. Her left arm looked broken with her hand bent at an unnatural angle. Three men were drinking inside the barn with her. The only other guards were the pair outside at the front of the building.

Roberts reported another dozen or so men milling about around the farm, all seemingly armed. There was also an open-back truck with a .50 caliber machine gun mounted on it. Deacon rubbed his hands over his chin and murmured, 'Shit four times as many targets as intelligence had found. Damn the CIA's estimates.'

Setting his radio to conference mode to include all his team, including Stockwell, Deacon said, 'Fuck it. Sorry guys, the intel I was given was crap. This is going to be a complete shit storm. Ideas?'

Four minutes later, they had a rough plan they all agreed on. No one was willing to leave the doctor there, but everyone knew the risks involved.

First, they needed to clear their exit path. Initially, stealth and silence would be the key to all of this. They needed to eliminate the opposition quickly and silently. If the alarm went up, they'd be overwhelmed just by numbers as well as being boxed in.

The five of them headed back to the clearing at Raya and set themselves up in the surrounding trees. The rain stopped almost as suddenly as it had begun and within seconds the entire place was alive with the sound of nighttime insects. Between the screeches and calls of the monkeys and added to the constant buzz and humming of insects, although their rifles were all automatics and had suppressors attached, Deacon did wonder if even any regular shots would be heard.

Deacon knew the South American jungle has always been an inhospitable place for man to exist in. Between just about every biting insect known to exist living there and finding westerners tasty, the number of dangerous things roaming or crawling about was beyond belief. From poisonous snakes that blended perfectly with the tree branches, to deadly scorpions and spiders with venom strong enough to kill you in agony within seconds. Even many of the plants were poisonous if you should brush up against them. The complete team had carried out various training exercises in jungles, but none of them enjoyed jungle warfare.

With their NVGs fitted, the surroundings took on a ghostly green glow. The moment the rain stopped the land had started steaming, the heat was back, and the humidity was off the scale. Working on the combination of surprise and speed they each sighted a man wandering around, along with a spare or second, and then waited until all five of them had confirmed targets in their sights. Then on Deacon's command, they loosed of two shots each before quickly switching to their secondary targets and firing again.

Nine of the twelve went down that way, silently, and before the remaining three knew what had hit them. One of the remaining started to shout before two shots, one from Martock to the head and another from Roberts to his chest cut him off.

As the two remaining guards rushed out of the small hut and raised their weapons trying to find a target to aim for, a fusillade of silenced shots from all five of them ripped their chests open, and they quickly joined their dead comrades, having not fired a shot in anger.

Swiftly checking the tents and huts to confirm they'd not missed anyone, Deacon heard the soft plops of suppressed handguns from his team making sure a couple of the wounded wouldn't pose a problem.

Radioing Stockwell to bring one of the Land Cruisers up as far as the Raya clearing, but without using headlights and keeping the revs low to reduce noise, the five of them headed back up the track towards the farm at a sprint.

The two guards standing outside were still smoking with the sweet smell of burning coco leaves drifting around. It was now totally dark, but the red glow of their cigarettes gave them away. Setting Martock and Roberts one each as a target, the other three approached the barn from the guard's blind side.

On Deacon's command, Martock and Roberts fired one shot each, and with two puffs of pink mist, two more were down. Quickly running to the double doors just as a woman's scream was heard loudly, Deacon raised his goggles and peered through the gap between the doors.

The woman was awake and crying. She had multiple cuts and grazes, but most of the blood on her body had dried. She had tears running down her face as one of the kidnappers was pressing the lit end of a cigar to her breast. Every time it touched her skin she screamed, but when he deliberately puffed it to a bright redness and placed it on her nipple, she screamed and passed out.

Of the two other guards, one had his back to Deacon and was just enjoying the show. The other was also enjoying watching the doctor being hurt and was leaning against the wall, smoking and holding a bottle of what looked to be whiskey in one hand while gently rubbing a growing erection with the other.

Gently sliding the blade of his knife into the gap between the doors, Deacon raised the thin wooden beam holding the doors shut. As the doors swung open, Canetti and Maričić fired twice each at the two next to the doctor. Both went down instantly, and Maričić swung around to take out the third and last man. This one, half out of his mind on coco leaves and whiskey, and with his mind full of the rape he was about to have had his mouth open in total surprise as the first shot entered his forehead, followed by a second to his throat.

Keying his bone mic, Deacon radioed, 'Target secure.'

Ripping the shirt off one of the dead kidnappers, Deacon and Martock used it to wipe off some of the blood that had sprayed onto the semi-conscious doctor before cutting her down.

'Nina! NINA! We're here to take you home. We're Americans. Lisa Kingman sent us. You're going home,

Nina,' Deacon said while rubbing her good hand to try and get her attention.

'Hom . . . home?'

'Yes, Nina. You're safe now. We're taking you home!'

Her eyes were trying to focus, but she was still only half-conscious and obviously in immense pain.

Her clothes were nowhere to be seen, so wrapping her up in a blanket from his backpack, Canetti shouldered his weapon, and, carrying her in his arms, they all moved out and headed back towards Raya and a waiting Stockwell.

Carrying her as gently as he could in his open arms, Deacon wrapped another blanket tightly around her and Canetti, before taking up defensive positions as they headed back to safety.

They'd gone less than a hundred yards when a burst of automatic rifle fire somewhere in front of them towards Raya added to the chattering, screeching night.

As they glanced back behind at the farm, the doors crashed open, and heavily armed men started running out.

9

Trapped in the middle between two parties, the staccato sounds of an assault rifle firing from in front of them echoed again through the trees, with at least a couple of rounds coming close. Rushing ahead, Roberts took off at a run before turning and crashing through the undergrowth shouting and firing as he did so.

Having drawn the fire towards him, Roberts now turned, dived behind cover, and laid down a withering fusillade in the general direction of where the shooting was coming from, while Martock tried to identify the target through his 'scope. Finally seeing what looked to be the outline shape of a person moving, Martock loosed off a number of shots below and to the left and right of it.

Calling on the others to cease firing, Roberts crept towards the possible target, weapon at the ready. As he neared it, he could hear gasping for breath. Circling around, he came in from the rear and found the armed man on his side, almost unconscious with blood escaping from large chest and leg wounds. Removing the injured guy's rifle, Roberts removed the magazine before throwing both further into the trees. If the guy didn't die in the next few minutes, at least he wouldn't be causing them any more harm.

While Roberts had been running for the trees, Stockwell had heard the gunfire. Jamming his foot on the gas pedal, and with the engine screaming, he roared into Raya before slewing the Land Cruiser into a one-eighty turn and reversing at speed up towards his colleagues, ready for a quick getaway.

Canetti and Stockwell tried to look after the doctor after laying her in the Land Cruiser. She was awake but not lucid. Shock had set in, and she was trembling and shivering. Wrapping another blanket around her, they tried to make her as comfortable as possible. All of the team had varying levels of rudimentary medical knowledge, with Canetti and Stockwell having more than the others, but now was not the time to clean and dress her wounds or reset bones.

Telling Stockwell to head on down and they'd all join up with the other Cruiser, Deacon ordered the others to set up a defensive position in the trees against the thugs pursuing from the farmhouse.

Their first shots started peppering the ground around them with one or two hitting the rear of Stockwell's Land Cruiser as it sped away.

With Martock, Canetti, and Roberts in the trees firing at the attacking kidnappers, Deacon and Maričić ran for cover to the right. As some of the kidnappers broke cover, the concentrated firing from the three of them brought down almost half of their pursuers. Suddenly, the truck with the .50 caliber roared into life and came hurtling down the track. Stopping, it raked fire back and forth along the tree line the three were hiding in. The amount of firepower the .50 caliber could lay down was incredible. Smaller trees and saplings were literarily blown apart. Wooden splinters flew dangerously in all directions while they could only cower under cover and watch on in horror as they lay face down in the undergrowth.

With all return fire from the tree line ceased, the truck rolled on after the escaping Land Cruiser with the remaining kidnappers running in pursuit.

As they ran past, Dean and Maričić in a crossfire position let rip, and another four went down with a fifth injured.

Leaving their other three colleagues to fend for themselves because the safety of their hostage was paramount, Deacon and Maričić sprinted along the wet slippery track towards Raya. Maričić climbed into the still warm truck that had arrived earlier, while Deacon clambered into the rear. Chasing after the .50 caliber truck, Maričić floored the accelerator, and their vehicle bounced and jolted down the track lurching and careening from one pothole to another as Deacon tried to take aim over the cabin roof.

Deacon was still hanging on for dear life as they quickly closed the distance between them and the truck. The lead driver hadn't realized he was being chased, and the guard on the machine gun had been so intent of getting the Land Cruiser in his sights he hadn't thought to look behind.

The shots from Deacon went wild, but close enough for the gunman to take note. Shouting something to his driver, he began to swing the heavy weapon around just as Maričić got close enough.

Deacon yelled for Maričić to bear away as the barrel of the .50 caliber swung dangerously close, and he pulled the pins from two grenades.

Almost dropping one as Maričić turned sharply left into the undergrowth, Deacon tossed both to land at the feet of the gunman. With a look of terror in his eyes, the gunman tried to scramble down and grab the grenades as they bounced and rolled around the metal base of the truck. Deacon merely smiled, waved a mock salute, and rapidly dropped to the floor of his truck to protect himself from the blast.

Maričić had driven less than twenty feet away when the two grenades exploded within a fraction of a second of each other. The blast didn't just wreck the other truck – it disintegrated it. There must have been other explosives stored, which added to the explosion because Deacon and Maričić's vehicle was lifted almost a yard off the ground before crashing back down, almost throwing Deacon out with the impact. Luckily the angle of their truck while in the air saved both of them from the heat blast, but their engine failed, and they bounced to a stop as a black cloud rose from all that remained of the other truck.

Eventually, after repeated turning over, their engine started again, and they turned and raced back towards their other colleagues. Miraculously all three had all survived the .50 caliber gunfire. Martock and Canetti had small wooden splinters embedded deeply in their arms and legs, but Roberts didn't have a scratch.

Climbing aboard, Maričić turned and headed down the track towards where Stockwell would be waiting along with the second Land Cruiser.

Five minutes later, after abandoning their damaged vehicle and shooting out its tires for good measure, both Land Cruisers were making as fast progress as possible while Deacon called Hank and ordered him to get immediate flight clearance for when they arrive.

The radio in Deacon's ear suddenly squawked, and Roberts said, 'Uh ho boss. We've got company.'

Glancing out the bullet-scarred rear window, Deacon saw two more Land Cruisers had joined the pursuit and were opening fire.

Kicking out the rear window, Martock and Roberts returned fire at the lead vehicle and smiled as their rounds found its target. While some entered the engine bay, at least half a dozen entered the cab. With the driver dead or seriously injured, the vehicle crashed off the track before hitting trees and catching fire.

The second chaser started opening fire, but both of Deacon vehicles were now on a better section of track and were almost back in La Coromata. Just before they entered the village, the road snaked sharp left then right. Stockwell's Cruiser was in front, along with Deacon and the injured Nina. Maričić was driving the second with Roberts, Canetti, and Martock. As they raced around the blind corners, Maričić slammed the brakes on, and he and Roberts ran to the left with Canetti and Martock to the right.

As the second chasing Cruiser came racing around the corner, the driver saw Maričić's vehicle in front, blocking the track. Jamming on his brakes he stopped just in time to be hit by concentrated crossfire. The driver and colleague in front were killed instantly. The three in the rear were all injured.

Climbing back into their own vehicle after disabling the other vehicle by shooting out its tires, Maričić soon caught up with Stockwell before both Cruisers continued racing back along Highway 12.

With tires screeching as they rounded the last corner, they juddered to a stop just feet from the aircraft steps. Hank was waiting. The engines were already warm and on tick-over. Stockwell and Roberts careful carried Nina up the steps and moved her to the rear of the aircraft. Hank had already altered two of the leather seats into a makeshift bed and had a first-aid kit, towels and warm water standing by.

As the others raced up the steps, Hank had the Gulfstream ready to roll, and the moment the last foot was inside the fuselage, he hit the button to fold the stairs up and close the door.

Near the airport entrance, two police cars suddenly put their flashing roof lights on and headed towards the aircraft just as the control tower radioed Hank and rescinded flight clearance. By now, the Gulfstream was already moving towards a taxiway, and without a moment's pause, Hank shouted, 'Hold on,' as he opened the throttles and the aircraft leaped forward before almost skidding into a turn onto the main runway.

With throttles jammed to the stops, the aircraft thundered along the runway until Hank gently pulled back on the yoke, and the wheels left the blacktop.

Once safely airborne and climbing rapidly through the clouds heading north, Maričić began cleaning and dressing Nina's multiple cuts and burns. He then gave her strong painkillers before taping up her wrist to minimize movement. She would need the arm and hand X-rayed before trying to reset the bones. In the meantime, Roberts was warming chicken soup for her.

Deacon sat quietly talking to her as she ate.

'What happened? How did you get found out?'

'I don't know. Nothing really. Nothing different. When I first arrived just over five years ago, the locals were very wary. They didn't trust outsiders and especially Americans. They knew I was American Latino, but gradually they realized I was here with the church on a mercy mission and here to help. I started just working with women and children. The local priest knew nothing about the CIA, so he fully supported me.'

'Go on.'

'Then one of the village elders became ill, and I tended him, along with the priest. Saved his life, and I think that helped break the ice. Soon I was getting people from the adjoining villages coming for help, but still only the

70

women and their children. I was reporting back anything I heard about drug shipments. All in code and covered under certain drug names and quantities. Then there was the fire.'

'Fire? What happened?'

'The chemicals the drug people use are highly flammable. Never knew exactly what happened, but one day about a year after I'd arrived there was suddenly an explosion in the jungle. Turned out one of their processing plants had exploded and caught fire. Over a dozen workers killed, and almost two dozen burned and injured. I ignored the guards waving their weapons around telling me to leave and started treating the injured. It seems one of the injured was the son of one of the leaders, and overnight I became trusted. Never told anything officially, but suddenly any males who were injured would turn up for treatment. The medical hut was paid for by the CIA but funded through the local church so was seen as Red Cross money. I was always so very careful. I never asked questions, even though sometimes it made it hard to work out how an injury had occurred for me to treat it.'

'So where did you get your info from,' Deacon asked.

'Usually, from the kids and their mothers. The kids would often hear what the men were saying and would repeat it to me, but I always pretended not to show any interest. My cellphone is modified and records everything said. At night I would listen to the recordings and delete those not interesting. Then I'd type and send text messages to my parents supposedly living in Puerto Rico. The phone never displayed the 'hidden' recordings and would only send them as an encrypted message when sending a standard 'clean' message. Both would be sent at the same time, and the encrypted one would be immediately deleted, so would never show on the phone.

My parents actually live in Connecticut, but they would still get my genuine texts, while the recorded messages were passed directly to Langley.'

'So what changed, and did they seize your phone?'

'No, the phone is still in the hut I think, so it wasn't the reason for their suspicion. And I don't know what changed. There wasn't any change in routine, everything was just normal. I was arranging new vaccine shots for the kids in the villages when suddenly everyone started cold-shouldering me. I really have no idea why. That was about three weeks ago. Then I was presented with a 24-hour guard outside the medical center. For my own protection, I was told. Then I was questioned by Raul, the local leader. When I didn't answer his questions properly and admit anything, I suddenly had my arms pinned to my back and slapped hard across the face. I think I must have passed out because when I awoke, I was naked and tied to a post.'

'Were you raped?'

'Not while I was conscious, no. Although I was tortured and kept naked to intimidate me. The guards would come close and leer. Some would touch and grope my breasts and touch me down there,' she said, looking embarrassed. 'The leader, this Raul, he was the worst. He kept threatening to rape me and then pass me to his men for their pleasure. I was smacked and beaten. Every so often, Raul would grab my breasts and sometimes bite them. He really hurt, but it seemed to excite him. Then they burned me with cigars. Once I must have passed out because when I woke up I was being pulled back upright and tied to the post again. I don't know what they'd done, but I was sore down there, and one or more of them might have raped me while I was unconscious, but I'm not sure. They pulled some of my fingernails out, and they kept saying I was a CIA bitch, and they were going to kill me. They twisted my arm behind me until I felt my wrist snap. I fainted when that happened. Today was another cigar session, but I don't really know what happened.'

'Well, just relax. You're safe now, and rest assured Raul won't be hurting anyone again. In fact virtually all of them there won't be hurting anyone again. Try and get some sleep,' Deacon said before tucking the blanket in close to her, turning the overhead lamp down, and moving away.

10

Washington

The tension in the air at the mission review meeting the following morning was palpable. The Admiral, Mitch, and Charles Ingram were present, and Deacon wasn't holding back.

'You fucked up!' he directed to Ingram. 'Your department's intel was lousy, and you almost got us killed. You claimed there were six or so kidnappers? Try thirty-five, pal!'

'How dare you speak to me like that! I'm the direct––'

'I don't give a fuck who you are. Your department supplied bullshit information, and it almost got a number of us killed, along with your agent.'

Raising his hands in a pacifying gesture, the Admiral tried to quell the heightened tension in the room. 'Okay, let's all of us calm down. As always, John, you and your team have exceeded expectations. You are all home safe and sound, and I'm glad to say your mission was a complete success,' he said, looking towards Deacon. Turning his head towards Ingram he continued, 'Charles, it seems your intel was badly lacking and only by the grace of God did the mission go according to plan. I think you owe the team an apology.'

Standing abruptly, Ingram snarled, 'The fuck I will,' before grabbing his briefcase and walking towards the door, muttering *'I was against this fucking mission from the start. Go fuck yourselves,'* before slamming the door behind him, leaving the three of them looking on, open-mouthed.

Finally, the Admiral said, 'Well, he's having a number of issues in his department. He's due to retire shortly, and I guess that date can't come soon enough.'

With the tension now eased, Deacon gave a detailed account of precisely what had taken place.

After he finished, Mitch took to the floor to update them on the latest updates concerning the ice station. He said, 'Simon Clark has reported our friends in Swedish intelligence have confirmed there was no evidence or even any suggestion of anything wrong at the last communication call. The call was between the ice station and its base in Trondheim and was being monitored routinely by them. There was a lot of static and interference in the air that day, but no more than was expected as there is always a lot around the equinox. Whatever happened to them must have happened quickly. There was no alarm raised at all. However, the Swedes did report a sudden increase in intense static that they couldn't explain. Lasted for a little under five hours then quietened down again.'

'Man-made?'

'They report it could have been, but they can't be absolutely sure. One other strange occurrence. Might be completely unrelated, but at least two Russian senior experts in the field of strip mining seem to have disappeared. Two completely separate companies are now advertising open positions to be filled. Assuming, as we were informed before, that some sort of undersea mining has been taking place, Clark said he started an investigation into how many companies in Russia have that specialist knowledge and capability. On first pass, it seems there are six that have undersea mining experience ranging from a little to a reasonable amount, and two of them are the ones now recruiting,' Mitch finished.

Just before the meeting ended, the Admiral confirmed he would be formally requesting the NSA, CIA, and the FBI look into each of these companies and report back as soon as possible.

Tired from his recent mission, Deacon was happy to be heading home. Arriving back at his Palisades apartment a short time later, he parked in his usual spot before grabbing the bag of groceries. Arriving very late last night, an empty fridge had greeted him, so he'd stocked up on the way home today. The quietness of his place suited him. It was an upper floor unit with two large bedrooms and a large lounge and kitchen. A full-length balcony gave excellent views across the Potomac.

Just as he was walking towards the main doors, he saw Mirabel waiting for him. Mirabel, a renter from the ground floor, was a little older than he was and divorced. They'd become friends soon after he'd moved in, and he left her a spare key to keep an eye on the place and water the plants when he was traveling. They would often have a meal together or drinks, but Deacon had made it clear he was happy to be a friend, but nothing more. She, on the other hand, being a good looking blonde in her mid-forties was always flirting with him and made it obvious she was happy to remain friends, but wouldn't complain if their relationship went further.

Flicking imaginary fluff away from his jacket, she looked directly into his eyes and said, 'Hi John. Back again. Can I persuade you to come down to dinner tonight? I cook a mean lasagna.'

Knowing her cooking was too excellent to refuse, Deacon agreed a time before sprinting upstairs to get a few hours shuteye before meeting her again later.

<><><>

The following morning Deacon was up and about early. He'd already completed a ten-mile jog along the river before showering and leaving for the office. The previous evening had been fun. Mirabel's lasagna was as good as any he'd ever eaten, and a couple of toasted ciabatta rolls and a green salad were the perfect accompaniment; washed down by a particularly good Cabernet Sauvignon. She was an excellent host, always cheerful and happy. She also had what seemed to be an endless pit of rude but hilarious jokes, and within an hour any tiredness he'd had was forgotten, and he'd had tears of laughter streaming down his face.

Smiling as he tried to remember some of the jokes to tell Mitch later, he drove in and parked in his usual place under the Phylax office. Today would be all business.

Only his secretary and office manager, Gina Panaterri – an extremely experienced ex-Secret Service agent, and Martock – a close colleague from his time as a Navy SEAL knew the truth of how Phylax worked. Gina had taken on more and more of the management role, and he was happy to leave as much as possible to her. Two months prior, he'd suggested taking on an additional receptionist to assist, and Gina had interviewed three, all young females, but all security cleared. Cindy Holt was the best and had started three weeks ago.

Cindy had settled in well, and everyone seemed to like her. She was always helpful and eager to learn. She was only aware of Phylax's 'normal' business role, but John could already envisage needing to tell her more soon. Today she was being dropped off by her boyfriend, Garry Moore. Same height and build as he was, he reminded John of himself a number of years ago. Even a few of his colleagues said Garry looked like a younger version of the boss. He seemed a nice guy. He was a keep-fit personal trainer. Initially the guy had been a bit jealous of the attention Cindy had been getting from some of the men at Phylax, especially as most of them were quite fit, but John had taken him for a beer after work one day and made it clear he had a strict rule for all employees of no work romances. Since then, Garry had relaxed, and Deacon was hoping on employing some of his services to keep his team fit.

After a long, boring day completing paperwork and returning missed phone calls, the phone rang again at a little after four. A few seconds after answering it, Deacon's face lit up.

Two hours later, walking briskly through the lobby, Deacon entered the Quadrant Bar of the Ritz-Carlton Georgetown hotel. Sitting at the bar with a glass of William Heavenhill 5th Edition bourbon in his hand, talking with the attractive female server, was Major Patrick Hythe of Her Majesty's British Special Air Service (SAS). Walking over quietly, he stood behind Hythe and could hear him sweet-talking the hostess.

'Don't trust a word he says,' Deacon said loudly, 'he's riddled with gonorrhea, and his dick has already dropped off.'

Laughing, the hostess stood watching as Hythe swung round off his stool, his face like thunder before it broke into an immense smile. They hadn't met for almost five years, but within seconds it was as if they'd never been apart.

After a couple of enormous handshakes and back slaps, and with both grinning ear to ear, Deacon finally managed to say, 'Patrick, you son-of-a-gun. You're looking well. So what brings you here?'

'John, you bastard. I had her in the palm of my hand.'

'Well, that's payback for the time you did the same to me in that bar in Hereford.'

'Ah, but that little redhead was a wee bit of a lass, and anyway, she was teasing you. So, what'll be?' he said, looking back towards the server.

Asking for a glass of the same as Hythe's, Deacon waited for the first insult from Patrick.

'I see you've hardly changed a bit. Well, maybe a bit. Is that a gray hair I see?' Hythe said, pointing.

'Fuck you, pal. Anyway, you're older than me,' Deacon replied, laughing.

'That I am, mate, that I am. Would that be older and wiser?'

'Don't push it, pal. But seriously, what are you doing in my neck of the woods?'

'Currently on escort duty. One of Her Majesty's senior diplomats is headed to the British Embassy for meetings tomorrow at the White House. Normal escort staff are tied up with some royal duties, so the word went around Credenhill they were looking for a volunteer for a couple of days jolly. I thought it would be nice to get away for a few days and maybe see an old friend or two.'

'So are you free now?'

'Yup. Dropped my charge off at the embassy and don't have to be back there until noon tomorrow to escort him to the House.'

'Well, my friend, tonight the drinks are on me,' Deacon said, as they moved away from the bar to find a booth.

The next few hours passed in a flash. They had met a number of times in Iraq and Afghanistan, usually on base, but they'd also carried out numerous joint US/UK missions together. Hythe was shorter than Deacon and a few years older, but the SAS were equally as tough as Navy SEALs. In fact, many US Special Forces cross-trained with their European counterparts and vice versa. There would always be the expected inter-service rivalry, but all Special Forces knew and appreciated they were the cream of the crop – better trained and better equipped than their regular soldier counterparts. They also knew they were usually given the toughest jobs and invariably suffered the worst casualties.

Slightly unusual for a Brit, Hythe was a keen bourbon drinker, preferring the fine US version over conventional Scottish whiskey; and William Heavenhill 5th Edition was some of the best in the world. He was also one of the best field planners Deacon had ever met, and he had a black sense of humor. When they'd originally met, almost eight years before, Deacon had thought of Hythe as a typical stiff-lipped Brit, and Hythe had seen Deacon as a loud-mouthed American. But a couple of rigorous joint training exercises together, followed by a few beers at the base O-Club soon helped the friendship to grow.

'So lately I've been based at SAS HQ at Credenhill, close to the England Welsh border. Where you came. Assigned more to running training exercises due to my experience and rank, I also get to do masses of paperwork,' Hythe said. 'I find some of the former excitement now missing, and often I reminisce about the old life,' he continued, 'and because I'm available to be called on, I often get tasked with senior diplomatic or royalty protection cover in and around London. But with most of it occurring within the UK, when a foreign trip came up, I jumped at it.'

The conversation then moved on to the official version of Phylax before progressing to how life was treating them both. Eventually, they discussed what had been happening in the Arctic, with Deacon confirming the FBI was looking into suspicious activity in Russian mining companies.

After jointly completing their second bottle of Bourbon, Hythe confirmed he'd be in Washington for two more days before returning to the UK, then taking four weeks leave owed to him.

Finally, at close to midnight, they eventually left the bar, with Hythe heading up to his room and Deacon taking an Uber home.

11

Deacon was up early and on the road before six the following morning. His inner circle team would meet him at his shooting range out towards Leesburg, about a one hour drive northwest from Washington. Previously, it had been an old isolated farm of thirty acres, with various rundown buildings.

When Deacon's father was still in the Navy and often away for weeks or months at a time, and his mother working full-time as an accountant, his parents had employed Jim and Betty Huxham to help around the house. Jim was gardener and general 'fixer-upper' while Betty cooked, cleaned, and kept the house together. To Deacon and his two sisters, it was like having extra parents. When at home or on leave, his father taught him everything he knew about sailing and navigation, while Jim taught him woodcraft. By the time Deacon and his sisters had grown and were planning on leaving the family home they had needed to say goodbye to double the family most children grow up having. After Deacon's parents finally retired, Jim and Betty moved on but always stayed in touch. When Deacon started Phylax he wanted and needed a private shooting range. The disused farm at Leesburg suited him perfectly. Remote and not too large to manage, the farmhouse needed restoring, but overall it was in reasonable condition. Close to Washington, it was a perfect find.

One of the outbuildings was easy to convert into a training room with part of it equipped with weights and exercise equipment, with over half being turned into martial arts fighting area along with padded flooring. One of the other outbuildings was converted into accommodation, with showers and sleeping arrangements for use when required. The farmhouse itself took slightly longer to restore and modernize, but again it was worth it. With a ten-year exclusive lease on the property, all that was needed lastly was someone to live there, manage it, and keep strangers away.

Jim and Betty considered it an honor and happily became the landlords of the farm with Betty eager to cook for all her men, as she liked to consider them. Like the other employees of Phylax outside the inner circle, Jim and Betty knew Deacon and his colleagues carried out various security work and also worked with the government, but didn't know or ask for details.

All arriving in time for breakfast, Betty already had bacon, eggs, and pancakes simmering on the stove. She knew each of the inner circle well, even down to how they individually liked their coffee. After greetings all around and later with stomachs full, they went off for a couple of hours target shooting along a purpose-built shooting range hidden amongst a mass of trees ensuring privacy. All used a mixture of weapons, ranging from the M4A1 standard issue assault rifle through to various submachine guns, with targets set at various ranges.

They also used conventional terrorist weapons such as the classic Kalashnikov AK-47 and the newer AK-74, and AK-15, and a multitude of pistols – some with, and some without suppressors. Three of them, Martock, Deacon himself, and Stockwell, were also good snipers, ranked in order of ability. The three of them would usually have a target shootout match at 800, 1000, and 1200 yards. At the shorter distance, all three were very similar, but their skills begin to show at the farthest ranges. As usual, Martock won with Deacon and Stockwell managing an equal third. After whistles, backslapping, and promises by the two losers to pay for that evening's beer, they headed into the indoor fighting area. First, they spent an hour on the exercise mats covering conventional hand-to-hand combat practice, including disarming someone with a gun or knife. Later, by the use of movable wooden walls to simulate various-shaped buildings, they could simulate various attack and hostage rescue scenarios. Changing to customized weapons firing rubber bullets, they all suffered multiple impact bruises, but Betty over-delivered that evening as she always did with an enormous beef roast dinner that any top restaurant would have been proud to serve, and any aches and pains from the day were quickly forgotten or washed away with a beer or two.

The following morning after another hearty breakfast, he split his men into two teams with one person from each team called the fox and given a thirty-minute lead to head off into the woods and evade capture. The teams would try and track down their targets, and the winners were the team to capture the opposing team's fox first. There were no prizes for this, just bragging rights, but both sides were determined to win.

Finally, after a lunch of sandwiches, meats, cheeses, and dessert, washed down with copious amounts of coffee, and stated as 'light' by Betty's standards, but filling by anyone else's, they each returned home.

Deacon headed into the Pentagon for a late afternoon update meeting with Mitch and the Admiral.

'I've collated the information back from the CIA and FBI,' Mitch said, taking his cue from the Admiral and opening the meeting. 'Out of a total of over a hundred mostly legitimate mining or mining-related companies identified previously there are six with the experience and knowhow for undersea strip or surface mining. Two of them are currently advertising for mining staff, which would typically make you think they might be involved, but being the two missing experts are from those same two companies we believe that clears them.

'The two others that stand out are the Ural Mineral Company Ltd and its partial subsidiary Poteryannoye Sokrovishche OOO – a Russian Limited Liability Company. A further small subsidiary company – Lost Treasures – is partly owned by the Ural Mineral Company Ltd, and various other investors and shell companies, but we can't trace whom. Both these two – Poteryannoye and Lost Treasures – need more examination. Both have registered addresses in Moscow, but these seem to be just small offices. Probably just a dummy plaques on wall type address used for mail drops, or similar. General Dreiberg has attached a note to these reports stating both companies seem legitimate on paper, but something doesn't feel right about them. He has asked our Embassy in Moscow to request information from the Russian government – normal investor type information – but so far, Moscow is blocking them.'

Turning to Deacon, the Admiral said, 'John, the president has asked if you would go in and have a look? We have to be careful. Any use of military forces would be quickly stamped down on, and quite rightly so. Moscow knows we are interested in these companies, but they are civilian-run, although we are trying to discover what ties and links there are back to the Russian government. But we do need to keep this particularly low-key, and he really doesn't want to involve any Embassy staff more than he already has. The worry is the Russians are currently looking for any reason to make us reduce our staffing levels over there, and any form of diplomatic incidence allows them to revoke some of our people.'

Stroking his chin while deep in thought, finally, Deacon answered.

'Please tell the president I'll be happy to take this on, on our standard terms, of course. Two heads are better than one, but I'll come back to you on that,' he said.

12

Moscow

Sitting in the Air France Business Lounge in Charles de Gaulle airport, Deacon was sipping a beer. After meeting with Mitch and the Admiral, Deacon had called Patrick Hythe at the British Embassy. After waiting almost fifteen minutes to be connected, Hythe finally came onto the phone.

'Sorry pal, was in a meeting. What can I do for you?'

'You said you're bored with routine paperwork and running training exercises, and you also said you had vacation time coming up. Yes?'

'Correct.'

'Four or five days all expenses paid trip to Moscow in three days' time of interest?'

'Where do we meet?'

'I'll get Gina to send you the details. Bring a coat – it's snowy there,' Deacon finished before hanging up.

Getting Hythe on board had been a simple choice. Both he and Hythe spoke passable Russian as well as some Arabic – essential skills considering both the UK and US Governments expected the SEALs and SAS to be deployed sometime either to the former Soviet Union or to the melting pot of trouble collectively known as the Middle East. Both governments ensured their warriors had at least rudimentary basic languages skills for use in the event of injury or capture. Arabic was a much harder language to learn, and Hythe could speak it far better than Deacon, but that was unlikely to be put to the test on this mission.

Now having flown in overnight on Delta from Washington, he was just killing time waiting for Hythe's flight to arrive from Heathrow before they would take Air France to Sheremetyevo International Airport, located only 18 miles northwest of central Moscow.

Ninety minutes later they were sitting in business class in seats 4A and B, on the three-hour forty-five-minute flight. Initially stopped and questioned by Russian Federal Customs Service as to the nature of their visit, they were finally cleared after supplying their pre-planned cover story of attending Securexpo, the international exhibition of fire and security systems, based at the All-Russian Exhibition Center in downtown Moscow. Deacon also had meetings already arranged to promote Phylax with two Russian companies with an international presence and executives that occasionally traveled to the US on business.

With the relevant entry stamps in their passports and after donning their heavier coats against the cold Moscow spring chill, they grabbed their bags and headed to the taxi cab rank before catching a cab downtown to their hotel, the Ritz-Carlton, located close to the Kremlin and Red Square.

Within ten minutes of arriving, after a quick and efficient check-in, followed by dropping their bags in their rooms, they were striding out to find somewhere for a late lunch.

They planned to attend the exhibition and spend most of the remaining time acting like tourists. Deacon would attend his two meetings, but otherwise, the idea was to do as little as possible to raise any interest in themselves. Lunch over, they spent the remainder of the afternoon looking around the usual tourist sites of the grounds of the Kremlin and Cathedral Square, Lenin's Mausoleum, and the incredible St Basil's Cathedral.

Dusk comes early to Moscow this time in the year, and by six o'clock, the sky was black except for the clouds full of snow. Heading up to Lubyanka Square, they saw the floodlit Lubyanka building, the massive yellow brick structure in the neo-baroque style, now looking slightly less menacing than when it housed the headquarters of the famous KGB.

Even the name of the KGB struck fear into most Russians. It was one of the concerns Deacon and Hythe had long carried, the fear that any action inside the former Soviet Union could end up, if captured, in the torture rooms below ground in this famous structure. Once detained, few ever left alive.

The KGB translates to the Committee for State Security. Its remit covered internal security, intelligence, and the secret police. Its powers extended to every citizen of the former USSR and it was famed for its tenacity and ruthlessness in hunting down subversives and both internal and external threats to the motherland of Russia. The organization was finally disbanded in 1991 after the dissolution of the Soviet Union, being converted and absorbed into its new form, the Federal Security Service (FSB), or Federalnaya Sluzhba Bezopasnosti.

For almost twenty minutes, the two of them walked around like any typical visitors often backtracking and regularly looking around. Although this made them stick out to some as tourists, it allowed them to carefully check they weren't being followed or under any type of surveillance.

Secure in the knowledge they weren't being shadowed, they headed towards the northern area just inside the ring road first by taxi and then by bus before walking the remainder. Dressed as they were like locals wearing jeans, hats, and heavy-duty coats, they blended in quickly, and nobody paid them any attention.

'This is at least the twelfth time I've been to Moscow, and it's amazing how much the place has changed,' Patrick said. 'Everybody used to keep their heads down and stay as private as possible when walking along. It was so drab and miserable. No color. Everything just drab and gray. Now it's so different and so much better. Apart from some of the shop and street signs still in Cyrillic, you could be in any major city anywhere in the world now. But only here in the central business district. Head more than a few miles outside the ring road, and you go back in time at least fifty years.'

'It's my first time here. What were your previous visits for?'

'Only once expecting trouble – we'd had tangible evidence an attack was planned against the Embassy, so a squad of us was sent to help protect it. Luckily, nothing came of it. The other times were in my current role as a diplomatic escort – escorting the Foreign Secretary or the Ambassador to the Embassy,' Hythe continued. 'It's great to see how the place has changed.'

After changing direction twice more, they arrived at a nondescript carriage gated entrance on Ulitsa Kuznetskiy. Walking past, they glanced in through the closed black wrought iron gate at over two hundred small brass plaques, each measuring roughly four inches by two, seen mounted against the gray cement wall of an entrance to a small office inside a dirty courtyard.

Standing there at the paper-strewn gateway from the sidewalk, the office looked unused. There were no lights in the windows, and a large number of envelopes lay on the step outside. Opening the outer gate, the hinges creaked as they stepped into the dimly lit courtyard. Approaching the office door all that could be heard was a dog barking. Twice Deacon knocked on the door to no effect. Hythe grasped the door handle and tried to turn it.

It was locked solid. Deacon clenched his knuckles, ready to knock one final time when a guttural voice close behind them made him stop.

13

'What do you want?' a deep voice said in Russian. 'This is a private area. Get out.' They both turned in time to see a tall, muscular guy dressed in drab gray, holding a baseball bat in one hand and the lead of a ferocious-looking guard dog in the other. The dog had its teeth bared and was straining against his harness, but wasn't making a noise. It looked extremely dangerous.

Hythe addressed the man in flawless Russian, 'We are looking for the offices of the Ural Mineral Company Ltd or for Poteryannoye Sokrovishche Obschestvo.'

'Not here.'

'But this is their address?'

'Not here, now go,' he said menacingly extending the length of the dog's lead and gently swinging the bat.

Neither Deacon or Hythe was carrying any sort of weapon, and although both knew they could easily overpower the guard, the dog was another matter. It just stood there, teeth bared, poised, and watching their every move. These dogs were trained not to bark or growl, merely to attack and kill. Once let loose, it would attack the soft tissue of stomach and throat – areas where it could very easily cause significant bodily damage and death. Without even a club or knife between them they both knew they didn't have a chance.

Walking away, Deacon said, 'Well, it did seem too easy that he'd let us in. We need to get into that office. The guard answered too quickly. He's hiding something.

You don't happen to have any drugged meat for the dog in your pocket, do you?'

'I didn't get a full view of the door lock, but it looks to be a pretty tough one to pick. By what I could see it looks to be one of the latest high-security versions. Fancy a little trip? I think I've got just the man for you,' Hythe said.

Heading west, they walked to the Pushkinskaya Metro station and caught the Tagansko-Krasnopresnenskaya Line east, signposted to the final destination at Kotelniki. This was away from the regular tourist areas, and the metro train reflected this. Just about every square inch of the carriages was covered in graffiti, mostly against the current government and its leader, President Viktor Kalygin. Some of the paint and markings had been partly erased, but it looked to be a never-ending job for those tasked with keeping the trains clean. The seats were cloth-covered, with many rips and tears, and the floor was awash in discarded rubbish and fast food containers. It reminded Deacon of the worst aspects of the New York underground. The further from the center of Moscow they traveled, the filthier and more dilapidated the stations became. This was clearly not the Moscow advertised in the colorful holiday brochures.

Twice en-route, they stopped and waited for a subsequent train, making it easier to check if they had a tail, but none was apparent. By the time the train reached the end of its route at Kotelniki, twelve miles south-east of Moscow center, most passengers had already left. The elevators were not working, and the two of them walked up the filthy steps, stepping out into a dark semi-residential area into a mixture of falling rain and sleet.

It took Hythe a few moments to orient himself.

'This way,' he said, gesturing along one of the darkened streets to the left. They now had a three-mile walk to a particular tenement building near the center of the Kapotnya District. With few working streetlights, it was awkward to see where they were walking. The sidewalk was pot marked with loose flagstones and holes, and often they stumbled and almost fell. The 18 or 20 story high tenement apartment blocks all looked identical in the dark. All were an unpainted concrete gray. Many had large areas of mold showing. Most were very dark and dismal, with few lights showing. It reminded Deacon of the worst examples he'd seen in old Soviet propaganda films. Everything was completely colorless. Even the few lights shining through windows appeared dim. Most windows were blocked by dark, heavy curtains – some possibly to keep the cold evening out, others to offer a modicum of privacy. A few of the lower ones with curtains parted gave a moment's insight into the lives of their inhabitants – a smoky, tobacco filled atmosphere where the furniture and walls all had the same nicotine-yellow staining.

Looking around, there were only a few modern cars parked. Most appeared to be beat-up old Russian models. Deacon couldn't help thinking how different this area was to the plush westernized central financial district they'd been in earlier, where every second vehicle was a BMW, Audi, or Mercedes and the shops were full of the latest British, American and Japanese products. The chance of finding an Apple store here was as remote as finding one on the moon. He couldn't believe how similar this looked in real life to the stereotypical version usually portrayed by Hollywood.

However, the lack of working streetlights in this rundown area made checking for a tail easier. One method was for one of them to wait in a darkened doorway while the other walked on. Anyone following would come into view eventually. Another way was to stop and light a cigarette. Neither of them smoked but standing in a doorway pretending to smoke allowed the luxury of looking around without looking suspicious, but the only sounds they heard was the distant hum of traffic and stray dogs barking in the distance.

Wearing dark clothes, a woolen or flat cap, along with smoking a cigarette ensured they blended in thoroughly. Crossing a darkened deserted but rubbish-strewn park, they finally arrived at the eighteen-story block they wanted. Kicking aside rubbish, used condoms, and discarded plastic syringes, Hythe said, '12th floor' and they climbed the damp, stinking stairwell. On the fourth floor, they passed a male and female heavily into each other. Both were in their teens, and the girl was leaning against the wall, a half-empty bottle of vodka in one hand, and her raised skirt and a pair of panties clasped in the other. One foot was on the floor while the other was hooked behind her boyfriend's back. He was totally oblivious to the two of them walking up the stairs as his pants were around his ankles and he was fucking her as if his life depended on it. Two male colleagues stood there watching him.

'Ah, young love,' Hythe said, 'how romantic. There she is, half out of it on gut-rot vodka with him banging her for all he's worth against the wall, feet scrabbling for purchase amongst the vomit. And look, two of his best friends waiting to have a go as well. Oh, and she's holding her panties in her free hand. Her mother must be so proud. Moscow's answer to Romeo and Juliet. And there was me thinking young people of today had no idea of romance.'

The boys hadn't noticed them at all, and the girl just smiled drunkenly at them.

Shaking their heads and laughing, the two of them carried on climbing the stairs. Reaching the fifteenth floor, they stopped and stood in the shadows of the stairwell for almost fifteen minutes to ensure they hadn't been followed, the smell of urine and vomit still ever-present in the cold air. They heard a commotion from lower down and glanced over the railings to see the three boys and girl staggering away, passing the bottle back and forth between them.

Finally, Hythe quietly said, 'If I'm not back in five or you hear any shouting, get the fuck out of here,' before silently moving off along the landing to the last apartment. With only two out of the six overhead lights working, he soon disappeared through the falling sleet.

Four minutes later, Hythe's smiling face reappeared. 'C'mon, I'll introduce you.'

As they approached the last apartment, Hythe tapped twice on the door. It opened, quickly and they were ushered inside with the door being closed and triple-locked behind them immediately. The apartment was dark and smelled of mold. A small, weasel-faced guy wearing loose-fitting clothes with a pointed nose and small-round Harry Potter type glasses squeezed by them and led them into what could loosely be called a lounge.

Hythe looked around and said, 'Lonely. This is my friend Mister White. Say hello, Lonely.'

Offering a sweaty handshake, he extended a limp hand after saying, 'Yes, Mr. Callan.'

'I didn't say shake his hand, did I? Just say hello to Mister White,' Hythe said again.

'Hello, Mister White,' the weasel-faced guy nervously said.

'Now go and put the kettle on, will you?' Hythe continued.

When they were alone again, Hythe continued, 'His real name is Sergei Dimonitrov. Best lock-smith come safecracker in all of Russia. Been on MI6's payroll for years. Does various jobs for MI6 when requested. Opens doors, safes, strongboxes, etc. Disables alarms. Quite a talent is our Sergei Dimonitrov.'

Looking around initially the apartment seemed bleak, but on closer inspection Deacon could see the entire place was covered in a fine mesh of copper wire. The walls, the ceiling, everywhere. There were also four very powerful looking computers up against one wall.

'A Faraday cage?' Deacon asked.

'Yeah, an extremely effective one. Covers the entire apartment. It's even under the flooring. All electronic emissions are contained. None can get in and none generated from any of the computers can get out. Makes the room electronically a black hole. Sergei here also has a collection of the latest high-tech electronic security locks operating either by hand or fingerprint, iris scan or other biometrics. He stays here devising ways to spoof or fool those types of locks,' Hythe says as Sergei walked back into the room with two cups of black coffee.

After explaining what he wanted him to do, Hythe drank his coffee while Sergei looked on unhappily.

'It's too soon to do it tonight, Mr. Callen. Too soon. We need to reconnoiter and examine everything first to make sure we don't get caught,' he said.

'No time for that, Lonely. It needs to be tonight. Don't worry, you'll be paid well,' Hythe replied.

At three o'clock that following morning, Deacon and Hythe were downstairs waiting for Sergei to get his old Moskvich 408 sedan car from his locked parking garage.

Scratching his chin after thinking about it for a while, Deacon finally asked, 'Why does he call you Mr. Callan, and you call him Lonely?'

'It's an old joke. Back in the sixties and seventies, there was a black and white TV series in the UK called Callan, my father used to watch. Starred Edward Woodward. I've watched old repeats of it. It was good in its time. Callan's unwashed little informant and helper called Lonely looked like Sergei does, so the name stuck. Also means he doesn't know my name. Just saves me using yet another alias.'

Just as he finished speaking, Sergei appeared driving his nondescript faded black car. It looked ready for the breakers yard, but the engine sounded ok, and the electrics mostly seemed to work. Climbing in, Deacon took the back seat while Hythe sat next to Sergei.

They headed back towards Moscow central through very light traffic. Light enough to not cause traffic delays, but busy enough, even at that hour, so as not to stand out. Like many large cities nowadays, Moscow never fully closes down overnight. After making various diverts to check they were not being tailed, they parked four streets away from Ulitsa Kuznetskiy, before exiting the vehicle and locking it. Heading on foot towards the target building, Deacon couldn't help thinking even the buildings around were grim. All very functional, but bland and boring, with little architectural difference between any of them. They appeared to have had no money spent on making them look attractive.

With few working streetlights, the entire street was quite dark. Across from the gated entrance, Deacon kept a lookout. A quick visual look confirmed the gates were now chained and padlocked. But at least the local guard was no longer there. Using a small night vision binocular pulled from his backpack, Sergei could see a small security camera located high in a darkened corner. Moving over to the gates, he clipped a small pen-like device to the gate frame, aimed it roughly at the camera and pressed a button. The device emitted pulses at a similar frequency to those generated by the camera, causing the signal to scramble. Aligning the pen device more accurately, a small but powerful infra-red laser overpowered the optics of the camera, freezing the image in its memory as a 'still' photo. Anyone monitoring the camera remotely would have seen a person walking by followed by a few seconds of interference but now a clear, non-moving picture of the courtyard.

Working on the heavy padlock, it took Sergei less than 30 seconds to open it. Passing a can of spray oil to Hythe, he instructed him to spray the hinges to stop them squeaking. Seconds later all three of them were in through the gates, while Sergei looped the chain back around to make it look undisturbed. It wouldn't pass a close inspection, but to a casual observer, the chain now looked in place.

As they approached the main door, Sergei confirmed to Hythe, 'As I thought. It's the latest Torterolo five-bolt. That's a really tough lock. These people know what they are doing'.

'But can you open it, Lonely?'

Without bothering to answer, Sergei set to work. It took him eight minutes to pick. Twice they had to stop and hide in the shadows due to people passing on the sidewalk. But the passers-by were office cleaners, tired and exhausted. Head down against the falling sleet they were just hurrying home to bed.

Finally, with a click, the lock opened. Before opening the door, Sergei ran a small ultrasonic imager around the frame. A tiny screen showed two pairs of miniature magnetic contacts in the frame structure and door. One pair were at the top, the other six inches below the lock. Using another small unit to check on polarization he commented the top one was normally open, while the lower one was normally closed. Getting two magnets from his backpack, he carefully placed them in each position with Blu-Tac.

'What's that for?' Hythe asked.

'When the door opens, one contact will close, the other will open. These magnets will stop that happening. Those contacts are connected directly to the alarm system. Any change will trigger it.'

Finally, Sergei opened the door, and all three of them moved inside.

Leaving the lights off, each of them placed a small LED light on a strap to their foreheads. Looking around, the small entrance hall contained just a table and chair. There was an alarm panel on the adjacent wall. Sergei placed a small box over the keypad. Red LED's ran through a flashing sequence, and within twenty seconds, each one changed to green. With the alarm now off, they could move around freely.

Two doors led off the entrance hall. One was already ajar and led to a toilet with a sink, faucet, and dirty floor. The other door was closed. Sergei used his ultrasonic imager again to check there was no secondary alarm before opening it.

The inner office contained a desk with telephone, two chairs, and a picture of the current president on the wall. There were no bookcases or filing cabinets, and the desk had coffee drink rings on it and smudges of food.

Sergei guessed a safe would be behind the picture and again used his ultrasonic imager to confirm there were no connections behind the picture frame. He then connected a small endoscope to a smartphone and used the images it produced to look carefully behind the edges of the picture frame. Satisfied, he finally lifted the picture off its hook, exposing a safe door, a twelve key electronic keypad, and a fingerprint scanner alongside an illuminated red LED.

Taking another spray can from his backpack, he sprayed a fine mist on the fingerprint scanner. The chemicals in the spray turned black on the small scanner screen where grease or sweat from fingers was present. He then opened a sheet of skin-colored paper with a clean plastic film attached and pressed the plastic against the scanner. He removed it and wiped the scanner surface clean, before folding the paper and plastic together.

He placed yet another small box with a screen over the keypad and activated it. A small laser traced each of the twelve keys and showed which six were commonly used, along with the star and hash key. It identified which six keys were being used, but not their sequence. Sergei stuck a small plastic disc to the safe door adjacent to the keypad and connected a wire to the box. He pressed a green button and waited. It took almost ten minutes to cycle through up to a million combinations before getting the correct one. Finally, the red LED turned amber. Sergei then took the fingerprint paper, reversed it back-to-front, and pressed it against the scanner. Two seconds later, the LED became green, and with a barely audible click, the safe door swung opened slightly.

Sergei stepped away from the safe, allowing Hythe and Deacon to move in closer, saying, 'This was very secure for just an office.'

Instructing Sergei to keep watch, Hythe leaned forward and opened the safe door.

Inside was a large wad of Russian roubles, and two larger ones of Euros and US dollars. There was also a Makarov 9mm pistol with two spare magazines. Next to that were a dozen or so Manilla-colored folders. Pulling them out, Hythe passed them one by one to Deacon. After glancing at them, Deacon placed them on the desk, careful to keep them in order. The first few were thick with paper with Cyrillic lettering on them.

The next folders each had a company name on each. Three of them meant nothing to Deacon, but the fourth had Poteryannoye Sokrovishche clearly printed on its cover. There were only five pieces of paper inside. Deacon quickly photographed each page on his phone before putting them back in the same order. About to pass the folder back to Hythe, he was just turning as the partly open office door was flung open, and two men brandishing automatic weapons burst in.

14

The taller one in front yelled, 'Zamorozit, pridurki!'

Although not totally fluent in Russian, they both knew it meant 'Freeze, assholes!'

With a blur of motion and a hand flick, the folder hit the gunman in the face, the papers spilling out everywhere as Deacon grabbed the barrel of the weapon and pushed it aside and up while slamming a closed fist repeatedly into the gunman's throat, crushing his larynx and blocking his windpipe. He'd be dead through suffocation within a minute. A second, harder blow to the neck, just underneath the ear ensured almost immediate unconsciousness as the guard's life drained. Before Deacon needed to worry about the second gunman, Hythe had drawn and thrown a six-inch bladed knife, and the second gunman slowly sank to the floor, the black hilt of the knife jutting out of his chest directly over his heart.

'Shit,' Deacon said. Then turning to Hythe, he continued, 'So much for Lonely's guard duty. Check if there's more out there.'

Hythe picked up one of the fallen weapons and headed out. Thirty seconds later, he was back and confirming they were alone before striding directly across the room to Sergei and grabbing him by the collar.

'How the fuck were we discovered?' he hissed.

'I don't know, Mr. Callan. Maybe they were suspicious of the camera just showing interference, or they might have just had a routine inspection, Mr. Callan. That's why

I like a few days to reconnoiter first. If they're police, we're in big trouble.'

'Look at their clothes, Lonely. They're not the police, just local thugs,' he said, picking up the fallen folder and passing it back to Deacon. After putting the five pages back in the order he remembered, Deacon handed it to Sergei, who replaced it in the safe.

'Do we take the money and make it look just like a robbery?' Sergei asked.

'No, we'll leave it as planned,' Deacon confirmed. 'Only someone with specialist skill could rob this place due to the high tech systems. That would set the scene as an organized gang. We need to clean up and leave as if nothing has happened.'

Commanding Sergei to stay there, Deacon went outside to speak with Hythe after rummaging through the dead men's pockets for their car keys. 'We've got what we came for. Tell Sergei to fuck off home after we lock up. We'll take and dump the bodies in their car.' Tossing the keys to Hythe and telling him to bring the car out front, he went back into the office. Sergei had already locked the safe and replaced the picture and was stood there looking down at the bodies.

'C'mon Sergei, move it.'

Deacon lifted the gunman he'd killed up and put the body over his shoulder before heading out towards the gate where Hythe had arrived with the car. Opening the trunk, the body quickly disappeared into the large storage space. Rushing back into the office for the second body, Sergei started to help and went to lift the legs, asking, 'What about the knife?'

'Leave him plugged, less blood.'

Together they moved him out and placed him in the car alongside his colleague. Sergei packed the rest of his electronics into his backpack, reset the alarm and closed and relocked the main door. He removed the magnets from the door once the alarm had been set. Finally, Deacon laced the chain back through the gate while Sergei relocked the padlock and removed the pen device.

Grabbing him by the shoulders to ensure his attention, Hythe said, 'Lonely, go home. This never happened, but I'll wire five thousand Euros to your Swiss account, as usual.'

'Ten, Mr. Callan. There was never meant to be any killing. Ten.'

'Six, now fuck off before I change my mind,' he said before shaking his hand and slapping him on the shoulder. As Sergei half walked, half ran back to his Moskvich a few streets away, Hythe leaped into the passenger seat as Deacon started the car and drove away.

Almost nine miles to the northeast of their location, just on the outer sections of Moscow itself, is Elk Island, a large forest and national park. Few roads traverse the park, and it was easy to follow one of the narrower tracks until deep amongst the trees. It was already gone four-thirty, and early morning traffic was already quite heavy, meaning less chance of being stopped.

Within a half-hour, the two of them were walking swiftly back towards the city center, blending in with the other early pedestrians heading to work. Their clothes matched the locals heading the same way, and the thin layer of falling sleet meant most people kept their heads down and just ignored any passers-by. They had driven the gunman's car with the bodies inside deep into one of the many small lakes dotted throughout the park, and it would be many weeks before the bodies and vehicle were discovered.

Later the same morning, they both flew back to Paris and then directly on to Washington.

The same morning the office manager, Gleb Lubov, arrived for work at his usual time of 07:30. His was a simple job, but that was all he wanted at age fifty. He'd worked hard as a child and youngster, before being conscripted into the Red Army. He'd been in the army for almost twenty years, rising from conscript to corporal, but life hadn't been easy. Injured twice in Afghanistan, he'd finally left with a small pension and a back and leg still peppered with shrapnel from a massive IED on a lonely hillside in a place without even a proper name. The truck he'd been in had held twenty soldiers, and he was one of the lucky five that had survived. Doctors had removed the worst of the shrapnel but hadn't bothered with the smaller, more delicate pieces. It pained him to walk, and it pained him to sit. In fact, just about any movement pained him, but he'd learned to grit his teeth and just try and blank it out. That's why he liked this job. Any mail arriving for any of the two-hundred-and-fifteen registered companies at this address needed to be sorted. He would then, using a list kept within the safe, telephone the relevant company or individual to arrange for someone to come and pick up the mail.

But not yet today. The mail wasn't due until mid-morning. Sitting back in the chair, he began pouring a steaming, thick, black coffee from a thermos flask into its cup lid. He also broke off some black bread he'd bought from a small stall on the way in. Something didn't feel right about the room, but he couldn't put his finger on what exactly. His desk chair was an inch or two too far to the left, and the phone seemed slightly too close to the edge. He'd just taken a mouthful of bread when the phone rang. It was rare he received incoming calls, especially this early.

Quickly swallowing, he grabbed the handset and answered, 'Da?'

The voice the other end was brusk, but he didn't recognize its owner. The caller said, 'Two security came to you last evening. Are they there?'

'No, no one was here. It was all locked up when I arrived as usual. I'm here on my own. Gustaf doesn't arrive until 08:00.'

'Gustaf? Who the fuck's Gustaf?'

'Gustaf is the muscle on guard outside. He's here from eight to six in the evening.'

Without another word, the call ended, and Gleb found himself listening to dial tone. Replacing the receiver, he muttered some curse words in Russian that roughly translated to a suggestion of what the caller should do with his mouth to a donkey's genitalia. He relaxed, ate some more bread, and took some gulps of his coffee. Shortly after, he heard a knock on the reinforced glass window, indicating Gustaf had arrived for work and was saying hello. Standing and moving towards the door, he noticed two small spots of blood on the dirty floor. Usually, the floor would be too dirty to notice, but these two drops had landed on one of the few cleaner floor tiles. Rubbing his shoe across it, one of the drops smeared slightly. Slowly bending through the pain in his back, he placed a finger in the larger spot. It wasn't really wet and looked dry. The surface had skinned over; however, the pressure of his finger broke the surface skin, and the dark red blood was still moist below. From his training and days while in Afghanistan Gleb knew the characteristics of blood drying and estimated this to be just a few hours old.

Beginning to panic now, he headed over to the safe and removed the picture hanging there. With trembling fingers, he keyed in the six-digit security code and opened the door. He sighed with relief when he saw the three bundles of cash still sitting there. Looking around the room, he wondered if he'd just imagined the few things slightly out of place. Finally, turning back towards the files, he removed the top five and carried them to his desk. The first few looked fine. They were quite thick, with over forty sheets of paper each. One of the sheets was his paper record of mail arriving for this client. Moving onto the next folder, he flipped it open with his thumb before suddenly feeling a chill and the hairs on his arms raised. He checked all five sheets, his breath now coming in short puffs, before quickly sitting down and picking up the phone, his fingers trembling so much he had trouble dialing.

15

Washington

Deacon and Hythe were waiting at the inner reception desk within the outer ring of the Pentagon. With the seven-hour time change between Washington and Moscow, they'd arrived yesterday evening. Deacon had put Hythe up in his spare room, and they'd chatted until way after midnight. Now in the Pentagon, although Deacon had an access pass allowing him to wander within the outer three rings of the building, his access level didn't allow him to escort a visitor. And this wasn't just any visitor. This was Major Patrick Hythe, of 22 Special Air Service 'A' Squadron and his first visit to this famous structure.

Lieutenant Stringer walked purposely toward them. After introducing himself to Hythe, he escorted them to Admiral Carter's office on the top floor. The five concentric rings in the Pentagon are designated from the center out as 'A' through 'E'. 'E' Ring offices are the only ones with outside views and are generally occupied by senior officials including Admiral Douglas Carter - Chief of Naval Operations, and close confident to the president.

Deacon always enjoyed meeting the Admiral in his office. Instead of just the standard drab pale cream color, the Admiral had made the room his own. The view out of the long picture window was of the Pentagon Lagoon Yacht Basin with its luxury yachts and then beyond to the Potomac River. With the walls adorned with photographs of the Admiral's history, Deacon always found something new to look at.

Rising to his feet from behind his large wooden desk, the Admiral stood as Deacon and Hythe saluted. Returning the salute, he took Deacon's hand and shook it warmly.

Turning to Hythe, he extended a hand and said, 'And you must be Major Patrick Hythe of her Majesty's Armed Services. Welcome.'

'The honor is mine, sir. I've heard a lot about you from John. It's a pleasure.'

With a level of warmth already growing between them, the Admiral motioned for them to all move over to the comfy chairs while Mitch ordered coffee and biscuits.

Over the next thirty minutes, Deacon and Hythe explained what had happened.

'So as was suspected, the office was merely a mail-drop for PSO, along with another two-hundred plus companies. When we opened the safe most of the larger companies had fairly thick files there, but PSO's was paper-thin.'

'So who exactly is this local asset you used?'

'Sergei Dimonitrov,' Hythe said, 'He's a British asset I became involved with a few years back. The Embassy uses him whenever we need something delicate opened and can't afford to take the risk we might be exposed. He's Ukrainian, motivated by money, and one of the best locksmiths I've ever met. Totally hates Russia and its government, and will do virtually anything to do with breaking and entering if the price is right. In fact, I think he sees it as a challenge.'

'You trust him?'

'No reason not to. He's done so many break-ins if the local police or FSB caught him he'd be lucky not to be shot. He makes quite a good living working for our Embassy, and he fills his spare time stealing jewelry from the rich. I agreed to pay him for his help. I'd be grateful if you would care to underwrite it. And so would Her Majesty's Government,' Hythe said.

Turning to Mitch, the Admiral said, 'Get the payment details from the major and arrange it, please.'

After nodding a thank you, Hythe continued, 'The building security was far higher than needed for a simple mail-drop office. They had some of the latest hardware locks and alarm system fitted. We couldn't have gained entry without him. Those thugs were armed and ready to kill - not normally expected at a standard legitimate office.'

Deacon said, 'The PSO folder only contained five pages all in Cyrillic. One looked to be phone numbers. We could have asked Sergei to translate, but I thought the less he knows, the better, so I photographed them and emailed them over.' Turning to Mitch, he asked, 'Any feedback yet?'

Picking up a folder Mitch replied, 'Yes, the translated copies are back. The first four pages seem to contain nothing of particular interest - just a record of when mail arrived and the date and cost of forwarding it - but no address as to where it was actually forwarded. However, the fifth with the phone numbers is more interesting. All four are mobile numbers, and one number is American. The Admiral spoke with General Dreiberg and arranged for the NSA to try to identify the location of each of the numbers. Three of them were dead, including the American one, so we suspect those are just burners. However, one was live.

'The NSA traced it to an area of Russia out towards the Komi Republic - an area just north of the Arctic Circle. It's one of the major coal mining areas. Biggest town in the region is Vorkuta. The NSA pinged the number, and it responded, but they couldn't isolate it closer than within a two-mile radius. When they tried again it had been disconnected and has been dead since.'

The Admiral cleared his throat and said, 'I got General Dreiberg to chase up Charles Ingram over at the CIA. The General's getting the CIA and NSA to pool resources to look into it. To see if the exact building or company can be identified. However, the CIA does already have some information on file. Ingram passed me information on one of the largest company's in Vorkuta, which, surprise, surprise, is the Urals Mining Company. Nothing much on its subsidiary, PSO though. However, Charles did send over some details from a Russian mining press release of news reports concerning the use of unmanned robotic diggers for underground coal mining. It claimed the uptime warrants the additional costs involved. These machines are operated by umbilical connection back to the driver, who sits in a control pod outside on the surface. Obviously has a much-reduced downtime for shift changes or lunch breaks etc.

'Whether these could also be used under the sea, I don't know, but it's obviously similar technology,' the Admiral continued. 'Also, the Urals Mining Co are the parent company and part-owner of PSO, so anything's possible. Ingram's lot couldn't find an address for them, but it's likely they have an office there. Anyway, he'll keep us posted.'

With their meeting basically over, the Admiral rose and excused himself to attend another meeting, leaving just the three of them together.

After Deacon and Hythe promised Mitch to come over for dinner that evening, the two of them headed out.

Heading back towards Dupont Circle to show Hythe around the Phylax offices, Deacon was unusually relaxed and failed to notice a black SUV with tinted windows tailing them.

16

Washington

That evening the four of them got on like old friends. Helen cooked one of her favorite meals, a large beef roast with loads of fresh vegetables, giving Mitch great pleasure in carving chunks of meat off. As usually, Deacon brought two bottles of Gravel Road Pinot Noir to complement the meal and, not to be outdone, Hythe brought along a bottle of Knob Creek nine-year-old bourbon.

After the meal had been finished and the table was cleared away, Hythe stood and, putting on an upmarket plummy British accent said, 'Knob Creek bourbon is crafted in limited quantities, aged 9 years and placed in only the deepest charred American Oak barrels to fully draw out the natural sugars. A *purrrfect* end to a *purrrfect* evening,' all to the amusement of the others.

Once the laughter started, the jokes began, and the evening got better and better.

Mitch and Helen had heard stories before involving Hythe's and Deacon's exploits together in Afghanistan, and before that, in Iraq, but Deacon had only ever given basic facts. Now they had a chance to uncover the real stories, and they took great pleasure in doing so.

'So Patrick, tell us more about yourself. What made you become a SAS Special Forces soldier?'

'I think it was always in my blood,' he said. 'I was born into a family of British Military heroes. My great-grandfather was cavalry in WWI and stayed in after. He rose through the ranks, and my grandfather joined during

WW2. They both received medals for bravery. My father joined as it was expected on him, I think. He helped keep the peace in Northern Ireland and was then involved in the Falklands War, the Gulf War, and the various conflicts in Yugoslavia and the Balkans. After the Falklands he joined the SAS and was there until he retired. I joined the British Army seventeen years ago as an Officer Cadet and completed all my initial training at the Royal Military Academy, Sandhurst. I was then promoted to Second Lieutenant and held that rank for a little over two years. I was in Afghanistan, and then Iraq from 2003 and various skirmishes got me promoted to the rank of Lieutenant. My long-term ambition had always been to join the Special Air Service Corps. I did so in 2007 and never looked back.'

Originally formed as a regiment in 1941 during the height of the Second World War, the regiment was changed into a corps in 1950. The corps undertakes many roles, including covert reconnaissance, counter-terrorism, direct action, and hostage rescue. Similar to other Special Forces operations, much of the information and actions regarding the SAS is highly classified and is not commented on by the British Government or the Ministry of Defence due to the sensitivity of their operations. Currently made up of three regiments; the 22nd Special Air Service Regiment, the 21st (Artists) Special Air Service Regiment, and the 23rd Special Air Service Regiment. However, they are commonly referred to simply as The Regiment. Successful candidates undertake extensive physical and psychological training, and with a pass rate of less than 10%, many fail. However, failed candidates return to their regular army positions without any form of black mark against them. Similar to the US Navy SEAL selection process, only a few very best candidates succeed. There is always rivalry between the two forces with the SAS regularly taunting they are better trained than SEALs, better disciplined and better soldiers, and, strangely enough, the SEALs taunt the exact opposite. In practice, SAS and SEALs often share training at their UK or US bases and join forces for many missions. Any rivalry is usually forgotten about over a couple of beers in the mess.

'Now what about some of the stories John has told us about the two of you working together. Tell us more,' Mitch asked.

With a glint in his eye Patrick then spent the next hour waxing lyrically about how the two of them had saved the world on multiple occasions. How much was true and how much was the product of a fervent imagination Helen and Mitch would never discover. Many times Deacon smiled and looked away when Patrick was explaining some incredible feat either he or Deacon had managed, but Helen and Mitch just sat back and enjoyed the stories. Finally, after the last few drops of Knob Creek dripped from the empty bottle, Deacon turned to Patrick, said, 'You are so full of shit. C'mon, we need to go. You stay at my place tonight,' amid the roars of laughter from the other three before calling a cab back to Deacon's.

With another half bottle of Jack Daniels shared between them back at Deacon's apartment, they finally headed to bed complete with that rosy feeling of anything was possible.

As always after a night when too much alcohol is consumed, the morning came too quickly for those affected. Thick-headed and with a furry tongue, Deacon climbed out of bed at a little after six. Two more hours, he thought. One. One more hour. Half-hour? He realized he had to keep moving, so he slurped back scalding black coffee, and then hammered on the door to Patrick's room and shouted, 'Spare trainers in the wardrobe. Shorts and shirts in the drawer. Coffee in the kitchen. Five minutes,' and staggered downstairs.

Ten minutes later, the bleary-bloodshot eyes of Major Patrick Hythe also staggered into view.

'Fuck, and we're meant to be America's and Britain's finest,' Deacon joked.

Looking at each other, all they could do was laugh as they set out for a 5-mile run in the cold morning air to clear their heads. It was middle spring now so cool nights with warmer days, but today a rain front had covered the entire East Coast. It wasn't just raining, it was hammering down. And it was cold. But it had the desired effect, and within the first mile their heads had cleared, their tempers had reduced, and they were almost back to their normal selves. Almost.

Thirty minutes later, shivering with cold, but without even a hint of the previous night's over-indulgence remaining, they clambered back into Deacon's place.

Showered, dressed, and complete with another coffee, Deacon drove them to the office, saying, 'Sorry pal, but nothing edible at home. I'll pick up some bagels in the office.'

The rain was still a torrential downpour, and the journey took longer than usual. Eventually, Deacon pulled into the multi-story parking garage, and they ran to the office. Deacon often picked up bagels and coffee for himself, Gina and Cindy in the office, but he was usually in by 7:45. Being later, he expected others to also have arrived, so wanted to count heads first.

Gina was at her desk having already checked the mail, and Cindy had just been dropped off by her boyfriend, Garry Moore. They'd arrived via the subway and Garry was only wearing a lightweight jacket. Deacon said to give him ten minutes to check email then he'd go out and pick up bagels and coffee for the five of them.

Looking around, Garry said, 'My first client isn't until 10:00, so I'll go and get them now if you want?'

Deacon gave him two twenties and a ten and said, 'Get two each for Patrick and me, and whatever you, Cindy and Gina want. But take my coat, pal - it's thicker than your jacket, and it's a real downpour out there.'

Slipping it on, Garry put a cap on his head and headed out to Bellini's Bagels three blocks away.

Within moments, the phone rang, and Deacon and Gina became engrossed in business talk.

Ten minutes later, they heard multiple sirens approaching. Two Metropolitan Police cruisers raced by, lights flashing, pursued by an ambulance from the 13th St Firehouse. Additional police cruisers followed, all with screaming sirens.

Thirty minutes later, there was still no sign of Garry. Cindy tried calling him on his cell, but as soon as she dialed, she could hear ringing. Turning, she saw his jacket hanging on the hook with his cell phone ringing in the pocket.

'There's obviously some sort of emergency going on out there. He might be stuck behind a barricade or in a crowd or something,' Gina said, helpfully. 'Why don't you go and check?'

Just as Cindy was putting on her coat before heading out, the door opened, and two men in crumpled suits walked in.

The older guy flashed a badge and said,' I'm Detective Rissolini of the Metropolitan PD. This is my colleague, Detective Whitley. Does a John Deacon work here?'

Fearing the worst, Cindy cried, 'Oh my god, what's happened?' as Deacon walked out of his office.

'I'm John Deacon. What's happened?'

'You're John Deacon?' Rissolini asked incredulously. 'You got ID?' he said brusquely.

Pulling his driving license from his wallet, he passed it over, saying, 'What's this about, officer?'

Rissolini examined the license before passing it to his colleague, Gail Whitley, eyebrows raised. To Deacon, who was still waiting for an answer, Rissolini reminded him of a typical 'seen-it-all, done-it-all' kind of cop. Maybe in his mid-fifties, wearing a gray suit that had seen far too many hours in a car, and a tie that had been put on as an afterthought. Politeness would be unlikely.

'You loan your coat to anyone today?'

'Yes, to a colleague, Garry Moore, to pick up bagels. What's happened?'

'Well, I'm sorry to inform you, but your colleague seems to be the injured party in a shooting.'

'How bad?' Cindy blurted out crying, and obviously completely upset.

'Are you a relative, miss?'

'Yes, yes, I'm his girlfriend.'

'Well, I'm sorry, Miss, but it was a fatal shooting.'

Hearing that, Cindy collapsed crying onto the floor. Deacon quickly ordered Gina to take her into the meeting room and stay with her. Beckoning the detectives to follow, he and Hythe went into his office.

'Can you tell me what happened?'

'Was this Garry Moore involved with any gangs? Was he into drugs?' The Detective Whitley asked.

'No, not that I know of. He's a personal trainer and the boyfriend of my receptionist. I loaned him my coat due to the rain. Here's his jacket,' Deacon said, passing it over. 'Why?'

'Well, it looks initially like a gangland execution. Three in the back of the head from close range. Was he getting

118

coffee?' Rissolini asked while searching through the pockets.

'Yes, coffee and bagels for us.'

'Looks like they waited until he was walking out of Bellini's and got him just outside the entrance. Never stood a chance.'

'Any witnesses?'

'Plenty, but no one saw a thing. All too quick. Plus, no one heard the shots, so we think the perp used a silencer.'

'A suppressor.'

'What?'

'A suppressor. They're called suppressors, not silencers. Only Hollywood calls them silencers.'

'How the fuck do you know that?' he said angrily.

'Well, I'm sort of in the business.'

'OK, asshole. This guy gets whacked up close and personal. The store owner thinks it's you from the coat, but you just happened to loan your coat to the target today. So you know what I think? Either this guy was a target all along, or you was the target and maybe you set him up to get whacked. And you know all about weapons. I think we'd better continue this downtown,' he said, slipping his cuffs off his belt, while Whitley slid her hand gently towards her sidearm.

Hythe said, 'There is another possibility, Detective Rissolini. John here was the target, and Garry Moore was mistaken for him and not set up at all.'

'Yeah, well, we'll sort this out downtown,' Rissolini said, turning to his colleague. 'Cuff him.'

Pulling a business card out of his wallet, Deacon passed it to the detective. There was no name or details, just a local Washington number. Rissolini looked from the card to Deacon and made an impatient gesture.

'What the fuck is this?'

'Call it.' Deacon said. 'The person who answers will vouch for me.'

Reluctantly getting his cell out, Tony Rissolini told Whitley to 'watch him' while he dialed the number. When it answered, Deacon heard him say, 'This is Detective Tony Rissolini of the Metropolitan PD. Who the fuck is this?'

Deacon smiled very gently to himself as the person at the other end of the line identified himself. The detective straightened up and stood noticeably taller while uttering a few 'Yes Sirs', and 'No Sirs'. At one stage, Deacon heard him giving the name of John Deacon and the address as Phylax. Two more 'No Sirs', followed by three 'Yes Sirs' before he finally closed his cell, by now red in the face.

'The Chief! You got the fucking Chief of Police's private cell on speed-dial? Who the fuck are you?' he gasped.

In the meantime, Hythe moved closer to Deacon, and said, 'Likely it was meant for you, pal. You got any enemies? Like he says, you are both the same or very similar build, even the same hairstyle and hair thickness. And he was wearing your coat. It was raining hard. In poor light, from behind, you could easily pass for one another.'

Scratching his chin, Deacon stood there momentarily, deep in thought.

Suddenly turning around, Deacon said, 'Can we go and see the body now, detective?' while taking Rissolini's arm to lead him out to the waiting cruiser. Detective Whitley followed, looking bemused, while Rissolini was still muttering 'The fucking Chief....'

Garry Moore had died quickly and without even seeing his attacker. The three shots had been in quick succession and were spaced less than an inch apart. They'd been fired from around three-foot distance as the entry holes had gunshot residue around them, and stippling of the skin had occurred. Without closer examination Deacon couldn't be 100% sure, but the entry wounds looked to be from a nine-millimeter fired upwards from a slightly lower angle.

Turning to Hythe, Deacon said, 'Execution style.'

Hythe nodded in full agreement, saying, 'Poor bastard never stood a chance.'

The explosive force of three nine-millimeter rounds entering the enclosed head cavity less than a second apart had caused the pressure build-up to explode, along with the spent rounds, out the front of the head. This meant Garry Moore's face was completely gone. Blood, brains, and flesh were splattered over the sidewalk and side windows of a car parked close by. Not only would it need to be a closed casket burial, but Cindy and Garry's parents wouldn't even be able to see his body to say goodbye.

It wasn't a surprise no one could remember what they'd seen. From experience, Deacon knew when anything this violent happened close-up the human brain couldn't take it all in and just blanked everything out. All most people would ever remember would be the nightmare images of blood and brains everywhere.

The Italian store owner, used to seeing and speaking with Deacon most mornings, and seeing a similar-sized body in the same coat had assumed it was him.

While they were there, the medical examiner finished his initial examination and released the body to be removed for autopsy.

After confirming the body wouldn't be released for burial for a number of weeks until the investigation was closed, and still unsure what relationship Deacon had with his Chief, Rissolini agreed to keep Deacon in the loop as and when information became available. The two of them also decided it would be best for the police to contact Garry Moore's family and break the bad news.

Back at the office, Gina had left to take Cindy home to her place. The doctor had been called and given her a shot to help her sleep. Checking her personnel file, Deacon found the mother and father were divorced, with the mother, Hazel, living just outside of Raleigh, Virginia. But the father's address in California wasn't known. Picking up the file, Deacon went into his office, shut the door, and took a seat. This wasn't the first time he'd had to make a call like this to unsuspecting parents, but before it always had concerned people in the military where this type of call is feared and often half expected.

When Hazel answered, Deacon explained who he was and what had happened to Cindy's boyfriend. The relief in Hazel's voice that her daughter was safe and sound was palpable. Deacon finished the call by reassuring her mother that Cindy's position would be held open for as long as it took her to recover. He then arranged for a car to drive Cindy to her mother's house.

After three days' investigation, the police were stumped. No evidence had been found, nor any witness had come forward apart from those already known. Rissolini reported the gang crews were all saying there was no particular trouble at the moment. There didn't seem to be any take-overs, no acts of revenge, no one trying to become king, and when a couple of gang informants had been asked, no one knew anything about a Garry Moore. The police case was dead-ended.

17

CIA Headquarters, Washington

The meeting commenced the following morning at 08:00 sharp in meeting room C.46 at CIA headquarters, Langley. Present was General Dreiberg, Charles Ingram, Lisa Kingsman, General Mansfield, Admiral Carter, Mitch Stringer, and Deacon. After a special request, Patrick Hythe of Her Majesty's SAS was also admitted. There was also a dark-haired person Deacon didn't recognize.

Standing, General Dreiberg said, 'I have asked Enzio Polowski, who runs our Russia Desk, to give us all a thirty-minute overview of the current state of Russia. Enzio, over to you...'

The dark-haired man to Deacon's right stood up and addressed the group.

'Thank you, sir. Now I will keep this as brief as possible but need to cover some significant historical aspects. After World War II the Soviet Union stole, or kept hold of, almost $65 billion of war booty. However, it had been ravaged by the war itself; deaths, famine, disease, typhus epidemics, and political purges. Although it rebuilt, it put most of its effort into an improved military – not surprising considering the losses it had taken during the war. However, its people didn't prosper. Most of the public was unhappy, and it took organizations such as the KGB – the Committee of State Security – to keep the public in a state of fear.

'The union was actually made up of fifteen republics and was the first country to adopt a planned economy, whereby production and distribution of goods were centralized and directed by the government. However, corruption was rife, and for many years production fell well short of what was predicted, and tens of thousands or even millions starved. In the early sixties, the US sold grain to the Soviets to stop their people starving. By the early seventies, the Soviets needed so much grain, but the then President, President Nixon, put so many restrictions and caveats on the sale, the Soviets dropped out. The following year, in 1972, the Soviets had another bad crop failure year, and, through various surreptitious means, they legally purchased over twenty-five percent of the US crop. This forced world prices to skyrocket. 1975 was another bad year for Soviet food production, but this time President Ford controlled the situation better, and proper deals were arranged. These deals stayed in effect until 1979 when the Soviets invaded Afghanistan.'

He stopped briefly to take a drink before continuing, 'By the early 80s, the Soviets had spent so much of their resources on their military build-up there was little money available for the country to improve itself. The quality of everything Soviet-built was laughable. In 1987, Mikhail Gorbachev was elected into the role of General Secretary with the power to make changes. He tried to reform and revitalize the economy with his programs of glasnost – openness; and perestroika - restructuring. His policies relaxed state control over enterprises but did not replace it by market incentives, resulting in an even sharper decline in output and political instability. In 1989, Soviet satellite states in Eastern Europe overthrew their respective communist governments, and in 1991 there was an internal coup d'état attempt while Gorbachev was away in the Crimea on vacation. Boris Yeltsin, the President of the Soviet Union, and below Gorbachev, held firm and located himself in the White House, Russia's parliament building. Addressing the nations' public by radio and television, supporters came and barricaded themselves inside the parliament building against repeated attacks. After three days of aggression, the coup began to fade, and when Gorbachev finally arrived back in Moscow, it suffered its death knell. Realizing he'd lost the respect of his colleagues and public, Mikhail Gorbachev resigned as General Secretary on August 24th but continued on until 25th December as President. The day following Gorbachev's resignation as President, the Soviet Union was formally dissolved, and it became the current Russian Federation with Boris Yeltsin at its head.'

Ingram raised a hand and interrupted Enzio, saying in an exasperated voice, 'This is all old history. Is it really relevant?'

Dreiberg looked sharply at Ingram and said, 'Charles, it's useful as it sets the scene. Enzio, please continue.'

Exhaling heavily, Ingram slumped back down in his chair as Enzio again spoke.

'Yeltsin continued the work Gorbachev had started and managed to transform Russia's socialist economy into a capitalist market economy; implementing economic shock therapy, a market exchange rate of the Rouble, nationwide privatization, and the lifting of price controls. However, due to the sudden total economic shift, a majority of the national property and wealth fell into the hands of a small number of oligarchs. To make matters worse, the KGB had also been disbanded when the Soviet Union was dissolved. This left an enormous number of spies, intelligence experts, and government-sponsored thugs looking for work in the open market. A new intelligence organization was formed, the Federal Security Service, but it went through a number of changes before finally becoming known as the Federal Security Bureau, or FSB, in June 1995. Although a number of key former KGB staff were recruited to the Service, many were not, and many saw the value of the data they had previously gathered and stored on behalf of the KGB as valuable bargaining chips. The ingress of American and European companies into Russia under perestroika became easy pickings and allowed organized crime to grow at an incredible rate to where it has remained today. The Russian Mafia, or Solntsevskaya Organized Crime Group as it's known locally, is now the largest organized crime syndicate in the world.' Enzio took another sip of water and looked around the group.

'Yeltsin cared little for his countrymen and continued the Gorbachev path of selling anything of value to foreigners. Oil prices slumped, and the Russian economy was close to collapsing. For many weeks and months, the army and many state-owned enterprises were never paid, leaving many people to exist in a pitiful condition. Eventually, on 31st December 1999, under enormous internal pressure to leave, Yeltsin announced his resignation, leaving the presidency in the hands of his chosen successor, Viktor Kalygin, who was Prime Minister at the time.

'One of the first things Kalygin did as president was to make the FSB directly accountable to him. To say he is corrupt is a vast understatement. The Russian constitution limits its Presidents to only two consecutive terms in office. To get around that, in 2008 he swapped roles with his then Prime Minister but kept strong hands on the controls of office. In 2012, under a cloud of secrecy, he swapped back and extended the time in each role within the constitution. Initially, Kalygin was seen as a savior to his people. He advertised himself as a tough-guy who wouldn't put up with corruption. He came down hard on a couple of tax evaders and won even more public support, but gradually his glow faded. His tough-guy image was augmented by pictures of him shooting and exercising in unarmed combat, all carefully staged. But he's overstretched himself and Russia. The rich still love him because his policies have helped them get richer, with a little extra each time for him personally, but the gap between rich and poor is now wider than ever. The working class is poor. They were captivated by him initially, but the glow faded quickly. They see corruption everywhere. Drug and alcohol use is almost at epidemic proportions, and street gangs run the local crime syndicates, reporting and working for the Russian Mafia. For many of the average 'joe' over there, they remember the times before glasnost and hanker for the old days when everything seemed more peaceful. Most of it is 'rosy-eyed' memories as times back then were much harder, but you know how fickle the public can be. He's begun to lose supporters by the truckload and knows that if he lets Ukraine go to NATO, he will lose even more. As with many leaders, he is trying to get the public behind him by rallying support through military strength.'

'And is that working?' General Dreiberg interrupted.

Polowski nodded, saying, 'It has to a certain extent. Most leaders find their country gets behind them in times of adversity. It happened to Margaret Thatcher in the UK back in the early eighties with their Falkland's war. It happened here under President Bush after 9/11. When a country is under threat, everyone rallies around, and past issues are forgotten. For a while, at least. So that's what he's working on in Russia. He's trying to build Russia up, promising new fantastic weapons to keep adversaries at bay. But if he can't make Russia stronger, all he can do is make other places weaker. It's human nature. People want the lives of people they hate made worse. It's inbred jealousy. However, he doesn't care about Russia or its people. He only cares about staying in power and milking the system for personal profit.

'As an example, his identified wealth is approximately US$3M. Yet his estimated wealth is between US$120-150 Billion, virtually all from ill-gotten gains. He has instructed all major deals must cross his desk for his personal sign-off. But most include an extra percentage for himself. He's totally corrupt both for money and power. Many of his political opponents have either disappeared or suffered fatal accidents, and elections are rigged so far in Kalygin's favor, it's laughable.

'Finally, for years Russia has played the 'destabilizing' game. The more disquiet they can sow into Western Europe, the better it suits them. In 2014 they began their annexation of Ukraine that continues until today. In November last year, three Ukrainian naval vessels were fired on before being seized by Russian forces while in international waters. Three crew members were injured, and all twenty-four crewmen were detained in Russia. The Kremlin is also heavily involved in geopolitics. The internet and social media were and are still being extensively used to undermine the EU, to cause confusion and unrest by promoting Brexit, and influence both Brexit and the US political scene. It's heavily in Russia's favor if Britain leaves the European Union. Britain is one of the central five core countries and is part of the 'Five Eyes' network, the USA led intelligence network of the USA, Great Britain, Canada, Australia, and New Zealand. Britain leaving the EU would have a detrimental effect on security throughout Europe. Here in the US, the more unrest raised, the better they see it. Many of the white supremacy groups here receive underground funding surreptitiously from Moscow.

'To help public opinion see things 'their way', the Kremlin uses full English speaking users pretending to be British or American on various social media platforms. In the 2016 US elections, Kalygin wanted Thomas Wexford to win, who was a much better choice for Russian foreign policy than his opponent. Again, a heavily funded, but totally secret and deniable 'nudging' of Americans to vote in Russia's favor. Nothing can be proved, of course, but the weight of evidence is that President Wexford was 'helped' to win the Presidency. As you can imagine, Kalygin and Wexford don't get on too well, although the president seems to think they do.'

Thanking Enzio for the overview, General Dreiberg continued, 'So bringing this all up-to-date with what we believe has been happening underwater in the Arctic Circle, we believe the answers may lie somewhere in Vorkuta, but we can't send anyone official in. We've asked questions through State, but they haven't answered yet, and we believe they are unlikely to. So, our hands currently are a little tied.'

General Mansfield cleared his throat and said, 'Where exactly is Vorkuta?'

Mitch said, 'Out in the far ass end of nowhere in Russia, sir. The region is called the Northwestern. It's out where it turns into the Urals. Almost 2,000 miles East from Moscow.'

The Admiral then turned to Deacon, smiled briefly, and said, 'The President has asked you to go there and get into the offices of the Ural Mineral Company in Vorkuta. Find out what you can about them and the subsidiary company, Poteryannoye Sokrovishche. If you can find proof the Russians are mining in Danish waters illegally, the President, along with the Danish Prime Minister, can take Russia to the International Court of Justice in The Hague. Likewise, if you can uncover what happened to the Arctic Drift Station. However, we need proof. Can you get us that proof? We could send in the CIA, but if detected, it would become a major embarrassment to the

President, and we'd lose any chance of a criminal conviction.'

Coughing slightly, he then added, 'Of course, if you're caught the President can deny all involvement.'

After looking at Hythe for a few moments, Deacon said, 'What's our excuse for being there?'

The Admiral nodded towards Mitch and said, 'Mitch?'

'Vorkuta is a town closely associated with Vorkutlag, one of the most notorious forced labor camps of the Gulag, the Soviet forced labor camp system. Vorkutlag Gulag was established in 1932 to exploit the resources of the Pechora Coal Basin, the second largest coal basin in the former USSR. The city of Vorkuta was established to support the camp. The mines had a perfect source of free labor from the Gulag, and the town grew. As with all Gulags, nobody really cared whether the prisoners lived or died, and many were worked to death. Eventually, Vorkutlag closed in late '62. The town carried on with mining, but gradually, many of the smaller mines closed, and the largest, the Komsomolskaya, finally closed in the mid-1990s. The town still exists and has a population of around 50,000, down massively from its heyday of almost 200,000. There are a number of smaller mines that support the town, but it's slowly declining. Back in the late '80s and early '90s, there were labor actions across the entire region as many of the miners hadn't been paid for over a year,' he said.

'So what is mined there? Just coal?'

'Coal is a generic name. The region produces a mixture. Anthracite - is classed as the king of coals. It's a hard variety made up almost entirely of carbon. It burns with very little flame meaning it gives the most energy with the least pollution, making it ideal for power stations. It's also the least plentiful. Also produced is coking coal - also high in carbon and used extensively to make coke, necessary for iron and steel making. Unfortunately, the region has low prospects of development due to high costs overall of coal production. The production conditions are difficult due to caving-in, bending, and breaking of formations.'

Speaking for the first time at the meeting, Hythe asked, 'So why would the Urals Mining Company be set up here if all they can mine is low quantities of various types of coal?'

'That's what we'd like you to investigate,' the Admiral said.

Nodding, Deacon said, 'And our cover story?'

Charles Ingram smiled, nodded in Lisa Kingman's direction, and said, "Lisa will set you up as TV scriptwriters and planners. You will be doing a major series on the Gulags with approval from Moscow - all part of the new, open Russia. What was Vorkutlag was partly knocked down, but most of the buildings were reused. It then became the home of the Vorkuta Infectious Diseases Hospital. We believe it's empty and shut down now, but it was an excuse to keep hold of political prisoners under the excuse they had infectious diseases after the Gulags were officially closed during the '60s. It was also used for experiments on prisoners. Mind-altering drugs, surgical and chemical lobotomy's, electric shock treatment, open brain electrode stimulation, all types of horror stories. Unfortunately, Moscow won't allow any of that to be discussed, but you would be able to talk about the good the hospital did against diseases. Paperwork will show you working for a Hollywood production company. Just scouting around for rough shots of the old Gulag - bits of fence remaining, where the trains stopped, you know the sort of thing ... brief glimpse into the old days, but nothing anyone now can be held accountable for. That sort of thing. Gives you the excuse to ask questions around there without anyone becoming suspicious. New names for you for this, but all genuine if checked out.'

'2,000 miles from Moscow, you say. How do we get there?' Hythe asked.

Before anyone else could answer, Deacon said, 'Hollywood production company, eh? Hollywood is rich, pal. So I think a private jet directly into Vorkuta, via clearance in Moscow.'

18

Central Russia

Two days later a Gulfstream G650 touched down at Vnukovo Airport, just 17 miles southwest of Moscow city center after a 10 hour 20 minute non-stop flight. Hank Pechnik had been the pilot. Having cleared customs with paperwork showing they worked for the fictitious production company, Red Pepper Productions, Inc, and using fake names of Bruce Wintergreen for Deacon and Charles Fortescue for Hythe, they traveled by taxicab to a local hotel, after arranging for the aircraft to be refueled.

Although spring had progressed since they were last in Russia, it was still gently snowing with the air temperature only just above freezing.

After checking-in and freshening up, the three of them met in the lobby before heading into the restaurant and then on to the bar. Always aware they could be being observed, they centered their conversations about the forthcoming film production.

The following morning, after an early breakfast, they checked-out to head back to the airport for the two-hour flight to Vorkuta, just above the Arctic Circle. As they stood outside their hotel, the fifth taxicab in the rank suddenly pulled out and accelerated, screeching to a stop in front of them, much to the rising anger of the other waiting taxicab drivers. With waving fists and loud cursing from the other drivers about what this driver and his mother must get up to at night, the three of them clambered in.

The aircraft had already been quickly searched by Russian Customs on arrival at Vnukovo as part of the normal immigration clearance procedure so wasn't searched again, but Deacon and Hythe knew they would never have been able to get clearance to take weapons into Russia, especially not the sort they needed.

Although they'd had one overnight bag each, there was a fourth large holdall already in the trunk of the taxicab. Carrying it onboard Deacon waited until the access door was closed and locked and Hank was taxiing out to the runway before opening it.

Inside were three Russian Makarov pistols with suppressors, three UZI submachine rifles, a Dragunov sniper rifle, a VHF/UHF Scanner & Jammer, two sets of night vision goggles, three satellite phones, and some other useful gadgets. One advantage the Gulfstream G650 had over the earlier model was more storage access compartments. Some were easy to find, but others were harder to access and ideal for safely storing items of importance. Or illegal items away from prying eyes. Deacon and Hythe quickly stripped the weapons down into their component parts before stashing them in various compartments. Even if the police came on board, it was unlikely they would find anything.

With clearance granted, and after racing down the runway, they soon broke through the thick cloud into a crystal blue sky above for the duration of the short uneventful flight.

Vorkuta Airport was made up of a single runway with a small taxiway alongside. Although busy in its heyday, the airport was quiet and rarely received unknown visitors. Especially foreigners, so their arrival caused some interest. Part of Lisa Kingman's arrangements had included a hire car at the airport. Booked locally, they were expecting a Chevrolet Cobalt or similar, as arranged.

The website advert showed a shiny, new example with automatic transmission. In reality, it was a stick-shift with a front fender broken, the windshield cracked in three places, the passenger door mirror snapped off, the hood dented, all doors dented, the seats ripped and badly scuffed, and the entire inside coated in a heavy overture of yellowing nicotine.

However, it finally started on the third try, the heater worked, and the tires looked reasonable. Well, as Hythe said, they at least had some tread on them and held air.

This far east and north the weather was severe at minus -12C (10F), and there was heavy falling snow. After hiring a hangar and getting the Gulfstream moved inside and refueled, they headed off. The vehicle wasn't much better to drive than look at. It had a severe wheel wobble over 30 miles-per-hour and both passenger-side doors had gaps around them from collision damage. However, once started the engine settled down and seemed to run well.

Heading into town along Ulitsa Transportnaya they were confronted by a stark, decaying town. Partly due to the weather, everything looked dead or dying. Every building was cement gray with no color, with many looking dilapidated and unused. The town showed minimal signs of life. Between the multiple empty buildings with windows and doors missing, there was graffiti and broken glass everywhere. What few people were out were huddled in thick overcoats, heads surrounded by fur hats, faces hidden in the fur. They all seemed to have the slow stumble of the totally despondent.

Hank summed it up when he said, 'It's as if they've accepted life is tough, and this is as good as it's ever likely to get. Just going through the motions of work every day and then waiting to die.'

Turning into Ulitsa Yanovskogo, they approached the three-star Hotel Dmitrov - a ten-story unpainted concrete block – and parked up. The hotel reception was as downtrodden as the rest of the town and Hythe casually said, 'Three stars? Someone was smoking some serious shit!'

The female booking clerk tossed their keys over the scratched counter after taking their passports and checking them in for two nights. From what looked to be the bar, four hookers looking as rough as the surroundings wandered out to the reception. Smiling, and not wanting to cause any offense, they said 'Maybe later, ladies,' before heading up to drop their bags in their rooms.

After leaving Hank in the hotel watching TV, Hythe and Deacon wandered out towards the deserted hospital, just 800 yards from the hotel. The three of them agreed the rooms were likely bugged and even possibly video recorded. Also, they assumed their bags would be carefully examined and any data probably copied from their laptops. However, the CIA had also expected this and set the laptops up as genuine from Red Pepper Productions Inc to help hold their story together.

Vorkuta was a typical Russian town built in the former days of the USSR. Most buildings looked identical - all were ten or eighteen storey concrete blocks in gray. With large, wide roads because all land was government-owned and therefore free, the street lighting every three hundred yards or so was never adequate. As the overcast sky darkened further, the weak yellow street bulbs shined dimly through the falling sleet and snow. Twice stopped by groups of men offering drugs or women or both, after approaching the run-down old hospital they turned and headed back towards the hotel.

Hythe quietly mouthed, 'We have a tail,' as a dirty police car slowed down and followed them at a walking pace. Eventually, it overtook them and pulled in front, blue lights flashing.

Two overweight police in rumpled uniforms stepped out. The driver stayed back with his hand near his sidearm while the other officer spoke fast in Russian. Although not fluent, both Deacon and Hythe understood what was being asked, but chose to play dumb.

Deacon smiled and held up his hands. 'American - do you speak English?' Both officers spoke with each other, the driver still keeping his hand near his weapon. Finally, the driver said, 'Papers! What for here?'

Smiling to keep any tension as low as possible, Deacon said, 'Papers Hotel Dmitrov,' and pointed in the rough direction of the hotel. After more urgent talking between the two of them, the driver reached into his car and used the radio.

Turning to Deacon, Hythe said quietly, 'He's just called for support, saying he has foreigners here.'

Two minutes later, two more police cars came racing through the falling snow, blue lights flashing. Once surrounded, they were pushed onto the car hood and frisked before being bundled one each into the back of two of the cars. Driven off to the local police station, they were then held in individual cells. One of the officers must have called the hotel because less than an hour later, Hank arrived with all three passports.

An English speaking senior officer arrived and introduced himself.

'I am Police Captain Medvedev. Who are you, and what are you doing here?'

Deacon carefully explained the planned story. He also supplied more paperwork showing their permits approved from Moscow. After keeping them waiting another couple of hours, Captain Medvedev confirmed the paperwork seemed to be all in order. He also confirmed they'd known of the flight arrival but not about who was aboard. Finishing, he told them to be careful as visitors in a strange town could get in trouble.

Hythe, yet to speak, thanked the Captain and asked if he'd be willing to partake in the TV program when they came back to film it. He explained how they needed someone who knew the history and area and had the gravitas to hold attention on camera. He went on to say that everything filmed had to be vetted by Moscow Central before being allowed to be broadcast, but having someone of his status and authority would add to the content.

Suitably impressed, Medvedev was quick to release them, even getting one of his officers to call them a taxicab after he personally stamped their paperwork.

After taking a couple of head and shoulder shots with his phone and a promise to forward them to their producers in Hollywood, Hythe led them out to the waiting cab. Sitting there a few minutes later, Hythe said, laughing, 'Thought that would get us out of there. One thing I've found is most Russians love to feel important. Couple of minutes of bullshit saved us an hour or two of more questions. He'll be telling his friends and maybe his wife that he'll be Russia's answer to Robert Redford next. Now at least we can have a beer in the hotel.'

19

The following morning after a minimal breakfast of porridge and black bread, the three of them headed back to the airport hangar to check on the aircraft. They had left a miniature security camera running, and reviewing it showed no one had been on board. Taking and reassembling some of their hidden gear, Hank took the handheld VHF/UHF Scanner & Jammer over to the car. Seconds later, he found the tracking bug located under the driver's side front wheel arch, placed there by the police.

Leaving it in place, they headed over to the old, deserted hospital and wandered around, taking notes and still photos. Together, they drew up plans of what to shoot and what camera angles would be required, to have something to show if stopped again. They also headed over to the only remaining working mine and took multiple photos around the entrance and gates. At each stop, Hank stayed by the car. After double-checking he was not being observed, Hank removed the plastic cover in the trunk and pulled out the stoplight and reversing light cable. After cutting the cables, he fitted a small toggle switch to both exposed cable ends. With the switch in the normal position, the stoplights and reversing lamps operated as normal. However, a simple flick of the switch would isolate the circuit and stop these bulbs from lighting.

Heading back to the airport, they dropped Hank off. He would now stay onboard the Gulfstream until they finally left; in the meantime checking systems and making sure everything was ready for a quick departure if required. The aircraft had electric heating, a full working galley, and a freezer full of top quality meats, as well as access to just about every US and European satellite channel, so Hank had better comfort than at the hotel.

Driving through the backstreets of Vorkuta, Deacon and Hythe hunted around until they found a run-down bar where they ordered two beers from a scruffy, but well-built barman. There was only one other person in the bar – an old man with gray whiskers and three days stubble who seemed intent in staring into his near-empty glass.

Beckoning the barman over Deacon asked, in Russian, where everyone worked now the mines are mostly closed? As expected, the barman merely grunted: 'Why?'

Taking his wallet out, Deacon counted out two $50 notes and placed them on the bar. Still no response. Adding a final additional $50, he still had no response, so he said to Hythe in Russian loud enough for the barman to hear, 'We'll find someone else to ask.'

Slipping his hand over the notes and sliding them into his pocket in one slick movement, the barman eventually answered, 'Many work at the compound.'

'What compound? What's it for?'

Just a shrug, so Deacon tried again, 'Where is it?'

Finally, the barman said, 'Two miles north towards Severnyy. By railway track. Compound is by group of ruins.'

Leaving another ten on the counter to cover the beers, they headed back to their car and Hythe drove. What they didn't see as they drove away was the barman picking up the phone and having an animated conversation with someone on the other end.

Driving as slow as feasible without looking suspicious, they approached the compound. The area itself was set three-hundred yards or so off the main highway and seemed to be about two hundred yards square surrounded by an eight-foot fence topped with barbed wire. The compound contained what looked to be almost a dozen individual buildings. The approach road and the surroundings were bare of trees or cover, and there were tower lights located at each corner of the fence. A small sign attached to the fence stated 'The Ural Mining Company - No admittance.'

Looking as they drove passed, Deacon said, 'Shit that's approximately forty-thousand square yards.' Carrying on past the main entrance, Hythe could see a power line running parallel to the railway before both entered the compound near the far corner.

Heading back to the hotel, Hythe parked their car opposite the hotel entrance. Deacon slid in under the car, pulled the tracking bug off the underside of the wheel arch, and dropped it in a mound of snow just falling off the underside of the vehicle. By not damaging it or tossing it away, he made it look like it just fell off and they'd simply lost it.

Approaching midnight, they headed back out to the car. The area was deadly quiet, with just a few wild dogs wandering around. With snow still falling and the poor street lighting, they were invisible from more than twenty feet as they checked again that no more bugs have been secreted in or on their car. The reading showed only the one lying in the snow. Trying the ignition, on the third turn the engine finally caught, and Deacon and Hythe headed north out of town.

A mile away from the compound, Deacon killed the lights before coasting gently to a stop. Ahead on the right was a dirt track exit approximately five-hundred yards before the compound's approach road. This track led to an old, abandoned encampment of deserted, disused buildings. Deacon kept the engine ticking over while Hythe scouted the area out using night vision goggles. After a long minute, Hythe gave him the all-clear thumbs-up, and with the kill switch for the stop and reversing lights now activated, he turned and reversed the car deep into the shadows of the old buildings.

Grabbing what gear they needed, they crossed the deserted road and approached towards the fence. Staying in the shadows of a large bush, they waited and observed. The compound itself was floodlit, so they waited in the shadows on the icy ground for almost an hour, watching. A two-man guard duty patrolled every twenty minutes, but luckily without dogs. Keeping to the dark shadows, they headed on foot towards where the railway and power line passed through the fence. Fifty or so yards before the junction and outside the loom of the floodlights, the power line was partly obscured by another large bush. Stretching up, Deacon strapped a thin strip of C4 around the power cable before setting a detonator and a simple radio receiver. With a simple press of a radio transmitter, he could kill all power entering the compound with the bush hiding the break.

Heading away from the main road towards the rear of the settlements, they found some bushes growing closer to the fence line offering a little more cover. There was no activity to be seen inside the compound between the twenty-minute guards passing, and they were parallel to where the railway track terminated. The cover was minimal, but after completing a full 360 lookout, Deacon used a pistol and suppressor to take out three lamps each approximately 100 yards apart. The falling snow muffled the soft pops of the suppressor, but the sudden shadows and darkness might have been observed. Laying in the snow, they waited for more patrolling guards, but after another forty-five minutes, all they saw was the standard twenty-minute walk-by. Approaching the wire fence they clipped a small meter to it to check if there was power running through the steel mesh before cutting a section out just large enough to crawl through.

Once inside, they quickly taped the cut section back in place. It wouldn't pass a close inspection, but a cursory glance wouldn't show it had been cut. The building they wanted was the upper rear section of the front main office. By keeping to shadows, and with weapons drawn, they finally approached it from the rear. Hythe flipped open a small wallet, pulled out some miniature metal picks, and started on the lock. Half expecting the alarm to sound as the door was opened, they were both surprised when nothing happened. Quickly checking the frame and edge of the door to confirm whether a silent alarm had been triggered, they heard the patrolling guards approaching and managed to hide inside just as the guards walked by. Breathing a sigh of relief at their narrow escape, they moved along empty corridors and up the stairs. Finally, they arrived at the manager's office on the second floor. Everything was in darkness, and they couldn't afford to use the lights, so, pulling a black cloth out of his jacket, Deacon placed it over the computer screen while he plugged in a USB data drive and pressed the power button. It was unlikely the glow of the screen would be seen by anybody from outside, but they didn't take any chances. Hythe moved over to the wall where the dark outline of a safe could be made out. This one also had a keypad, and even using the latest gadgets and electronic gizmos 'Lonely' left them, it still took almost fifteen minutes to crack the code. In the meantime, Deacon had finished the data dump, and he pocketed the USB drive and powered off the computer. As the safe door swung open, a red light began to flash on a LED display inside the safe, and a thirty-second timer began to count down.

'Fuck. What do we do now?'

'Quick. Plug in Lonely's box again. If that doesn't work, run like fuck in twenty-eight seconds. Pass me those folders.'

Glancing at the names on them, Deacon tossed them aside one by one until he saw the one with Poteryannoye Sokrovishche OOO stamped on it. Jamming it up under his jacket while counting down the seconds in their heads, they both picked up their weapons and were about to run towards the door just as Lonely's gizmo box bleeped and the red light in the safe stopped flashing and turned green. Breathing a sigh of relief and laying the contents of the PSO file on the floor, Deacon photographed every page by shielded torchlight. Apart from the other folders, there was nothing else of interest in the safe, so after putting all the folders back, he closed its door before unplugging Lonely's gizmo.

Their exit back out was the exact reversal of entry. With the aid of their NVGs, they passed around the other dark buildings towards where the fence wire was cut. Pushing the wire back together, Deacon held the cuts close together while Hythe clipped small staples over the cuts. It wouldn't hold if anyone pushed hard against them, but the staples were more permanent than the tape and would pass visual inspection.

Back away from the fencing, and with Hythe keeping watch, Deacon unplugged the receiver and detonator and removed the C4. Tempting though it was to have blown the power and to have gone in shooting, discretion was obviously the better choice. They hadn't taken anything, merely copied it, so the longer their intrusion stayed undiscovered, the better.

Knowing if they were stopped they couldn't explain away their weapons; they hid their gear and armaments in the empty buildings before heading back to their hotel rooms.

With a chair wedged under the door handle for added security, Deacon uploaded the photos from his camera and the contents from the USB drive using a secure remote encrypted server connection back to Langley, before deleting all evidence locally off them.

20

After another boring breakfast of more porridge and black bread, they checked out and headed outside. Two men were waiting by their vehicle. Both were mean looking and well built. Carrying just overnight bags and his computer, Deacon mouthed to Hythe, 'Trouble.'

Opening the trunk and dropping their bags inside, Hythe slammed the trunk lid closed, and the two of them turned to face the men.

For maybe ten seconds nobody spoke, then another eight thugs approached, four from each direction until the car, Deacon, and Hythe were completely surrounded. Two of the thugs were carrying pickaxe handles, one had a long chain, three were brandishing knives while the other four just stood there clenching and unclenching their fists.

'Rock, paper, scissors, comrades?' Deacon said, with a grin as he gently shook his arms and loosened his muscles, noticing Hythe was doing much the same himself.

Seeing the quizzical look on their faces from his comment, the two of them just waited for one of their assailants to make the first move.

One with a knife and one with a pickaxe advanced on Hythe, while the other pickaxe thug plus the chain guy moved towards Deacon.

Hythe feigned moving right while moving sharply left. As the pickaxe guy raised the handle above his head, ready to smash it down on Hythe, he darted in and delivered three rapid, hard punches to the guy's midriff. With a whoosh of expelled air, the thug almost doubled over, and Hythe almost gently lifted the pickaxe handle from the thug's fingers as he collapsed to his knees, gasping for air. Stepping back, Hythe swung it once, hard, at the guy's neck, connecting just below his right ear. The guy collapsed like a dropped sack. Following the swing through and upwards, Hythe brought the end of the handle down with enormous force onto the forearm of the second guy advancing with the knife. Both the ulna and the radius bones snapped under the tremendous impact; the guy screamed, went as white as a sheet, and promptly fainted.

Deacon's attackers didn't fare any better. The one with the chain started swinging it around his head, ready to lay into Deacon, but Deacon just kept moving backward. Waiting until the maximum amount of chain was behind the attacker, and at the height of its swing, Deacon leaped forward towards his pickaxe attacker while driving his right elbow towards the chain guy's exposed throat. When a pointed swinging elbow meets the soft throat tissues, there's only one outcome possible. Turning blue, the guy collapsed to his knees, gasping for air, the chain dropping to the ground. Catching the downward smack of the swinging pickaxe in both palms, Deacon spun and twisted, pulling it completely out of the other attacker's hands. As he continued spinning, he changed his grip and thrust the bulbous end directly into the stomach of the chain guy who was still struggling to breathe. He went down almost as quickly as Hythe's first attacker. Turning back he delivered two hard jabs into the pickaxe handle attacker's chest, and the third much harder jab resulted in the cracking of at least one rib, maybe two. As the guy partly collapsed, Deacon swung the handle like a baseball bat as hard as he could into the guy's kidneys, and he also joined his three other colleagues.

From start to finish, both attacks had taken less than ten seconds to quell. The ten attackers were now six and Deacon, and Hythe hadn't even raised a sweat. Retreating slightly and obviously unsure what to do, the remaining six moved backward until with a screech of brakes and blue lights flashing, three police cars came roaring into the hotel car park.

The female hotel receptionist came rushing out, shouting, 'Men have been attacked.' However, instead of the police grabbing the attackers, Hythe and Deacon suddenly found themselves facing nine very angry and highly excited policemen, all aiming their weapons at them and shouting in Russian.

With their hands forced behind them, both Hythe and Deacon's wrists were secured with cable ties. Their attackers were spoken to by the police but allowed to leave, half-carrying and supporting their four fallen comrades.

Deacon and Hythe were spat on by the police before being bundled roughly and separately into two of the police cars.

They were shouted at in Russian for the duration of the five-minute drive to the local Police Station, before having their phones confiscated, their coats removed plus anything that could be used as a weapon, including bootlaces and pants belt. Thrown into a cold, icy cell, they would be kept apart from each other for the remainder of the morning.

Four hours after their initial lockup, they were moved into another cell and interviewed by Captain Medvedev again.

He was sitting shuffling paper before finally looking up and saying, 'You are both charged with starting a fight in a public place. You have injured four loyal Russian comrades, and you are facing five years in jail with a twenty thousand U.S. dollar fine each. How do you plead?'

Keeping very calm, Deacon merely answered, 'Captain, this is total bullshit. They attacked us. Why would two of us set on ten of them? What could we hope to achieve? We demand to call the U.S. Embassy. We have your government's permission to be here. You are about to have a major international incident on your hands.' *Deacon knew their embassy wouldn't help them, this was the normal course of action for innocent people so not to have insisted would have looked suspicious.*

Looking at them for almost a minute, they could see the anger in the Captain's eyes. Finally, he stormed back out, slamming the cell door leaving them both together.

Held in the cell for the remainder of the day without food or drink, they were just beginning to get really annoyed when Medvedev entered the cell again.

'Do you plead guilty?'

'Fuck you, pal. We demand food and water and to call our embassy. The longer you stop us from doing that, the worse this will be for you,' Deacon replied. 'Your face will be all over the U.S. by this time tomorrow. How do you think your masters will take it when they see your face splashed everywhere and the story of how ten angry Russians attacked two innocent American researchers. How will that reflect on Russian Government business?'

Storming back out, the door was slammed again; however, this time, hot coffee and stale bread were supplied two hours later.

At 06:00 the following morning, the cell door opened, and Medvedev walked in and sat himself down before placing a folder on the desk. Deacon said to him, 'Captain, we both know we are innocent. We are only here researching for a film, approved by your government. This is going to get worse today, so what can we do to make this problem go away?'

After a moment's thought the Captain opened the folder and started tapping the top sheet of paper, saying, 'Yesterday morning I received this fax demanding the two of you be arrested and held indefinitely. I don't know where the fax came from, just from one of the offices in Moscow. It just said you two were to be arrested and held. I am just carrying out orders.'

After a slight pause, he continued, 'However, you are rich Americans. It is possible the fax arrived after you left and I missed you,' he said, tapping the paper beneath his finger, one eyebrow slightly raised.

Deacon leaned forward, glanced down, and thought for a moment or two. Then he smiled and asked for his satellite phone back. He said, 'Captain. I think I have a solution that will keep us all happy.'

Captain Medvedev just sat there looking at the two of them. Eventually, he stood, grabbed the folder, and walked out. Ten minutes later, a guard walked in with Deacon's satellite phone and handed it to him. Powering it up, he immediately called Hank.

'Boss, you've had me worried. Where the fuck are you?'

'At the local cop shop again. Listen, did you get flight clearance yesterday?'

'Yes, for a ten o'clock morning take-off.'

'How soon could we leave today? Could we go asap?'

'Uhhh, well it's not easy, boss, what with it being both a military and civilian base. We'd still need clearance.'

'Can you bluff it due to previous flight clearance?'

'Can all but try, boss.'

'Take 5 thou out of the safe and place it in an envelope and put it on the bottom step. Start and warm up the engines for immediate take-off when we get there.'

Finishing the call, he turned to the guard and asked to speak to the Captain again.

Medvedev returned a few minutes later, closed the door until just the three of them were alone, and said, 'Yes?'

'Captain, if you were to forget the fax for a while and let us get to our airplane, there would be a thank you gift of US$5,000 cash waiting for you.'

Smiling, Medvedev slowly nodded, and they both shook hands before Medvedev headed back out.

'It could be a trap, John?'

'Yeah, but in this case, I don't think so. We're in the middle of bumfuck Russia, and this Medvedev guy isn't exactly on a fast-track promotion here. Five grand is about eight-months' pay, and many Russian officials accept corruptness as part of the job. I don't think Medvedev is any different. It will be easy for him to bluff the phone lines were down, and the fax never arrived.'

Twenty minutes later, the cell door was opened, and both prisoners were escorted to the Captain's car. No other officers were present as Medvedev climbed into the driver's seat.

Arriving at the airport, the guard on duty recognized the Captain, saluted and waved the vehicle through. It was still just before seven o'clock, and the airport seemed deserted. The main parts of the small airport didn't open until eight o'clock unless inbound aircraft were expected. The night-duty flight controller was in the tower and had approved flight clearance. As they headed towards the hangar, they could hear the gentle whine of the Gulfstream's engines.

Driving into the hangar, Deacon noticed the wheel strops were removed, and he could see the shimmer of hot engine exhaust at the rear of the two engines. The only thing holding the aircraft in check were the brakes.

At the bottom of the aircraft steps was a white envelope. Picking it up, Deacon handed it over to Medvedev while shaking his hand.

Without waiting, they climb aboard as the Captain thumbed the crisp, fresh notes. Moments later, the stairway began to recline and fold as the brakes were removed, and the aircraft moved slowly towards the hangar doorway.

Before giving the Captain any chance to change his mind, as the nose wheel cleared the doorway, Hank opened the throttle a fraction, and the small aircraft almost jumped out towards the taxiway, the exhaust gases blowing back towards the Captain who was forced to hold on to his hat.

Opening the throttle more, the plane started to accelerate and head down the taxiway as Deacon was still in the process of locking the main hatch. Turning sharply onto the main runway, Hank pushed the throttles to their stops, and the business jet hurtled along the concrete, ignoring the snow flurries, before lifting her nose westward and accelerating up into the dark sky, still slowly brightening from the east.

One hour later, they requested flight clearance to alter course from Moscow to Copenhagen, Denmark. With permission granted, they headed towards the Danish city before refueling for the long flight back to Washington.

21

Admiral Carter's Office, the Pentagon

Sipping coffee, Mitch produced prints from the information they had obtained.

'Vorkuta appears to be the regional local center for the Urals Mining Company. They process the relatively small amounts of coal produced in that immediate region, before shipping it out by train. Here are lists of daily, weekly, and monthly tonnage shipments from there, broken down to types of coal, etc. They have many more sites around Russia and would seem, at least to the naked eye, to be quite legitimate,' he said, passing the copies across.

'These are files from the data drive you copied, and they all seem legit. The head guy is confirmed as Major Pavel Cherenko, but we knew that already. However, it confirms the tie-in to the military. A lot of the other data seems to be normal company stuff such as payroll, employee details and the like. However, Director Ingram over at the CIA is creaming over all of this – they're always looking for tidbits of info they may be able to hook into and use to their advantage. As to the company known as Poteryannoye Sokrovishche, there was nothing showing on the main directory of the drive.'

'But there was a folder. I photographed the contents,' Deacon said.

'Correct. And I said 'not on the main directory of the drive'. There were a number of hidden, password-protected sub-folders that were quite interesting.'

'Go on,' the Admiral said, beckoning Deacon to pour them all more coffee.

As Deacon grabbed the coffee pot, Mitch continued, 'We have broken the passwords to two of the folders. They refer to this company PSO. Officially, it doesn't exist. It's run by a Lieutenant General Dmitry Yermilov, which is surprising being it's a smaller subsidiary, but this guy Yermilov is four ranks above Cherenko. This site at Vorkuta is the central processing plant for what PSO supplies.

'And what they supply is,' Mitch stopped to take another mouthful of coffee, much to the annoyed look from Deacon, 'what they supply is standard minerals such as copper, fluorspar, cobalt, etc. as well as about a dozen of the seventeen classified rare earth minerals. They have also been processing significant amounts of silver and gold, and, in particular, diamonds.'

'Wow, they have a diamond mine,' Hythe joked.

'Well, that's where it gets interesting. All of these minerals and gold are shipped from their one working mine eighty miles north of Vorkuta that we knew nothing about. The heavy stuff, including silver and gold, is shipped under guard by rail, but the smaller rare earth items and the diamonds are flown to Vorkuta by helicopter, and they come directly from Amderma. None of this appears to be recorded officially. The quantity of standard minerals is added to the totals from the Vorkuta mines, while the rare earth, silver, gold, and diamonds never show up in official paperwork.'

Looking at the data, Hythe asked, 'How much are we talking about?'

The Admiral cleared his throat and said, 'Tens and tens of millions of dollars, possibly hundreds of millions. If our rough estimates are correct, we think Yermilov might have spirited away close on half a billion dollars' worth. The more important question is where has that money gone or what it is funding. We know the Politburo is corrupt and everyone is taking bribes, but Yermilov reports directly to Viktor Kalygin, so we know he's mixed up in something big. As you know, President Kalygin is one of the most corrupt presidents Russia has ever had the misfortune to have ruling over them.'

'So how big is this Amderma plant. It must be pretty massive, yet the recon boys over in the National Reconnaissance Office missed it?'

'That, John, is an interesting fact. Mitch, show them the aerials.'

Handing over a series of photographs, Mitch said, 'It's a piss-poor dump of a place. Population of about 700, down from 6,000 back in the '90s. Located in the north on the Kara Sea well into the Arctic Circle. There's a small airport, now virtually abandoned. Used to be a Mig-19 interceptor base in the cold war, but closed in the late '80s. Now an Antonov flies in once per week in winter with supplies. Most buildings look uninhabited. Google Earth shows it as desolate, yet this is where tens of millions of dollars' worth of diamonds and rare earth metals are coming from.'

With that, the Admiral turned towards Deacon and said, 'John, we've fully briefed the President and his team. I know you've only just come back from that region, but he's requesting you to go in there and have a look around. You can take your team if you require, but we believe a low-key approach is the best. Charles and Lisa over at the CIA can set up your legend, but as always, you'll be flying under the radar, so to speak. But something you need to know first. And this stays in this office! There was a U.S. number in one of the folders. More importantly, it was a burner phone, and it was last used by someone inside Langley. We don't know who used it, but it looks like we have a traitor or at least a double agent at the CIA passing them information. The President is aware and has ordered General Dreiberg at the DNI, and Clark at the FBI to investigate. Ingram at the CIA has not been made aware as we think this is someone at very senior level over there, and we don't want to spook them. We don't know how far and wide or how high this extends. But it means we cannot guarantee they won't know you are coming.'

After sitting there a moment in thought, Deacon said, 'Give me a little time, Admiral. I have a few things to complete here, and I need to sit with Mitch and Patrick to come up with a plan. Let me get back to you.'

Mitch commandeered a vacant meeting room, and the three of them spent the next two hours going over terrain maps, timetables, flight routes, and a hundred other items before finally agreeing on a basic plan.

From the aerials, they could see roads in this entire area were pretty non-existent.

'What about using the small airport at Amderma?' Mitch suggested.

'No, it's so small any unscheduled landing would become big news and let everyone know we are there. No, it will have to be a covert approach.'

'What about by sea?'

'Possible, but that entire coastline will be heavily protected by radar. Any approach by surface craft will be seen.'

'So what are you thinking? Submarine?'

'Again, possible, but the sub would have to be well inside Russian waters. There's a high chance it could be detected and attacked. That would be a major embarrassment to the government,' Deacon said.

'So what does that leave? A very long route across land or a parachute drop?'

'I'm thinking more towards a parachute drop,' he said, turning to the screen on his computer.

After calling up various web sites, he said, 'We'd need flight clearance over the area, but nearest commercial jet routes are over fifty miles south. I wonder . . . .'

Leaving him to think, Hythe and Mitch headed off to get coffee and sandwiches.

Thirty minutes later, Deacon was ready to discuss his plan.

'There's something niggling me about this. Why are we being asked to go check? This is something a local asset on the ground could check. Or overhead satellite imagery. We are not being given the full picture here. But, assuming we go, we could use a military flight along commercial routes and 'chute out, but that would leave us with a fifty-or-so mile hike over rough terrain. Not impossible, but a reasonable chance of being discovered.'

Turning to Patrick, he asked, 'Ever used a wingsuit?'

With a smile of evident fond memories, Hythe stroked his chin and said, 'Yeah, they're great fun, but I think you can only get about 20 miles.'

'A place in California is advertising ones with enlarged wings. They claim theirs will fly thirty to forty miles. What do you think?' Deacon said, turning the screen for them to see.

After another hour checking and rechecking, Mitch typed it up and passed it over to the Admiral for approval.

Finally, it was sent to the CIA for passports and associated paperwork to be produced, along with transport and weapons arranged.

22

At nine o'clock the following morning, after not having been able to reach the detective by phone, Deacon headed to the Metropolitan Police HQ in downtown Washington. Showing his ID, he was escorted upstairs to the detectives' pool for an update about the shooting of Garry with Detective Tony Rissolini.

Sitting at his desk, eating a hot dog with slaw, the detective raised a hand and summoned him over. 'Hey, Mister "Friend of the Chief," what can I do for you?' as Deacon approached and sat down.

Rissolini had tomato sauce on his chin and fingers, and the hotdog was dripping more onto the paperwork.

'So, Poirot, have you caught the guy or guys that killed Garry Moore yet?'

'Yeah, well, early days yet. Gotta few tips and leads. Been following 'em up, y'know.'

'So you've not just been sitting on your fat Italian ass doing nothing. I'm impressed.'

'What the fuck?'

'Look, you've got a murder in cold blood, in broad daylight, and all you've got is a few tips?'

'Who the fuck do you think you are? Eh? Nobody saw nothing, like. Just ghosts. All we's got is two men did it, possibly black. By the time anybody realized what was happening, they'd gone. OK? So lay off.'

Deacon slowly shook his head, saying, 'America's finest, eh?' before rising and walking out the same door he'd come in.

<><><>

Arriving at the office, he gave Gina a quick summary of his talk with Rissolini. Disappointed, she said she'd call Cindy and let her know about the lack of progress, and that it did look likely it was aimed at Deacon and just a terrible case of mistaken identity. Wrong time, wrong place. Wouldn't make it any better for her or take away the pain, but might help her come to terms with it easier.

Having been away, Deacon spent most of the day completing a mass of paperwork that had built up as well as partaking in a video conference call with Japan concerning a group of senior bank officials arriving the following week who wanted to employ the protective services of Phylax. For the evening, John had invited Helen and Mitch, along with Patrick, who, being back in Washington was working a couple of days at the British Embassy, and the Admiral, to come to his place for a barbeque.

Having purchased a stainless steel monster of an outside grill last fall, he hadn't had a chance to christen it yet, but tonight was the night. Leaving the office early, he headed to the local supermarket, where he picked up steaks and fish, along with cobs of corn, salad, and plenty of beer.

Driving home, he noticed a white Ford van seeming to keep pace four cars behind. However, after it turned off at an intersection, he put it out of his mind.

Pulling into his designated parking spot, he began to unload everything, ending up with three large paper bags just about grasped in one arm, with a 24 pack of beer in the other.

At his door, he was half leaning on the doorframe and trying to balance the pack of beer on a raised knee, while he fumbled for his keys just as his cell rang.

Suddenly willing hands grabbed the keys off him, placed them in the door, and unlocked it as Mirabel squeezed past him, smiling. 'Here, let me help,' she said, taking the beer from him and moving towards the fridge. 'I'll go on putting it away while you take your call now the fridge is fixed.'

Deacon was checking the calling party's number when something didn't sound right.

'Say again.'

'I said the fridge is fixed. I let the men in earlier, and they left about a half-hour ago. They said it was fixed now,' she said, reaching for the door.

As her fingers curled around the stainless steel handle and she pulled, Deacon screamed, 'NO! DON'T TOUC---

The blast blew the fridge door completely off its hinges, crushing Mirabel's hands, face, and chest. The over blast shock wave turned the soft tissues in her body cavity to mush. Milk, bread, eggs, and cold cuts were vaporized, and Deacon was flung backward back out through the entrance, his cell phone being ripped from his hands.

Crashing back against the wall winded him, and he glanced up just in time to see a table, or what remained of it, flying towards him and smash into what remained of Mirabel's body. She'd actually saved his life because he'd been standing almost eight feet behind her, and her torso acted as a partial blast shield.

Dazed and bleeding from his eye sockets and nose, and deafened by the blast, he tried to look for his phone to dial 911 as something wet stuck on the wall next to him began to drip on his arm. Sighing, he finally succumbed to the blast, gently sliding down the same wall into a welcome unconsciousness.

23

Face black and blue, he looked like he'd lost a round against Mike Tyson, but miraculously, he'd not suffered any significant damage or trauma. He had aches, pains, and severe bruising, but that was all. Kept overnight in a private ward in hospital he was X-rayed, CT, and MRI scanned before receiving a necessary certificate of health and well-being that allowed him to leave late in the afternoon. He still had a ringing in his ears and his hearing was down by almost half, but the doctors had said that would all clear in the next day or so.

Hospital rules stated all patients moving between locations had to be transported either by stretcher or wheelchair, so an indignant John Deacon was finally wheeled out to the visitor waiting center, cursing quietly under his breath that he was fine and needed to get back to business. Instead, he was held captive sitting in the black leather wheelchair until a worried-looking Gina blasted through the main entrance doors.

With his apartment a crime scene and uninhabitable anyway, Gina had already taken it on herself to look after him, but Deacon had other ideas.

Detective Tony Rissolini was waiting to interview him, but Deacon had already given full details to the evening shift the night before. Even to Rissolini, it now had to look like Garry had been mistaken for Deacon, and Deacon didn't feel like explaining to the detective why he hadn't mentioned his suspicion straight away.

Opening his cell, he called a worried Mitch.

162

'Hey pal, yeah, I'll be fine. A few more bruises and scars, but I'll heal. But laying here has helped me think and the more I've thought about this mission, the more I'm convinced something's not right here. Not only that, some bastard is trying to kill me, which may, or may not be connected to this mission. We're not going anywhere until we get the bigger picture. I want answers. Tell the Admiral it's the full picture or nothing,' he said before hanging up.

His truck was still outside his home, so he sat in Gina's passenger seat brooding and deep in thought all the way to her place while she chatted as she drove her Prius. Arriving at her home where he would stay for a couple of days until his apartment was finished with by the police, he insisted he would cook their evening meal. Two hours later and fortified with a cold beer in one hand, he was standing on her rear porch in front of a small brazier as he fanned the glowing charcoal with a folded piece of cardboard as lamb kebabs on the skewers slowly charred.

Gina was sitting, curled up, in a large rattan chair watching him. He was in the middle of discussing his feelings that something far more significant was going on that he didn't know about when his cell rang. The caller ID showed the call was from Mitch.

'John, I passed your message onto the Admiral. He wasn't happy. He muttered something about you being 'too damn smart' and shooed me back out of his office. I don't know whom he called, but he made over a dozen calls. End result is we have an eight o'clock tomorrow morning at Langley. Patrick is also invited. How about I pick you up at seven-fifteen from Gina's?'

The drive the following morning was quiet as all three men were deep in thought. After the previous evening's call, Deacon had called Hythe about the meeting before texting Mitch to pick Hythe up first from his hotel. Now they were driving north along the George Washington Memorial Parkway towards CIA headquarters at Langley. Occupying room C.46 again, Deacon, Hythe, and Mitch knocked on the door and waited.

Footsteps approached from within the room before the door was suddenly yanked open. Sitting waiting were General's Dreiberg and Mansfield, Melvin Tarrant, and Charles Ingram of the CIA.

Admiral Carter held the door and beckoned the three of them inside. 'Gentlemen,' he said, 'let's talk.'

After the three newcomers were seated, the Admiral started, 'John, we were only instructed to tell you the very basic of information unless you raised it to us.'

'Instructed to? By whom?'

'The order came directly from the White House. But last evening I spoke with the President, and he's authorized full disclosure. So tell me, what do you want to know?'

'This set-up . . . it's far too complex just for mining some coal. The missing scientific base, and all the potential deaths in the same region? There's something far larger than a bit of illicit mining. What's going on?'

General Tarrant stood up and walked to a whiteboard, saying, 'It's ok Douglas, I'll take lead,' before continuing to Deacon, 'I know you are civilian now, but I'll refer to your honorary rank, if I may. Lieutenant Commander; Major Hythe; what you are about to learn is of highest importance and carries a purple-level security clearance. None of this can ever be repeated outside of this room. Understood?'

After receiving nods of acceptance, Tarrant continued, 'What do you know about shooting down missiles?'

'Well, when you detect an incoming missile, you fire off one of yours to intercept, I guess. Never really thought about it in detail, but same as a shoulder-launched surface-to-air-missile, I guess.'

'Good answer, Lieutenant, but it's a little more complex than that. A shoulder-launched surface-to-air-missile is usually used against aircraft. They fly fast, but compared to an incoming missile, they're real slow. You fire towards or after an aircraft, and the in-built sensors take over. Usually heat-seeking, they lock onto the aircraft's hot engine emissions and steer the faster moving missile in to explode against the aircraft. Correct?'

'Sir.'

'Okay, now think of the old anti-aircraft ack-ack fire in World War Two. The gunners would spot the aircraft and fire their ack-ack by leading the aircraft. You see, they knew it would take a certain amount of seconds for their ack-ack shell to get to the same altitude as the aircraft, say 30,000 feet, so they would 'lead' the aircraft so their shells would get to the same three-dimensional point in space and at the same time as the aircraft arrived. Direct hits obviously brought the aircraft down, but ack-ack didn't need a direct hit. The shells exploded in close proximity, and the shrapnel would fill the sky as the aircraft flew into it. That's what usually brought the aircraft down. Even if the ack-ack exploded behind the aircraft, the speed of the shrapnel exploding was faster than the plane was flying so effectively it would catch up and still damage the aircraft.

'Now consider an ICBM or intercontinental ballistic missile. Most current designed ICBM's fly at between 6 and 7,000 miles an hour. That's between 8,800 feet to over 10,000 feet per second. Or, to put it into perspective,

165

almost two miles per second. Most missiles are relatively unprotected as weights for protection slow them down or reduce range, but if you managed to fire your ack-ack weapon at the missile and it exploded just as the incoming one passed it, by the time the shrapnel exploded out to fill the sky, the incoming one has moved past it at up to 10,000 feet per second. So what that means is you need a fair amount of computing power to track the incoming missile and work out how long it will take yours to reach the same height. You also need to estimate where both will need to be to intercept in all three dimensions and offset yours so that the exploding shrapnel has chance to fill the sky in front of the missile before it gets there, so as to cause it damage before the damn thing flies straight past it.

'Now consider having to do that on whatever track you detect the incoming missile. If the incoming one is approaching you directly, then you add its speed to the speed of your intercept missile. But if it's tracking across you, then it's all different equations. Even worse, if it's flying away from you, you end up playing catch-up. Clear so far?'

'Sir.'

'So now we come to lasers, or Directed Energy Weapons, to give them their full and proper name. We are just talking about lasers at this time. A laser emits a beam of light energy at the actual speed of light. The reason a laser is so powerful is it concentrates the power. Go outside on a sunny day with a magnifying glass, and you can focus the sun. Do it onto a blade of grass, and this focused power can cause a fire quite easily. What you have done is put a large amount of energy into a single, concentrated area. From a simplistic point of view, a laser works the same sort of way, but instead of having to move a magnifying glass to focus it, the tiny laser beam is

166

continuous. This is called 'coherent' light. Small lasers can be used for something as delicate as cornea replacements in the human eye, while bigger more powerful ones can easily cut steel. So the advantage of using a laser to shoot down a missile is you can aim it directly as the beam travels at the speed of light. No more having to work out where their missile will be by the time you get to it and planning an intercept course. All you need to do is see it visually or on radar, aim, and fire. Saves enormous amounts of computing power.'

'I sense a 'but' coming . . ..'

'Absolutely, Lieutenant. The downside is if you make the attacking missile very shiny, up to 90% of your laser beam might be reflected off elsewhere and scattered, not leaving enough power to destroy it. One solution is to keep the beam aimed at exactly the same spot until the weaker amount does enough damage. Very hard to do, especially if the incoming missile rolls or spins. Also, dust in the atmosphere diffuses and scatters the laser beam and the further the distance from laser to missile, the worst it becomes. Cloud affects it even worse. Back in the years of Reagan, we had the Strategic Defense Initiative or SDI. Its nickname was Star Wars if you remember. The plan was to have large, powerful lasers in space. That would get over the problems of diffusion in the atmosphere and clouds, but it's incredibly expensive and beset with technical problems.'

Stopping for a moment to take a sip of water, the General continued, 'One solution is an X-ray laser. X-rays are not easily blocked. The only real way of stopping an X-ray is lead screening, and you can't put lead screening around missiles as that is far too heavy. Shiny surfaces don't affect X-rays either - they just punch straight through. Same with clouds – no effect. Dust and atmosphere still has some scatter effect, but overall much less impact on an X-ray laser, too. The problem or downside is to make X-rays 'coherent' i.e. to line the X-rays up into a concentrated beam, you need a very intense X-ray reflecting surface to bounce them off. Much more complex than building a standard light-based laser. We have one under development, and it's almost thirty feet long. Silvered glass surfaces are just not pure enough. One theory is to use diamonds. But it would need lots of them, and their surfaces need to be cut extremely accurately so as to reflect the X-rays precisely. One Russian scientist claimed to have discovered the way to make X-rays not only reflect off the inside surfaces of a diamond, but each time it reflects somehow he's managed to make it increase in power. He claimed it is also possible to make an extremely powerful version by synchronizing multiple lasers together and their combined output would be more than the sum of the individual outputs. He literally means two plus two plus two would equal far more than six. That's his theory, anyway.'

'And the Russians are mining diamonds . . .' Deacon said, beginning to connect the dots.

'Not just that, Lieutenant, we believe they have put his theory to the test and developed a new laser capable of shooting down missiles and satellites, far more powerful than anything they had before. Far more powerful, in fact, than anything we have. The National Intelligence believe they have uncovered the reason and importance of the diamond mining. They believe the Russians are far ahead of us and in the final testing stages of an X-ray laser missile defense system, some 400-500 times more powerful than the most powerful lasers we currently have. No missile or satellite system known to man could withstand that amount of power. If true, our force of ICBM's and fleet of first-attack aircraft become immediately redundant, along with any satellite they

168

choose to take out. That's why we think they have been mining for diamonds. Now Russia is already the world's largest producer of diamonds by volume, and theirs are very high quality, but not high enough for this. The problem is political. Russia, combined with the various countries in Africa account for something like eighty percent of the world's diamonds, and the market is awash. Diamond prices slumped big time after the 2008 world recession and have never recovered. Russia currently stockpiles most of their production. There is good reason to cut diamond supply and push prices back up, but Russia literally cannot afford to do so for too long. The country's credit rating is faltering, and even at a depressed world market price, a diamond-buying spree would cost the government a massive $220 million each month. Their main diamonds mines are in eastern Siberia and any increase in production would be seen one way or another by the other diamond producing countries and cause prices to slump even more. But just mining extra diamonds is not the answer. These lasers need incredibly high quality stones and these specific diamonds are not coming from their standard mines in Siberia. We think they have found an easily mined source in Danish waters in the Arctic. It's been known for generations that the waters of the Arctic are full of minerals. Less well known is the region is also full of precious or rare metals used in the latest high-speed computers. Most of these metals and elements are contained in minute quantities in manganese nodules that lay just under the seabed at depths of up to six thousand feet. Up to now, it has been cost-prohibitive to mine those metals and elements in any great quantity due to the amount that would need to be mined to obtain enough payback, and the cost of operating in the depths of water these nodules are found in. The ice covering the area adds another hazard and cost element, but with global warming, the sea ice north of Russia is receding for longer periods each year. We estimate that within another five to ten years the waters of the Arctic will be one of the largest producing regions in the world. That's why every country bordering that region is making territorial claims, with Russia's claims being the loudest.'

'Now if they are mining, and in Danish waters, it's possible the people at Ice Station Hap stumbled onto something about it and were eliminated. We need you to discover if and how they are mining the diamonds and to stop their production.'

'So this place Amderma where the mining takes place. Is that where the X-ray laser is?'

'No. Our recon flights and satellites have identified a disused observatory in the very north of the Ural mountains about 220 miles southeast of Amderma. Very isolated and at high altitude with perfect horizon to horizon views out over the Arctic. We believe the actual laser is situated there. Any attempt by U.S. Forces to stop the mining or put the observatory out of action could be construed as an act of war by Russia, but we must get this mining stopped.'

'So does any of this have anything to do with someone trying to kill me?' Deacon asked.

Charles Ingram replied, 'Not that we're aware, Lieutenant. We think this is some sort of personal vendetta against you. I've assigned a team of agents to look into the names you've supplied, but there's no news yet.'

The group spent another hour or so going over exactly what was required and what equipment they could take with them.

Ingram said his people would take care of allocating their new names, arranging passports and travel documents, and confirmed the paperwork and cover stories would be complete before the end of the day.

Mirabel's funeral had been in the afternoon the day following. Her ex-husband attended, along with a large crowd of friends. The official story was an accidental gas explosion in the block of apartments. Deacon had attended in full Naval uniform and given the first eulogy. He'd kept it simple, saying she was a good friend and neighbor and would be missed terribly. In reality, he knew he'd miss her far more than he'd let on. In the last eighteen months she had always been a friendly voice to talk with. She was a massive flirt, an outlandish storyteller, and the recipient of some of the rudest jokes he'd ever heard. But, she had a heart of gold, was excellent company, and nothing was too much for her. There was no romance between them, just pure friendship, but Deacon valued friendship closely and someone had taken her life.

Although deeply upset by her murder, he kept his feelings to himself. Looking at her casket a final time, he vowed to find her executioners and seek revenge when this mission was complete.

24

Somewhere in the Arctic Circle

Two days later Deacon and Hythe were boarding an American Airlines scheduled flight to London where they were met by representatives of the U.S. Embassy before being taken to RAF Lakenheath in Suffolk, where a special delivery direct from California was waiting for them.

The following morning a near-empty C-17 Globemaster large military transport aircraft took off from Lakenheath before initially turning westwards, before changing its ident settings and reversing course, then heading northeast towards Norway and Sweden, before continuing by following the regular great circle route to Japan.

Meanwhile, the British Airways flight board in Heathrow showed flight BA0005 as delayed. An hour later, the status was updated to reflect 'Cancelled', with all booked passengers being offered refunds or compensation.

To all ground-based air traffic control systems, flight BA0005 was on time and underway, as each sweep of the ATS radar returned a response indicating the aircraft being monitored as BA0005.

Five hours after take-off, Deacon and Hythe climbed into their dark-colored thermally-insulated wingsuits and inflated some of the enclosed pockets. They couldn't hear the pilot talking to Finnish Air Traffic Control, instructing that BA flight 0005 was experiencing a technical problem with its port engines and was planning to throttle them back temporarily.

Flying at a little over 44,000 feet and almost fifteen miles north of their usual flight path, the reduction in engine revolutions allowed the aircraft to slow quite rapidly. The whine of the tailgate door opening and the rush inside of freezing air soon awoke everyone. The red light was showing, indicating three minutes to target jump. Completing a final visual check over each other to ensure the harnesses and helmets were correctly fitted, the air tanks they were wearing tested and face masks fitted, they both moved to the rear of the aircraft nearer to the ramp.

After a final inspection ensuring no bare skin was showing as it would quickly freeze in the minus 55^{0}C temperature outside the aluminum skin of the aircraft, they stood there immobile, deep in thought. Not only did they have to contend with severe minus temperatures, but they would need to breathe from air tanks until they were well below fifteen thousand feet. The extra weight and shape of the tanks and facemask would all increase drag and reduce the distance they could fly. After what seemed an age, the aircraft slowed suddenly, and the red light turned green. Carrying as little extra weight as possible, they high-fived each other before turning and stepping off the ramp.

Instantly the rushing noise ceased.

They fell head over heels at least five hundred feet before they could right themselves and start actually flying. Glancing up, Hythe could see the C-17 disappearing into the distance. Had it not been for its navigation lights drawing his attention, Hythe probably wouldn't have seen it at all, its dark outline already invisible against the stars. Having radioed the Finnish ATC again that the temporary fault had been isolated as a fuel starvation problem and had been resolved, the pilot increased engines to full power again and would continue its voyage to its destination in Japan, still transmitting its BA0005 ident code every time it was washed by the electronic pulses of the air traffic control systems.

Prior to landing, but well within Japanese airspace, it would return its ident code to its previous military designation before altering course slightly before landing at the Yokota USAF airbase just outside Tokyo.

Flying high above the icy waters of the Lincoln Sea between Greenland and the North Pole, Captain Bissett, flying his Air Force RC-135, heard the radio traffic between BA0005 and the Finnish Air Traffic Control.

As usual, these fourteen-hour missions were repeated daily and made to overlap, ensuring monitoring of the northern Russian territory was maintained at all times. Satellites helped, but you couldn't beat the old-fashioned look-and-listen techniques used since the sixties. The main improvements since then being the aircraft were now more comfortable and warmer and could fly more extended periods, both in time and distance. And the electronics were far more advanced.

The Captain listened in to the radio traffic with interest. Any pilot having problems with an aircraft was concerning. It didn't matter whether you were civilian or military, friend, or foe. When you were up in the air, things could go wrong, and if enough things went wrong, or they were severe enough, people could get hurt.
Luckily, this seemed to be a minor issue, and after hearing the pilot radio the fault had seemed to clear, Hank relaxed again and continued to view the ice sheets below him.

Checking his watch, he knew if the X-ray burst were on time again tonight, it would be sometime in the next forty minutes. Since the first, just over six months previously, approximately every two months at the same comparative date and time, the burst had reoccurred, each time being almost double the previous strength in power. More worrying, each time the target drone distance was also doubled.

This time, the powers that be had arranged a satellite to be traversing the area overhead. If the burst occurred as expected tonight, between them and the satellite, they would hopefully get a better recording of its exact power and, more importantly, its exact location.

So far, each time they'd recorded it, they had isolated its source down to within a few square miles, but it was so brief. However, with two-directional monitoring, the experts reckoned they could get it down to mere inches.

As the clock approached 02:00, he knew everyone on-board would be on full alert. At 02:26, just as everyone was wondering if tonight was the night, Senior Airman Travers again monitored a brief burst of high power X-ray energy being emitted. The Raytheon Command and Control system recorded the burst and, having communicated to the computers onboard the satellite flying high overhead, computed its power output and its exact source coordinates. The signal strength had again doubled in size and was now sixteen times as powerful as the first time they'd detected it.

From the exact GPS locations of both the aircraft and the satellite's position, the source was again pinpointed to have come from a small region within the northern Urals mountains, but now able to be isolated down to an exact building. As before, no other unusual signals were detected.

As with all data collected, a summary report was immediately passed up the channels to senior intelligence officers.

Colonel Dudko's smile was beaming. So far, everything had gone 100% according to plan. Every six weeks, a new batch of diamonds had been delivered and were fitted into a waiting pair of lasers. These newly activated lasers had to be synchronized to the existing ones, and extensive bench testing and adjustments would then take place. Once combined, a live test to shoot down a drone would take place. Tonight was that test with nine out of the full complement of ten lasers fully synchronized and working.

If successful, and the Colonel had no reason to doubt it wouldn't be, in less than another two months the final laser would be added, and Russia would have one of the most powerful and deadly anti-satellite and anti-missile weapons ever invented.

Checking his watch, he knew the drone would be on station in another few minutes. The target operator confirmed the drone was coming into view in the radar system, and he selected the target on his screen. The targeting computers crunched their numbers, and the motors and gears controlling exactly where the twelve-foot-long silver tube was aiming moved it slightly as the selected target changed from red to green. As the drone flew on its course way above the Arctic ice mass, the motors and gears moved imperceptibly to keep the target precisely in its crosshairs.

Colonel Dudko tapped the operator on the shoulder and gave him permission to fire when ready. With a calm voice, the operator counted down, 'Three, Two, One, Fire,' and pressed the trigger.

Apart from the distant small image on the radar screen disappearing, nothing appeared to change. In one five-millionth of a second, the burst of power from the nine combined lasers disintegrated the drone at six hundred miles distance.

In previous test shots, it had started by punching a hole clean through the reflective surface of the drone. As the power output increased, each subsequent test caused more damage.

The last test had exploded the drone. This time the amount of energy simply atomized it.

25

Having finally stabilized the free-falling after leaving the aircraft, Deacon maneuvered his arms and legs until the wingsuit he was wearing altered his course to almost due north. Now the ride was much more stable and comfortable.

Pressing the finger switch in the palm of his hand, he said, 'Blue 2, do you read me?' The answer came moments later.

'Blue 1, to your rear and above.'

Glancing over his shoulder, he could see Hythe just a few hundred feet away from him and slightly higher.

Neither had any worry of Russian forces detecting them. Not only were their suits made of heavily insulated padded nylon, anything metal, such as a pistol or air tanks, was covered in a thin wire copper-mesh cloth. This type of covering absorbed, not reflected, radar pulses, thereby making them invisible. The radio only had a range of two miles and was scrambled. It was also burst transmitted, meaning messages took only fractions of a second to transmit, making detection by the enemy listening stations extremely unlikely.

With their night vision goggles turning the darkness of the Earth below them to a ghostly green, they flew on, quickly covering mile after mile. This close to the Arctic Circle, the land was entirely covered in snow, but gullies and rivers showed as black. The snow-covered landscape was displayed as a pale green. Any man-made heat sources would show brilliantly in their goggles, but looking around, there were few to be seen.

Even now, still at over 30,000 feet, and able to see more than 100 miles distance, only the occasional distant pinpoint glow of a bright light showed. The entire area was one of the most uninhabited regions in the world Deacon had ever visited. Flying on in the freezing weather while trying to minimize any unnecessary movement as each movement of an arm or leg made them drop a few feet lower, Deacon realized he could see a large pale green area many miles in front.

It took him a while to realize it was the ice sheets stretching from northern Russia way up to the Arctic. By now, the pale area was almost as wide as the horizon. Thousands and thousands of square miles of ice as far north and east and west as they could see.

As they got closer to their destination and lower to the Earth, they also realized they'd have to pull up and open their parachutes soon. Checking his GPS, Hythe confirmed they had traveled almost twenty-nine miles since leaving the aircraft, but their altitude was dropping fast. The extra weight of their air tanks and few weapons was taking its toll, and minutes later, at the height of only 250 feet above the terrain below, they had to pull their emergency parachutes. Dark gray, they were hidden against the sky had anyone been looking, but in the deserted terrain they were landing in no one was looking.

Olga Douzhenko had worked as an Air Traffic Controller for over twenty years at the local Air Traffic Control center at Salekhard. Keen on her job, she was well-liked and popular. She had started as a junior and quickly passed her various exams, receiving promotions as they became available, up to her present position of Senior.

She had received BA0005's initial warning it needed to decrease power to its port engines, made a note of the statement, and stayed in contact until the aircraft had confirmed the problem had resolved itself. The ident and radar return of the aircraft seemed normal, but it was a little off track.

Olga felt uneasy. Something was wrong, but she couldn't put her finger on it. She had 'lost' over ten aircraft that had crashed over the years, and she'd developed an instinct for when things weren't quite right.

Aeroflot, the state airline, had two levels of maintenance. High for the aircraft flying internationally and to the West where European, American or British rules applied to safety, and far lower to the fleet that remained inside Russia. Those Aeroflot aircraft the Politburo used had 'гп' printed on the fuselage under the pilot's window, the first letters of the Russian word mean 'airworthy'. Many of the remaining aircraft received rudimentary maintenance only, and Aeroflot within Russia had the most unexplained crashes of any airline worldwide. All ten crashes had been internal Aeroflot flights, and every one of them still haunted her. On three of them, she had been talking urgently to the pilot when she'd heard their final expletives as they'd crashed.

Her instincts were troubling her again today. Something was wrong with this flight, but she couldn't quite be sure what. The aircraft was a little slower than usual, although engine trouble might explain that. It was also returning a slightly bigger and brighter radar return on her screen, she thought.

Coupled with it being almost fifteen miles further north than its standard course, she just felt uneasy. She checked the log again to confirm. British Airways had been flying this route for over ten years, usually using a 747 or one of the newer 787's. But in all that time, she'd never experienced a pilot more than a few hundred yards off the great circle course. Maybe it was nothing, and she was just overly cautious, but Russia still wasn't a place that forgave mistakes, so she went and reported her feelings to her senior, Major Yenko.

He instructed her to check the British Airways and London Heathrow websites. Both showed today's BA0005 as canceled due to technical problems. With Douzhenko's concerns now confirmed that something was amiss, but not sure what, Major Yenko immediately raised his concerns with Central Command, in Moscow.

Within thirty minutes of the message being received, secure calls went out to the Russian Embassy based in Tokyo to send people to Narita Airport to confirm if any type of flight bearing the ident code BA0005 was due to land. Russian contacts working within the Japanese Air Traffic Control Center later confirmed less than an hour from landing BA0005 changed its ident code to that of military origin, and a C-17 Globemaster bearing U.S. Air Force markings landed at Yokota Airport.

Moments after the data was received at Moscow Central, an alarm had been raised. The U.S. trick of taking an existing approved flight from somewhere in Europe and replacing it with a military one flying a fake ident could mean one thing. A clandestine mission was likely underway. Examining all the possible locations, and having already being informed of the two American investigators at Vorkuta last week, the General in charge of Moscow Central confirmed this deviation from the approved flight path indicated a potential imminent clandestine parachute jump by a force or forces unknown onto Russian territory. Following his orders, he picked up a phone and dialed.

General Dmitry Yermilov, Head of Poteryannoye Sokrovishche OOO in Vorkuta and Amderma, was a stickler for the rules. His rules. Each evening he enjoyed a few glasses of wine with his supper. This was *his time* while eating, and colleagues and subordinates knew better than to disturb him during this time. He let the phone ring for almost a minute before snatching up the receiver and snarling a curt "Yes!" down the line. However, any anger soon disappeared after a few moments on the call when the caller identified himself. Three minutes later, and after replacing the receiver, the merest hint of a smile broke out as he called for another vodka.

In the meantime, and still with almost twenty miles to their destination of Amderma to go, the two of them hastily buried their 'chutes and removed their bulky outer flying clothing. Underneath they wore regular dark work clothes and heavy work boots under a camouflaged heavily insulated 'cold weather' outer layer. Each slipping their backpacks on, they examined the electronic map, checked their position, and set off, their clothing making them almost invisible against the stark white snow-covered backdrop.

The terrain was harsh and unforgiving. The frozen layers of ice and snow quickly began to exhaust them. The snow wasn't deep, but an ice layer covered the marsh-like ground level, with a snow layer of two to three feet covering it. However, the ice layer wasn't strong enough to always support their body weight, and they regularly crashed through, soaking their clothing in the icy water up to their thighs. After an hour, they'd barely gone a mile when they could make out through their goggles a black line heading into the distance just ahead. Stumbling on, they reached the single-track railway line connecting Amderma to Vorkuta and on towards, finally, Moscow. Following the track north, they made far better progress, and their new far-faster pace helped warm their frozen limbs.

As they eventually approached the semi-derelict town, the first thing Deacon noticed was how neglected it was. The photos the National Reconnaissance Center had sent over had been accurate, but even those high-resolution images couldn't project the empty feeling of desolation Deacon experienced as they walked towards the disused and crumbling buildings.

Cold and tired, they picked the upstairs of one deserted shell of a former large store of some sort near the town's perimeter. Every window was broken, and the walls at ground level were covered in faded graffiti and waste. Upstairs fared little better. However, daylight was now only a little over an hour away, and they needed somewhere to rest.

The town was built on a slight incline, so almost all buildings overlooked the waterfront. Standing upstairs in darkness at the northern corner of their building, they could both look down toward the water and the small harbor itself. There was what seemed to be a large trawler against the quayside. There was no sign of life onboard and no smoke emissions from the funnel. In fact, the entire dock front looked deserted in the yellow glow of the sodium dock lights.

Needing to rest and regain energy spent walking through the snow, they settled down to make camp. Their backpacks contained microfiber sleeping bags, – rolled up tight with all air expelled these bags weighed just ten ounces but opened up and shaken free they generated the same warmth as any top-of-the-range duck-down-filled sleeping bags. Nestled down in the dark, they each cracked open a packet of self-heating, ready-to-eat meals.

Relaxed and fed, and out of the direct cold, Deacon stated he'd stand first watch of two hours with Hythe doing the same after.

Six hours later, refreshed and nourished, they ventured out into the cold again. The sun was up, and the weather outside was heavily overcast and gloomy, with snow still falling. They could wait until much later with total darkness, but both felt it would waste far too much time.

Exiting their building after removing their camouflaged top layer, they could see the sprawl of empty disused apartment blocks ahead. Many had roofs fallen in, and most had doors and windows smashed. The entire area looked desolate and downtrodden. They both agreed if film producers wanted an ideal location to make a zombie-cum-apocalypse film, then this would be a perfect location.

With just their dark work clothes and woolen hats pulled low down covering most of their faces, from a distance they looked like any other persons wandering around and blended in perfectly. As they approached the harbor, they identified two buildings overlooking the dock and looking better maintained than the rest. These had what looked to be small double or triple glazed windows, and steam was coming from the roof area, hinting at heating within. However, they didn't seem to be occupied currently as all internal lighting was off, and the rooms inside appeared to be in darkness. The larger of the two buildings was bordering the quay and was also abutted to the railway track.

The snow was falling more intensely now, and the wind was making the situation worse. The chill of the wind and the lack of visibility, which had dropped to yards, seemed to be keeping anyone indoors. The ship, the *Iskatel*, was moored directly against the quay, and its lights were still off. Quickly sprinting along the gangway, they were both hidden in the worsening gloom. Heading around to its port side, away from the quay, Hythe kept a lookout while Deacon checked the doors. Unexpectedly, the heavy doors into the bridge were unlocked.

Deacon whispered for Hythe to join him. 'It's unlocked. It might be a trap. Or it might be so fucking desolate here there's nobody around to steal anything.'

Gently sliding the door open, they both headed in before venturing down below. Although the outsides of the ship were covered in rust, the engine room was clean and tidy, and the two large Wartsila diesel engines looked well maintained. Moving through the various passageways, they found the empty crew's quarters along with the captain's cabin, also vacant.

A quick search of the desk in the captain's cabin revealed charts of the Lomonosov Ridge off the coast of Greenland with clear marker lines showing which waters belong to which countries. The waters of Russia, Norway, Greenland, Canada, the USA, and Iceland were clearly marked and color-coded. Multiple tracks and waypoints had been entered encroaching into Danish - Greenland waters. Looking more closely, Deacon could see where the Norwegian Ice Station Hap had been located. Next to it were directions and speeds of flow the ice sheet was taking. Around those markings were numerous coordinates, all clearly in Danish waters.

'It looks like here is where they were mining, Patrick. The ice shelf has now moved down this way, but for quite some time, this area where Hap was located would have been almost directly on top of their mining.'

Turning on the computer on the captain's desk, it booted up and then asked for a password. Opening drawers Deacon found a small notebook. Inside the rear cover were seven random letters. Typing them in, he was pleasantly surprised when the screen opened up. Plugging the USB drive in, Deacon waited almost five minutes until the red light glowed green before disconnecting it and powering the computer down.

As he turned to speak to Hythe, the door suddenly burst open, and three men carrying AK-74s stood framed in the doorway.

26

One of the guards lowered his weapon as an officer moved past him and stepped through the doorway.

'Gentlemen,' he said, 'we've been expecting you. Let me introduce myself. I am General Dmitry Yermilov, and you must be US Navy SEAL Lieutenant John Deacon and Major Patrick Hythe of the British Special Air Services. Please surrender your weapons.'

The three guards stood far enough away, aiming their weapons at them that any attempt to rush them would be futile. After being searched and disarmed of their pistols, they had their hands handcuffed in front of them and were marched out of the captain's cabin up to the bridge.

'So who told you we'd be here?'

'Ahhh, let me just say little happens that we don't know about. And you should be happy. You will be looked after well and made comfortable until your time is up.'

'And when will that be?' Hythe continued.

'Too soon to say, my friend. Too soon to say. One choice is to send you back to Moscow for interrogation and torture. Then death, of course. However, you have no strategic bargaining ability. Your respective leaders will deny knowing you are here and disown you, so you will die slowly in prison. The other option is to kill you here. It saves a lot of time and trouble and is easier for you as well.'

'Well, that's decent of you,' Deacon said.

With one armed guard in front and two keeping pace behind, as well as Yermilov, there wasn't much chance of any type of escape. On reaching the bridge, they all spread out a little. Yermilov made himself comfortable in the captain's chair while the three guards positioned themselves either side of Deacon and Hythe, again making any potential attempt at escape impossible.

There was an engraved wooden name plaque above the main windows – The *Iskatel*. Looking around, Deacon could see the ship itself was pretty old. Maybe built just before, or immediately after WWII, he decided.

'You see she is old, yes? But heart like of stone,' Yermilov said, slapping a bulkhead.

'So how do you complete the mining?' Deacon said.

'You typical American. Straight to business. Not cultured like your friend here,' he said, kicking out a leg towards Hythe. 'But OK, Mister American. We do it your way. We scrape the seabed surface taking just the top twelve to sixteen feet. It's filtered, passed, and stored here in the front storage. The water is drained off, and then we place the mud and sediment on a small moving belt – I think you call it a belt-conveyer and it ––'

'Conveyor belt,' Deacon corrected him.

'Thank you. A 'conveyor belt' where it is passed along inside the ship,' he said, pointing at the large hold outside. 'Here, any large sediment containing rocks is removed, and the slurry is piped over to the forward hold. There it's spun in industrial-sized centrifuges to separate all the heavier manganese nodules to the outside. Any magnetic metals in these nodules are attracted by electromagnetics for further processing. All the heavier items, gold, silver, etc, are left to drain. When we return to port here, the mixture is passed to the hut alongside where it is further sorted, by hand, and packed up to be sent away for further processing.'

'And the diamonds too?'

After raising an eyebrow, Yermilov said, 'You know more than my superiors realized. Yes, diamonds too. Some of the nodules contain diamonds. Very clear, high-quality diamonds. These are removed and used . . . elsewhere.'

'But I thought manganese nodules are only found at great depths. Four, five thousand feet beneath the sea or deeper. How do you get to them? This ship isn't big enough to drill to that depth,' Deacon said.

The General smiled before answering. 'Here in the Rodina, what you American's call lady luck has smiled on us,' he said using the old-fashioned word Rodina meaning Motherland Russia. 'The deepest parts of the Lomonosov Ridge are indeed almost six thousand feet below the surface and beyond reach. But, the edges of the Ridge are mere hundreds of feet below the surface, and Russian skill and ingenuity have found hundreds of tons of nodules in this area,' he continued.

'But this area isn't in Russian waters, is it? You're mining in Danish waters?' Hythe said.

'They didn't even know the riches are there, just waiting to be plucked from the Earth,' he said, directing them to walk towards the deck area.

'And what of Ice Station Hap. What happened there?' Deacon said.

'I can tell you as you are not going to be leaving this place alive. Somehow, the scientists in the Ice Station discovered what we were doing. They tried to raise the alarm, but we blocked it. Our soldiers arrived to arrest everyone, but unfortunately, it got out of hand. Somebody fired, and it became a massacre. The officer in charge of the Russian force overstepped his authority and has since been tried, found guilty, and executed.'

'What happened to the buildings and equipment?'

'At the time, people panicked. As I said, the officer in charge overstepped his authority. The buildings were dismantled and removed, along with all trace of life there. We put out the story of the ice sheet parting and suddenly sinking. It kept most people away. But not you, I think. Two people were seen traveling to the site by snowmobile, and two of our soldiers were murdered. Was that you?'

Choosing not to answer the direct question, Deacon said, 'What of the bodies, General?'

'They have received burials in accordance with their faith.'

'And of the survivors?'

At that, the General didn't answer. Pointing at them to walk out and down to the main deck, the guards covered them at every step.

Walking past the main hold, Hythe asked, 'So what type of diggers do you use?'

The General said something quietly in Russian Hythe couldn't hear, and the guards moved apart, each covering either Hythe or Deacon with a rifle before the General pointed them down into the hold. Sitting quietly in the darkened hold were two vehicles each over twenty feet long by fourteen or fifteen feet wide. Their height was similar to a conventional car, but these were unlike anything either of them had ever seen before. They looked like squat tanks with caterpillar tracks instead of wheels. Along the front at the bottom were movable jaws with large, steel, jagged rollers that would break up the seabed as this monster moved along it. Behind the jaws was a large opening that would suck up the loose rubble. From the rear, a thick umbilical tube almost eighteen inches in diameter connected the digger to the parent ship, for all the world looking like a hideous long fat tail.

'How far away from the ship can they go?' Deacon asked.

'Because the surface is mainly mud and the particles we scoop up are relatively small, we can extend the umbilical up to ten miles.'

'Don't you need a large crew?'

'No. Russian ingenuity has automated everything as much as possible. We only need a crew of twelve, including the captain.'

'But what about launching and recovering the diggers? I don't see a deck crane,' Deacon said.

'The *Iskatel* can take the ice. Her bow is solid, and she can break through over two feet of solid ice. But her hull opens at the keel. I believe you Americans call it a moon pool. The diggers are lowered through the hull by these winches you see here,' he said, pointing. 'So she clears a path in the ice before lowering her twin babies through the ice path she has cleared,' he continued, proudly presenting the achievement of Russian design. 'You are lucky. You will get to see the *Iskatel* operating. Unfortunately, you won't be coming back to tell anyone.'

With that, he said a few words in Russian, and the guards ushered Hythe and Deacon to a paint locker, before opening the door and pushing them inside. The door clanged shut behind them, and they heard the handles being pushed solidly home outside.

The light inside was controlled by a switch and timer from outside and was currently on, so looking around they could see this was a ten by ten feet square steel room with a small ventilation hatch. There was no window and only one solid metal door. As its name suggested, this was the paint store for the ship. Rust is a problem for any vessel and keeping the ship operational, and the rust at bay was usually a daily task, especially in the cold, wet weathers of northern Russia. Aside from the various tins of paint, there was paint thinner, cleaner, and multiple sheets and coverings.

There was also no heating in this storage locker, and the air was frigid, with their breath making crazy patterns against the dirty walls.

With nowhere proper to sit, they dragged some of the coverings together to provide some insulation against the icy cold steel deck before making themselves comfortable and huddling together to keep warm.

Within moments, the overhead light extinguished, leaving just a small band of dim daylight entering through the ventilation hatch.

27

Three hours later and shivering from the cold, they felt, rather than heard, the throb of the diesel preheaters adding to the constant background noise of the power generator. In the severe cold, the two large Wartsila diesel engines would never start unless preheated first.

Soon after, the main engines began, and the steady vibration caused the paint tins to rattle. Moving around now to warm up semi-frozen muscles, and with his ear pressed against the steel door, Hythe could hear people moving about outside.

The initial movement of the ship was so slight they hardly felt it, but shortly after, they felt the swell of the ocean rocking the *Iskatel* as she headed out the mouth of the harbor and into the Pechora Sea. Within a short while, the soft thump underfoot of small ice flows being broken by her bow added to the increased vibrations from her engines.

They knew they'd be brought out sometime, so they prepared the scene. Although searched for weapons, neither had been thoroughly patted down. Both each still carried a book of matches, but to start a fire now would mean certain death from asphyxiation. Their small cell would quickly fill with toxic smoke.

Deacon poured a mixture of brush cleaner and turpentine onto the deck in the corner. Covering it with two painting blankets, the fluid was quickly soaked up. Urinating on the blanket and folding it over on its self to keep it damp, they then pried the lids off various cans of paint by using the edge of his handcuff as a small lever. After removing the tops from more turpentine bottles, and laying them on an angle to slowly leak, they placed the damp blanket over the lot. Then they waited.

When they heard voices outside, and one of the doors handles started turning, Deacon quickly lit a match before igniting the two books of matches. As they flared, he dropped them onto the turpentine soaked blanket and quickly folded the urine-soaked part over it.

With the door fully open, they were ushered outside under gunpoint from four guards and moved aft. One of the guards closed the paint locker door behind them. As the turpentine soaked area continued to burn, the fire slowly spread through the damp blanket, creating smoke in doing so. Minutes later, the blankets caught properly, and the rising flames eventually caused the opened paint cans to catch alight, further fueled by the other opened turpentine bottles. As the heat within the tiny room built up, smoke began to seep through the ventilation hatch. Finally, enough smoke was escaping to trigger one of the fire alarms, and the klaxon began to shriek.

Leaving two armed guards on Hythe and Deacon, the other two raced back to the paint locker and opened the door. As regularly happens when a fire starts but is starved of oxygen, it smolders and stays small. The sudden inrush of fresh air as the door was opened was the equivalent of throwing gasoline on it, and with an enormous 'whoosh,' it exploded, with a blast of superhot flames leaping out of the doorway instantly engulfing the two who'd gone back to fight it.

The explosive fire blast initially stunned the other two armed guards, and they froze for maybe half-a-second. That was all Deacon and Hythe needed. Pivoting on one foot, Deacon pushed the rifle barrel away with his hips as he slammed his fists and the handcuffs just below the ear of the left guard. As the guard collapsed, Deacon raised his foot and stamped once, hard, on his throat. With his windpipe crushed and already unconscious, he would be dead within minutes.

Hythe brought his knee up into the other guard's groin, and as the guard doubled over in pain and surprise, he brought his wrists together and slammed them down on the back of the guard's head with as much force as he could muster. The handcuffs did the damage, and the crack of the guard's spine sounded like a tree branch snapping.

Four down, eight to go.

Grabbing both guards' fallen rifles, two more guards rushing to assist were quickly dispatched with double taps to their chests.

Six down, six to go.

As they raced towards the bridge, two more crewmen came running around a corner. Whether they were planning on helping the fallen guards or tackling the fire, Deacon and Hythe didn't stop and ask, but two three-second bursts tore them almost in two.

Eight down, four to go.

The captain was standing on the bridge wing open-mouthed in amazement. Moments before everything had been under his control, but now, less than a minute on, chaos was reigning. Turning to the sailor holding the wheel he watched, before he heard the chatter of automatic rifle fire, the red of bullet holes magically appear on the sailor's chest, as Hythe stepped in through the doorway and lowered his rifle before pulling the *Iskatel's* engine telegraph levers back to 'Stop'.

Striding up to the captain, Deacon slapped him across the face to get his attention, before asking in Russian, 'Where's Yermilov?'

Stuttering at the rapid turn of events, the captain managed to say, 'A . . . ashore.'

'Sit down and don't try anything.'

Nine-three.

As Deacon moved aft with his rifle pointed down towards the companionway suddenly, the captain's voice came over the Tannoy. He'd grabbed the microphone and was trying to reach for a pistol while shouting for help. Hythe turned and fired once.

Ten-two.

Positioning themselves at the top of the stairs, they waited. A few minutes later, both crew from the engine room came slowly up. One was armed with a pistol, the other with a wrench. Deacon took the one with the pistol out with a double-tap to the chest and shouted at the remaining one to surrender. Instead, he grabbed his fallen comrade's pistol and rushed towards Deacon. He'd only managed to move a few feet before a three-second burst from Hythe cut him down too.

Twelve-zero.

'Well, me hearties, the ship be ours. Where be we headin' to, Cap'n?' Hythe said in his best Captain Sparrow voice and with a smile on his face.

'First, let's find the keys for these handcuffs,' Deacon replied, heading back towards the first pair of fallen guards.

They had to keep the speed of the RIB down due to the floating ice but still made reasonable time back to shore. Although they'd been on the *Iskatel* a total of almost five hours, they'd only been underway a little less than two. However, due to ice flows, it still took nearly four hours in the RIB to get back.

As to the *Iskatel*, they'd placed all the bodies in the hold, opened its seacocks, locked the steering, pushed the throttles to the maximum, and left it heading further north. Whether it would fill and sink before it became stuck on the ice or would beach itself to sink slowly as the heat of the summer increased and the ice melted was unknown, but it was finally on its last voyage.

It was late evening, and the sky was dark as they approached the small harbor of Amderma again. They stopped the engine while outside the harbor wall and waited clear of the loom of any lights. This time, they were armed and ready, but there was no reception committee waiting for them. In fact, the entire waterfront area was deserted. Keeping to the shadows, they ventured to the first building. Here they found a team of four specialists grading, inspecting, and cutting a pile of diamonds. One of the four was using a powerful computer connected to a 3D printer. After tying the four of them up and securing them, Deacon gathered all the diamonds into one container.

Looking down at the glittering stones, he showed them to Hythe and said, 'I've never seen so many in one place before, but they really do look like little pieces of ice.'

'And likely worth more than we will both make in a lifetime. Ice in a country covered in it.'

Putting a lid on the container and placing it in his pocket, they both headed towards the other building.

General Yermilov was housed in the larger building of the two, along with the communications gear, computers, and weapons. Approaching it, the area was still deserted as they made their way to the darkened end. This was the main office but empty this time of night. Heading further along, they found the weapons store or armory. There were more AK-74s, some of the newer model AK-15's, a shelf full of Makarov pistols, ammunition, hand grenades, detonators, and timers, and over 30lb of C4 high explosive; as well as Hythe and Deacon's original gear.

The end room contained General Yermilov along with three guards. As he saw Deacon, Yermilov shouted a warning, and the guards grabbed their sidearms, but all three moved too slow and were quickly cut down by two short, sustained bursts from Hythe and Deacon.

With the hot barrel of his AK-74 jammed up into the chubby flesh of General Yermilov's throat, Deacon said, 'Hey pal, we're back. Thanks for the offer of the fishing trip, but maybe next time.'

'Wh . . . where is . . . where is the *Iskatel*?' Yermilov stuttered, the hot barrel burning his chubby flesh.

'Not sure, pal. Last seen heading north. Might be a bit bent by now.'

'Are you going to kill me?'

'Answer my questions, and you might live to see another dawn. Where's our gear you took earlier. How did you know we were arriving? Who told you?'

Pointing to the cupboard where Deacon's USB drive was stored, along with their weapons, Yermilov said, 'I received a message from Moscow Central.'

'Where did they hear it from, c'mon! answer!' he shouted, jamming the still hot barrel towards him again. 'All they said was Washington informed them.'

As Yermilov answered, he carefully slid open his desk drawer with the tips of his fingers. As Deacon moved to the cupboard to recover his drive and satellite phone, Yermilov grabbed the pistol lying there and aimed at Deacon's back.

The brief chatter of Hythe's weapon cut through the air as Yermilov flew backward, one round in his stomach, one in his upper chest by his throat and one in his face blasting his jaw off. As his bloated body slumped down the wall, Deacon's only comment was, 'Looks like you missed the dawn, pal.'

Deacon walked over and searched him. He wasn't carrying anything on him, but his jacket and peaked hat were hanging up. Looking through it, Deacon found his ID cards, a wallet, and a set of car keys. Flipping the wallet open, it contained a large bundle of roubles along with a Visa and American Express credit card.

Pocketing the wallet and taking the jacket and hat, he said, 'Goddamn it, even the Russkies have Amex. Anyway, they might come in useful.'

Heading back to the armory, they grabbed C4 explosives, detonators and timers. Planting the C4 throughout the buildings, they paid particular attention to ensure all communications gear would be wrecked beyond repair. Hythe went on connecting detonators and timers while Deacon connected his data drive up to their computers.

Logging on and connecting to Langley through a secret ultra-secure encrypted VPN, it took almost ten minutes before the red led on the drive turned green. At least Langley now had a copy of the data. Only three other guards appeared during this time, all chased off by withering fire from Deacon and Hythe. It was after they'd uploaded the data they realized most of the other occupants of Amderma were simple fishermen and their families just trying to eke out a meager living. Yermilov and his thugs had brought hope and money, but only for the few and only at the end of a weapon.

Looking around for any type of vehicle they could take, parked in a shelter opposite was what had to be General Yermilov's private vehicle. Even Deacon whistled in surprise. It was a Aton-Impulse Viking 2992 - a massive squat 4x4 off-roader only Russia could build. Similar in shape and size to a Humvee, it was better equipped and had larger wheels. With a smile as wide as his face, he called Hythe over to take a look.

'Let's have a little chat with the natives, set the timers, grab our gear, and then let's have a little ride.'

28

Opening the tailgate, Deacon forced off the plastic cover and severed the cables to the stoplights with his knife. He then did the same the other side and for the license plate. A red tail light could be seen at over eight miles distance on a clear night.

Heading back into the other building, they untied the senior diamond grader, took him back into the main room, aimed a rifle at him, and asked him questions.

'If you want to live, tell me exactly what you are doing here.'

'W . . . we sort the metals and diamonds. The metals--.'

'Just the diamonds. What are you looking for, and what do you do to them?'

'We scan each one into the computer. It grades it for purity, and--,' he said before stopping abruptly.

Grinding the barrel into his chest, Deacon said, 'Your choice, pal. Answer or die. I'm sure one of your colleagues will answer.'

Gulping, the Russian continued, 'The computer shows where we have to cut.'

'Why? Why do you need to cut? C'mon, answer,' he said, grinding the barrel again.

'They will kill me if I tell.'

'I'll kill you now if you don't,' Deacon said, moving his finger towards the trigger.

After a moment's thought, the prisoner relented and said, 'Each raw diamond is a different shape. Each diamond needs to have two flat surfaces cut precisely. The computer tells us where and how deep to cut and then labels the diamond.'

'Why? You're not telling me everything. Go on.'

Almost sobbing, the prisoner continued, 'The X-rays are fired into the raw diamonds through one of the flat surfaces. The X-rays then reflect off the inside of the uncut raw diamonds and come streaming out the other flat surface. They then go into the next diamond. I don't know how, but I believe the signal gets enlarged that way.'

'Then what happens?'

'Each diamond is labeled, and the computer prints a special container for them on the 3D printer over there,' he said, pointing. 'It's like a honeycomb. The computer program then tells us where to place each diamond exactly into one half. Once they are all placed, we clip the other half of the frame to the first, and they are set permanently in place.'

'And?' Deacon said, trying to goad more information.

'Then the General takes them to the observatory, and they are placed in the laser.'

'How many have you done?'

'Lots, but this is part of the last batch. The *Iskatel* is bringing us more in a few days, and that will be the last.'

'Where is the observatory?'

'I don't know. We've never been there,' he said, almost crying with fright, 'but I can show you where it is on a map,' he said, pointing.

His finger wavered over a particularly empty region of the Urals.

Noting that the area indicated was approximately the same as identified by the USAF, Deacon turned to Hythe and said, 'We need a copy of this diamond cutting program. That's the heart to this entire project.'

Patrick took the prisoner back to the others, untied them, and kicked all of them out into the cold, telling them he'd shoot them if they came back to the building within a half hour. Deacon plugged his VPN drive into the computer. While it was copying and uploading to the U.S., he ripped as many cables as he could from the phone system. After it had finished copying the contents of the disk drive, Deacon ripped the covers off the computer and removed the disk drive itself.

From the armory, they grabbed a sack full of grenades, two new AK-15 assault rifles, spare magazines of ammunition, and as much C4 high explosives as they could carry, before loading everything into the Aton. They also raided the well-stocked kitchen, along with six spare jerricans flush with fuel.

Placing some of the C4 throughout the two buildings and setting the timers on a fifteen-minute delay, they headed for their ride out of there.

Deacon was six-feet-two with Hythe five-feet-ten, but both had to stretch to climb up into the cab of the vehicle. Each wheel was the size of two regular vehicle wheels, and the tread on the tires was almost like those on a tractor. They were also under-inflated, so were quite soft, thereby offering excellent grip and were made of solid rubber mesh construction. They couldn't be punctured and could even be sliced open and would still work as effectively as normal.

Hythe took the driving seat, started the engine, and sat there revving the engine with a wide grin on his face.

'Which way, boss?'

'Pick up our gear first, then I think we owe the observatory a visit. Saves the Admiral sending us back a fourth time.'

Heading back to the empty site where they had made camp, they quickly grabbed everything they had left there.

Six minutes outside of Amderma, just as the snow-covered road began to falter and run out, two large explosions lit up the twilight sky behind them. The remaining explosives in the armory had then exploded, taking the roofs, and most of the walls with it. They'd made sure not to damage any of the infrastructures such as electricity or water, but had wanted to guarantee the diamond sorting was finished. They'd also made sure the complete state-of-the-art communications systems were included in the initial blast.

The journey was slow. Progress was little more than twelve miles an hour, rising to nearer twenty on flat, firm sections of land. The sky darkened, but night was short this time of year due to being above the Arctic Circle, but the snow kept falling, keeping visibility to a minimum.

There were few tracks to follow. The main one was little more than a dirt track leading straight to Vorkuta almost three hundred kilometers away. However, they had no intention of heading there again. The other option was cross-country. Setting a direction on the compass, Hythe turned, and they set off crossing the frozen tundra.

In the colder winter months, the landscape had been covered by up to six feet of snow, but now with the longer warmer spring days, some of the snow had melted, and small tufts of vegetation were breaking through in various places. The entire area was waterlogged and crisscrossed with small streams, some larger than others. However, the Aton had been built for this exact type of terrain. The doors fitted perfectly with water-tight seals meaning they could cross rivers and streams typically far too deep for a conventional vehicle. The heater worked so well within a few minutes of leaving Amderma both had shed their heavy, outer clothes. The headlights were ultra-bright and penetrated a long way in the crystal-clear air between snow flurries, and both were surprised to see the number of animals that existed in this barren, icy land.

Deacon had brought the last shipment of diamonds with him and showed them to Hythe.

'What a shame, but I guess we've gotta do it,' he said, 'We've got the data and can't let these fall back into the hands of the Russians.'

'We could just keep them,' Hythe said, as a mischievous smile spread across his face.

'No. If we get caught and these fall back into Russian hands . . .'

Seeing Hythe nod in agreement, Deacon wound down his window and was immediately hit by a severe blast of super-chilled air. Over a distance of a few miles, he scattered the diamonds into the marshy vegetation where they sunk without a trace into the cold, muddy ground.

This area was tundra - a treeless, marshy plain; frozen solid in winter, but turning to slush now. But even here, nature flourished. Vast herds of wild reindeer traversed the land safe from hunters, and the rivers were swollen with salmon. But time was short, and they needed to push on sharing the driving as each became tired. As they headed south, the land changed. From tundra, they moved onto what's known as taiga - denser underfoot with a lower water or ice content. Here traveling was faster, but the terrain was less flat, often with rocks and boulders protruding. Twice they saw lights in the distance. They extinguished theirs and kept well clear. These would be nomads hunting the reindeer, sable, marten, ermine, and moose prevalent in this area.

Strangers weren't welcome in this cold and unforgiving land. If they were discovered, they'd likely also be included on the nomad hunter's list.

The overall lack of roads and bridges over the broader deeper rivers meant they had to head further southeast than ideal. The maps in the vehicle indicated where bridges were located, and after fifteen hours, they came across their first main problem. The only way across one particularly deep river was at the dam. However, this would likely be guarded.

Heading further down the river, they finally approached an area where the water was no more than four feet deep, although it was almost a half-mile wide. Gingerly driving the vehicle out into the water, they watched with concern as the water level crept up the doors, across the hood, and half-way up the windows. Thankfully the designers had fitted an extended air intake to the vehicle roof, but they both knew if the engine should falter, they'd be in trouble. It was a strange feeling to be sitting lower than the height of the water, but Hythe kept the revs up, and the vehicle never stalled. However, both breathed a sigh of relief as the rubber wheels gripped the far side dry embankment as they climbed back to dry land.

Ten minutes later, they joined a paved road further on from the dam, and their speed and quality of journey improved. Within another four hours, they turned off this road onto a well-used dirt track that wound steeply up into the heights of the Urals. In all that time, they had only seen two vehicles approaching them. Luckily, the occupants of both had ignored them beyond a flash of headlights and a friendly wave.

After another three hours steadily climbing and making a mere ten miles per hour, they were now within striking distance of their final objective. Although the track was covered in a layer of snow, other vehicles had driven along here recently, their tire tracks showing clearly. Most of the landscape was quite barren, mainly rocky ground covered in a thick layer of snow. What few trees existed at this altitude were bent over from the constant buffeting of the wind, ending up looking like old people slowly shuffling along.

Stopping, Hythe found two bushes that he cut at their base and dragged to the vehicle while Deacon tied them to the rear fender. It was imperative they mask their tracks, so Deacon continued driving up the steep hillside with Hythe watching to make sure the branches disguised their tire tracks. The surface of the dirt track they were following gradually worsened with large ruts and holes. As it narrowed, it became impossible for two vehicles to pass one another. Occasionally there were areas where it widened, and as they neared the top, Deacon pulled off at one. Skirting various small rocks, he carefully drove the vehicle up behind a large outcrop and stopped. Climbing out, they were both relieved to find both they and their vehicle were completely hidden from view from the track.

Even through the falling snow, they could tell they were close to the top. They hadn't eaten since breakfast, so stopped and ate eating some of the food they'd brought with them. It would be a long night, and they needed to keep energy levels up. Revitalized, they rejoined the track with a renewed sense of urgency. The steepness of the dirt track increased further until as they neared the top and rounded the last corner they came upon a turning circle, and the track finally leveled as the landscape opened up in front of them.

The entire landscape was heavily covered in snow. As the clouds temporarily cleared, the distant cliffs could be just made out at least fifty miles away. Apart from the observatory itself and the various buildings near to it close to a mile distant no other man-made object could be seen, Quickly reversing, they moved back out of sight. Climbing out, they moved forward on foot but kept in close to the rock face where they could observe but not be seen.

In between more snow flurries, they looked at the observatory. It was built at the top of and into the cliff edge. Approximately fifty feet tall with the top dome able to swing around 300 degrees and angle from near horizontal to vertical, there was little sky it couldn't see. Approximately a half-mile away from the observatory in either direction were two radar domes, each between fifteen and twenty feet in diameter. Although these were enclosed within protective plastic spheres, it was likely the equipment inside would be mounted on gimbals and able to turn and move. It was apparent the initial detection of any hostile incoming missile or aircraft would come from Russia's early warning systems far out in the Arctic or by satellite. Once its path was transmitted and the target was within the horizon view of the observatory, these two localized radars would pinpoint it, and the observatory dome would be able to track it.

The observatory slider covering what previously would have been an optical telescope and was now thought to contain the X-ray laser was currently shut, so it was impossible to see inside from where they were.

'We can't get near without being seen in daylight. I don't mind a firefight, but all elements of surprise will be lost,' Hythe said.

'No, we need to wait until dark. We also need to get away after 'cus Mrs. Deacon's little boy doesn't want to spend the rest of his life in a Russian Gulag or full of holes, and I guess you feel the same. Let's head back down and look at the options.'

Their worry was the two buildings behind the observatory. These were obviously barracks for the scientists and guards. Slightly further away was a large 'H' specifying a small area designated as a helicopter landing pad. Not wanting to expose themselves on the turning circle, after heading back to the vehicle, Deacon reversed it while Hythe guided him. Luckily, it was only a few hundred yards back to their hiding place, and after some careful accelerator and brake pedal work, the Aton was soon hidden behind the rocky outcrop again.

The snow was still falling, and heavy clouds overhead reduced the daylight. Any vehicle coming either up the track or down from the observatory would shortly need headlamps on. Needing to know who or what they were letting themselves in for, Hythe took first watch.

Coming up to 23:00, the sky had darkened enough. The night would be short and the snow laying around would stop it becoming completely black, but every fraction darker would help. In the time since they'd stopped only one vehicle an old army truck had passed. The sides and rear tarp were missing allowing Hythe to see as it passed that only the driver was present.

They discussed the various options and had agreed on a plan. They would leave the Aton where it was and proceed on foot. There was much less chance of random discovery this way, but if they were compromised, they'd have to fight their way out back to safety on foot. After refitting their snow camouflaged outer gear, they headed back up the mountain path dragging one of the bushes behind them to mask their footprints. Both had their weapons primed and ready. In this one instance the lack of total darkness in the sky helped them. Although dark, the snow illuminated the track enough without having to use headlights or night vision goggles. As they approached the top they stopped at the previous turning point and reexamined the buildings through binoculars.

They'd already discussed the plan. Hythe would take a third of the C4 and split it for the two radar domes. Deacon would use the rest for the observatory building itself. They would go in armed and ready to fight, no idea of how many guards and how quickly reinforcements could be called in, but the plan was to set the radio-timers for forty-eight hours and leave. If discovered, they could trigger the radio-timers remotely and at least complete their mission. Currently in the center north of Russia, thousands of miles away from any border, and not able to call on any help, they also knew discovery was likely certain death. Plus, Moscow Central knew they were in-country, and the hunt wouldn't cease until they were captured or killed.

With a plan to meet back at the vehicle in two hours, they synchronized watches and set off.

29

Patrick Hythe gently sucked air through his open lips as he crept along the mountain, parallel to the track. Twice he stopped completely hidden in the dark shadows as he watched for roving guards.

Careful not to dislodge any loose shale, he kept at least one hundred feet away from the buildings as he moved past and along to the farthest radar dome. The sky became slightly darker as denser clouds rolled in from the West, and the falling snow turned more to slush and rain, all making it harder for him to be seen. At least God was on their side he thought as every extra bit of cover helped. Approaching the dome he could see it was unmanned. The fiberglass fixed outer sphere structure surrounding it kept snow and rain away from the actual radar dish, electronics, and moveable gimbal system.

Gently testing the door handle, he was surprised to find it unlocked, but then smiled when he thought why would anyone need to lock it being on top of a mountain somewhere deep inside Russia. Entering, his NVG's made it as bright for him as any external lighting would. After quickly checking he was alone, he closed the door behind him. There wasn't any way to lock it, but a shovel leaning against the wall of the dome quickly became an effective door wedge.

Looking around, the layout was much as they had expected. There was a circular toothed gearing ring with all the remaining equipment placed on it. This consisted of a radar dish, multiple geared motors, and a small control unit. A thick umbilical cable connected the control unit to a separate stand-alone metal cabinet housed against the outer wall of the site.

Placing a C4 charge at the main gear points after smearing it with grease to camouflage it, he then climbed down underneath the toothed gearing mechanism while praying someone didn't activate the motors at that exact time. The timer and detonator were small, but not so easy to hide, so he placed the timer as far down underneath as he could. The detonator itself was concealed by inserting it into the C4 as far underneath the gear mechanism as possible; after checking any movement of the gears wouldn't dislodge it. He hid the connecting wires under the thick, black grease.

Moving back slightly, he was happy it would pass casual inspection. Someone would need to climb down under the mechanism where he was to discover it. Setting the timer to forty-eight hours minus the time taken so far, he then moved over to the metal cabinet against the wall. This was the size of a two-drawer filing cabinet with three heavy cables protruded from its base over to the radar mechanism. The door was locked, but the key was still in the lock. Opening it, he could see this was crammed full of electronics. This was obviously the main control and communication unit. Leaning in, he placed another small C4 charge at the bottom rear, completely out of sight. He also set a new timer and detonator. Again, unless anyone was deliberately looking, the charge and timer were completely hidden. To make discovery even harder, he closed and locked the equipment door and pocketed the key. Anyone wanting to open the cabinet would assume the last person to do so had kept the key. After a final check, he replaced the shovel and opened the door a fraction. Looking around everything was as quiet as before, so he exited the dome and closed the door behind him. Keeping to the shadows he retraced his steps.

It took him almost a half hour to skirt the buildings and get back to the nearer radar dome. Twice he saw guards milling about, although their attitude seemed sloppy. They didn't seem to look around and were more interested in smoking than actually patrolling. After waiting for them to move on, he finally arrived at the second radar site and found, as expected, it was an exact duplicate of the first.

After checking he was alone, he made quick work in copying everything he'd done previously. Just as he was about to leave, he heard footsteps and quiet voices approaching, and he froze. He'd pushed the door shut behind him as he'd entered, but not closed it completely and it was now slightly ajar. Silently cursing, he realized it would be easy for anyone stood outside to see it was open. As quickly as he could, he moved over to it and gently pushed it closed while keeping the edge of his glove jammed on the latch to stop it clicking. Barely breathing, he pulled his suppressed pistol from his jacket, ready to dispose of whoever was there. Both of them had left their automatic rifles at the vehicle, since it was too much to carry and likely to knock against something and give away their position. The footsteps halted, and he remained frozen.

Suddenly there was a brief burst of brighter light showing between the edges of the door before the crackle of something burning and the smell of cigarettes wafted in. The guards stood there, less than two feet from him, talking and smoking something Hythe could only think was lion shit. Whatever tobacco they were using wasn't

Marlboro Light he thought, and he pitied their wives or girlfriends if they had to kiss those lips. He heard them move away a few minutes later but waited another ten before slowly cracking the door open a fraction to check. The entire area still looked deserted, so after carefully closing the door behind him, he kept low in the rain and slush and headed back to the vehicle, before tossing the cabinet keys over the cliff face.

It was now an hour forty-five since he and Deacon had departed, and he remained watching and waiting for his colleague to return.

Deacon was having trouble. When he arrived at the observatory building, he could hear people inside. He would have liked to set charges on the laser weapon itself, but that looked impossible now. The building had been built overhanging the cliff with a metal grating surrounding the outsides, with a thigh-high metal barrier around it. Deacon couldn't see why they hadn't just built it flat on the rock surface, but the designers had planned it right on the very edge; with the rear of it supported by the cliff itself, and the front by three solid concrete reinforced support beams built at an angle down into the cliff. Maybe it gave the original telescope an extra degree of angle or something, he thought. However, he hoped their design would make his job easier.

Careful not to be observed, he crept closer until he could climb over the metal barrier and, with his fingers supporting his weight through the snow-covered metal grating, ease himself forward to the first of the concrete beams. After what only took a couple of minutes, but felt far longer to his tortured fingertips, he eventually moved far enough forward to snake a leg around the closest beam. Easing some feelings back into his numb fingertips, he waited momentarily before gently sliding down the icy beam until he was underneath the observatory itself.

At least he was out of the rain and snow here. Looking down through his NVGs, the cliff face dropped almost vertically down at least three hundred feet with rocks and boulders at the bottom. It then shelved steeply down at least another hundred feet.

Shaping the charges and attaching them to the beams was relatively easy for the outer most two. Although the bases of the beams weren't joined, the angle they came down from above made it easy to move from one outer one to the other. The central one was more difficult as it was longer and entered the cliff face lower down. For this to work, he planned to use three small detonators, synced together from one remote timer. This would remove the need for any connecting cables that could expose them. Warming and molding the C4 in his hands, he pressed it firmly against the concrete beam before fixing the detonator. Sliding out from the relative safety and shadows from the building above, he had to hold onto one of the outer beams as he lowered his legs down until he could reach the lower, middle one.

He stopped.

Although it was dark underneath the observatory, Deacon would be stood clearly silhouetted against the cliff face, should anyone look, while balancing and standing at an angle, feet deep in snow.

Carefully sitting down with his back to the cliff face, he was now completely visible from above. It would be near impossible to get a good shot at anyone, and if the alarm went up, he'd be trapped. With his legs wrapped around the beam, he inched higher and higher until he was at the optimal place to set the explosives. Taking some of the remaining C4, he molded it and, leaning up and supporting himself on one arm, he pressed it firmly against the concrete pillar before fitting the detonator.

Just as he finished smoothing the snow on the beam to hide evidence of him being there, he heard the wrang of metal-studded footprints on the metal grating above.

Not moving an inch and barely breathing, he slowly looked up just as he heard a strange noise followed by a water spattering.

He could see a guard or someone had walked out onto the grating and was relieving himself. However, the wind was blowing the stream of piss back under the building. It wasn't actually hitting Deacon but was coming close. If Deacon moved or the guard looked down, he'd be seen. There was no way Deacon could get to his weapon if he needed to, and he was the perfect target if discovered. After what seemed more than humanly possible to piss in one session, the guard finally finished and zipped up. Just as Deacon was thinking he could begin to relax, another worker came out, and the two of them lit cigarettes. By now, Deacon's right arm was becoming numb. The way he was leaning, all his weight was being supported by his right hand and arm, and he already couldn't feel his fingers. As the feeling in his arms became less and less, he could feel himself sliding backward down the beam, but there was nothing he could do.

30

As his grip loosened and he began to slip down the snow-covered beam, he tried to keep quiet. His weapon was in his right-hand pocket, but his right hand was numb and temporarily useless. Luckily, the wind and rain masked any noise his clothes made sliding back down the beam, but when he hit the base where the beam was embedded into the rock face, something he was carrying in his backpack hit the solid granite with a dull thud, just as the wind and rain momentarily stopped.

Had the guards been another twenty feet away, or had the wind and rain not stopped, the noise would have gone unheard. Or if the guards had been talking. Annoyingly, that was the precise moment both guards had paused to take a breath and were drawing on their cigarettes.

'What was that?'

Looking down over the edge of the railing, all they could see was darkness. Deacon had quickly slid sideways until he was in an area deep in shadow but stayed frozen as any slight movement could give him away. He couldn't even afford to look up to see where they were looking, instead keeping his hood over his head and facing down. He'd covered his face in mud and dirt to darken his skin before setting out, but no camouflage is perfect, and today's attempt was rudimentary. In the darkness, any flash of white skin would give him away.

He could hear both guards moving around the grating, trying to get a better look when he heard one of them say, in Russian, he was going to get a torch.

With nowhere to go, he was stuck, and from his position he made a clear and perfect target. Rapidly glancing around, his only chance was a narrow fissure in the face surface of the mountain just over three feet away. However, to get there he'd need to let go of the support beam and hang on literally by his fingertips onto the rock face itself to pull himself over.

Not tied on and with a three-hundred-foot fall beneath him, he knew he had no other choice. If he was seen where he was, he faced either falling to his death, arrest, and sentenced to death as a saboteur or being shot off the beam. Either way, none of his options had a good ending. Stretching as much as he could, he managed to get his fingers into the cracks and fissures in the rock face and hold on. The feelings had partly returned to his hand and arm, but they were still tingling and not fully back up to strength. He heard the guard run back up and saw the loom of the torch as it shone down towards him. With a final lunge and pull, he managed to get his body and backpack into the opening just as the torch beam hit the middle concrete beam where he'd been sitting.

He was wedged in a crack in the rock face barely wider than he was, with his fingers and toes supporting his entire body weight. Impossible to move or even draw his weapon, all he could do was wait and hope nothing he'd done could be seen.

Silently cursing and praying there wouldn't suddenly be a shout of 'What's that?', all he could do was keep his face pressed against the cliff and wait. Again, after what seemed hours but was, in fact, mere minutes, the torch was extinguished, and he heard more cigarettes being lit. Ten minutes later, they finally flipped their cigarette ends

218

over the railing and watched them fall, before turning and walking back into the main building itself. Whatever noise they'd heard they had put down to a bird or bat or something.

Finally, Deacon felt able to relax slightly. He altered his hold and began working his fingers and arm to get some life back into the muscles. Gradually, as they came back to life and the strength in them returned, he felt able to move back onto the support beams. Climbing back up, he finished molding the C4 onto the central beam before covering the explosives as much as he could with dirt from the concrete and with snow. The remote timer was set and placed under the beams and totally invisible from anybody standing up top. Unless someone climbed down to where he was now, there was zero chance of detection. As Hythe had done, Deacon set the timer to explode simultaneously with the others and offset it to synchronize. Climbing back up to the cliff he pressed in close to the rock face directly under the edge of the observatory positioned on the cliff. The remainder of the C4 was pushed and molded into the cliff edge itself and timed to detonate ten seconds after the other three. The idea was to remove the front support beams first before blasting the rear of the observatory off the cliff. The weight of the building should ensure it would fall completely over the cliff edge. Finally, Deacon would have liked to place more explosives around the laser itself, but the two white coats were still working inside the building, and he couldn't risk it. Climbing back up to the edge, Deacon checked nothing could be seen and then set off back to their staging point.

Hythe was patiently waiting with an AK-15 nestled in his arms as Deacon approached.

'How did it go?'

'Best part of 20lbs of C4 should do the trick. Half the mountain should go up with it.'

Relying on their NVGs, they quietly half-walked, half-ran back to where they'd left the Aton. Climbing in, they headed down the track with lights off. Four miles on, just as the track was improving, Hythe could see the loom of headlamps heading up towards them. The vehicles the headlamps belonged to weren't yet visible, but within thirty seconds or so they would round the next corner, and the Aton would be caught fully in their glare with nowhere to hide. Yanking the wheel over, Hythe turned off, and they began crossing a lower part of the mountain range by following a slow-flowing stream, awash with melting ice. Turning into the middle of it and driving downstream meant they would leave no tracks, but due to the rocks and boulders, travel was no faster than walking pace.

Looking back, they could see the headlights of at least a dozen trucks slowly following the track up to the observatory.

'Fuck. Good call. If we hadn't turned off, we'd be nose-on with them,' Deacon said, thankful he'd disconnected the rear lights.

As they further descended the mountain, they discovered a disused cart track running parallel to the stream. Although full of pits and rocks, moving onto it allowed them to increase speed until after another thirty minutes or so they got up to almost 20 mph. In the distance, they could see the lights of a small compound that looked to be a small mining operation. Keeping well clear, they again went 'off-road' across country before passing the site at more than a mile distance and then re-joining the track which had improved and was wide enough for trucks.

A dozen or so miles further on the track became smoother still, and they were able to increase speed further. Within ninety minutes, they were approaching the larger mining town of Kharp. In this instance, they couldn't divert across country to miss the town as the map showed a small deep river flowing through it, so they kept their speed down and just drove straight through and across the bridge. Whether anyone would recognize their vehicle and report it was a chance they had to take, but it was still early morning, and they only saw one person who ignored them.

Three hours later, they drove into Labytnangi, a small town on the north side of the Ob River. The ferry was large enough to carry up to sixty cars or twenty trucks. There were only a few other vehicles waiting, so within thirty minutes, they were allocated space on board. The actual crossing took forty minutes across a wide and fast-flowing river to the sister city of Salekhard.

Having disposed of their weapons and anything incriminating on the journey, they parked in the small airport's long-term parking and approached the airline ticket desk to get one-way tickets to Moscow. The General's jacket was too tight on Deacon but fitted Hythe perfectly. In a gruff voice and in perfect Russian, Patrick ordered two seats on the next available flight to Moscow. The young female assistant asked for his credit card and ID.

Looking fiercely at the young girl, Hythe lowered his voice and hissed, 'ID? ID? Do you not recognize this uniform, you stupid girl? I am General Yermilov of the Russian Federation, and I have urgent business in Moscow with the President. Now give me two seats on this flight.'

Seeing her hesitate, he continued, with his voice rising in tone and anger, 'Perhaps you would prefer I call the

President himself to vouch for me? Would you like that? . . . No? Are you sure? . . . Well unless you want your parents to spend the rest of their days digging coal in Siberia, I suggest you give me the tickets right now and stop wasting my fucking time!' his voice raising even louder and booming on the last sentence as he slapped his credit card down with a loud bang.

The door behind her opened, and a nervous man rushed out explaining he was the sales manager, apologized for his 'silly young assistant' and, putting his hands on her shoulders, told her to issue the tickets immediately.

With her eyes filled with tears and gently sobbing, her fingers quickly flew across the computer keyboard.

Apologizing profusely and repeatedly saying neither of them meant any disrespect to the brave military comrades of the Russian Federation Forces and to the President, the tickets were supplied moments later, and the credit card returned.

With a final deep growl of, 'You have not heard the end of this,' Hythe snatched up the tickets and his card, spun on his heel, and they walked away.

Walking towards the bar and waiting area, Deacon had to work hard at keeping a straight face.

Keeping to only speaking Russian, it was a relief to sit in a quiet corner and enjoy a cold beer while they waited for the flight.

Smiling, Deacon said quietly, 'Don't you think you were a bit hard on that poor girl? She's only young.'

'Nah. Nothing like having a healthy fear of the military. Anyway, I am General Yermilov of the Russian Federation,' he said in a typical Hollywood Russian accent.

After checking they couldn't be overheard, Deacon used the encrypted satellite phone to call Shane Walker, the CIA spook at the US Embassy in Baghdad.

'Shane, John. Can't explain in detail, but in trouble in Bear country. Myself and a friend. Remember Patrick H from the good old days. You do? Good. Need a couple of travel docs from your office in the main town. New names. Can't call L, which I will explain later. In fact, can't let any of them know anything. Just between you and me, yeah? Something you can arrange on the QT? Will be there tomorrow for pickup at two whole ones before Gary Cooper. Can you arrange passage? I owe you, thanks.'

31

Salekhard, Northern Central Russia

The sales manager personally escorted Deacon and Hythe on to the Aeroflot flight, even walking them to their assigned seats. He'd upgraded them to first-class without charge and seemed relieved that they were on their way, and no more threats against him or his staff were made.

The three-hour flight was completely uneventful, and arriving at Sheremetyevo Airport as domestic passengers meant minimal security. Guards were walking around, but neither of them had to show documents. Hythe was wearing ordinary clothes again, having removed and discarded the General's jacket in the toilets. A cab from outside the arrivals hall took then to the center of the city before two more cab trips, then two local train trips saw them close to their destination. Another sixty minutes of back and forth walking to ensure they weren't being followed finally saw them arrive at a particular door.

Hythe knocked twice.

As it opened, he quickly pushed it open wider and stepped in before the occupier could complain.

'Hello again, Lonely,' Hythe said. 'We need a bed for the night.'

The following morning they retraced their steps before ending up at Bolshoy Devyatinsky Lane in the Presnensky District. They looked different, as well. On the way through town the previous evening, they'd stopped at a pharmacy. Deacon now had his hair a light brown and was wearing eyeglasses. Hythe's hair had been darkened to almost black. They had also swopped their clothes for some spare ones at Lonely's. Hythe's fitted quite well, but the pants were too short on Deacon, so he had them lower than usual, and his arms a little too long for the shirt. Luckily, the coat he was wearing masked most of it. After double and triple-checking they hadn't been followed, they approached the guards outside the US Embassy at precisely ten o'clock. After Deacon explained to the guard he was an American citizen and had appointments arranged, they were immediately ushered inside. They then went through the regular metal screening and were taken to a private room to wait.

A tall, extremely attractive brunette walked in.

'Which one of you is Deacon?'

'That's me, John Deacon.'

'I'm Linda. Linda Finch. Shane said for me to welcome you to Moscow, but I have to state your code skills are rudimentary,' she said, with a broad smile on her face. She then added, 'Did you get dressed in the dark?'

'And there was me thinking I looked quite fetching,' he said looking sheepishly at his clothes, 'as for the codes, it's all I could think of at the time,' he said, 'you know, Bear country . . . Russia; office in main town . . . Embassy here in Moscow; L . . . Langley; two before Gary Cooper – High Noon . . . ten o'clock. I thought they were pretty good in the heat of the moment.'

Laughing, she replied, 'Pretty basic. Schoolboy level, I'd say. Shame you're flying out today, I could have given you a few lessons,' she said, showing a little glint in her eye.

Seizing the moment, Deacon said, 'Why don't I give you my number, Linda, and when you're next in

Washington . . .' quickly writing his cell number down on the back of her hand.

With an even bigger glint in her eye, she said, 'I'm not sure my husband would be happy about that and I don't think your dress code works for me either.'

'OK, gentlemen, let's get down to business. I've got two passports, both used and genuine. You both work at Microsoft in California, and entry stamps show you have been visiting their campus here. Just need photos. You,' she said, turning to Patrick, 'are Ted Wallman, and you are Kurt Dreiberg,' she said, looking at Deacon. 'How long do you need these for?'

'Assuming we don't get stopped, twenty-four hours maximum,' he said.

'OK, let's go upstairs and get photos done, and these completed. Unless I hear differently from Shane, in forty-eight hours, I'll get these revoked,' she said, standing and walking towards the door. As they followed her up the marble staircase, Deacon couldn't help looking at her pert backside and tried to hide his smile, especially when he saw Patrick glance at him and mouth, 'Lessons? Hmmmm?'

Within an hour, and wearing business suits that fitted, Deacon was on a secure line to Gina organizing first-class tickets from Sheremetyevo to Warsaw for both of them on the afternoon flight, hotel rooms at the Warsaw Sofitel, and onward first-class tickets to London for Hythe and Washington for him.

The next morning was for goodbyes and hangovers. The previous night they'd sat in the restaurant of the 5-star Sofitel eating and drinking Bourbon until gone two in the morning, celebrating. The trip through Sheremetyevo Airport had gone smoothly. Although their passports were carefully examined, and they were both questioned, everything had been in order, and they were allowed on the flight.

Both had given silent cheers when the pilot announced they'd cleared Russian airspace, and Deacon ordered whiskey for them both. They agreed the recent trips had been fun, and they'd stay in touch, but both knew their jobs could bring them into danger at any time, so goodbyes were always 'so long until, and if we meet again'.

Today Deacon slept through most of the twelve-hour flight to Washington and quietly headed back to his apartment after landing. Gina had arranged immediate cleaning and repairs after the detectives had finished at his place, and it still smelled of fresh paint. At least it was livable now, and carpenters would be arriving the following day to put the finishing touches to the new kitchen units. However, exhausted after the recent trip, all he wanted was sleep.

The following morning, Deacon awoke bright and early before going for a five-mile jog. Returning to his apartment, he showered, had a quick breakfast, and headed to the Pentagon. He was still early and was sitting in reception drinking coffee when Mitch arrived.

Thirty minutes later, the Admiral arrived along with Generals Dreiberg and Tarrant. After heading up to one of the secure meeting rooms, the Admiral asked Deacon to give an overview of what had happened.

'The main thing, sirs, is they were expecting us. When we arrived at Amderma, we walked into a reception committee. Moscow Central had alerted them. Someone here in Washington is talking.'

Looking towards the Director of National Intelligence, the authority the CIA reports to, he said, 'Warwick, do you want to give an update?'

Clearing his throat, General Dreiberg coughed twice before saying, 'It pains me to admit it, but you're correct. We definitely have a leak out of Langley. We have narrowed it down to a small group of people who have access to this type of information. At this point, Charles Ingram is undergoing extensive scrutiny. He's due to retire later this year, and the President is pushing him to go sooner.'

With a genuine look of surprise on his face, Deacon said, 'Shit, Ingram! You mean the Director of the CIA's a traitor!'

'Let's not jump to conclusions. All I am willing to say is Ingram is currently a person of serious interest,' Dreiberg replied.

Deacon then spent over thirty minutes explaining in depth everything that had happened.

Finishing, he said, 'OK, so what about the data we brought back?'

'Now that is where your British colleague and yourself deserve a handshake. We've only deciphered less than half of the data so far, but have already confirmed a series of facts. Let me reconfirm to everyone around the table here; this information is beyond Top-Secret. Understood?'

Glancing around, he could see everyone nodded their heads in agreement. 'First, this Russian laser is formidable and very dangerous. Somehow, they have uncovered how to synchronize several lasers together. In doing so, they arrive at a power output level higher than the collective sum of those lasers by almost three-hundred percent. We're not sure yet how they accomplish this, but the data contains the laboratory results from multiple trial scenarios and is being passed to our best lab boys as it's being deciphered. We believe some of the increase in power relates to the way the diamonds are cut that bounces the power back and forth, but our experts are still looking into that.'

Turning to Mitch, he said, 'Lieutenant, do you have the satellite footage?'

Mitch nodded and pressed 'Play' on the remote, and the screen came alive. The aerial satellite image showed the harbor area of Amderma. It still had the same number of sunken vessels in the harbor, but now the two long buildings near the dock were just burnt out shells. The picture then changed to the area close to the observatory. It was now a complete mess. Both outlying radar dome installations had been destroyed, one completely disappearing over the cliff.

As to the structure housing the laser weapon, the entire area the observatory was on had disappeared, leaving quite a large crater.

'Where has the observatory itself ended up?'

'Good question, Lieutenant,' Dreiberg said, 'What's left of it is about 300 feet down the side of the mountain.'

'Any of it recoverable?'

'I very much doubt it - certainly not this year with winter only a few months away. And as to the laser itself, well someone will need to dig and find what is salvageable if anything, after a fall like that. The edge of the mountain came down on it as well, so I don't give much for their chances. Either way, an excellent job, Lieutenant, excellent.'

'We were surprised we didn't encounter any direct opposition,' Deacon said.

'We think you managed to confuse the Russians,' Dreiberg continued. 'The NSA intercepted a call from General Yermilov to Moscow Central stating you had been captured. The orders he received were to get rid of you, and Yermilov confirmed you'd been taken aboard the *Iskatel*. After you escaped and killed him and blew up Amderma, the Russians seemed on the back foot. After communication was lost with Amderma, we think they assumed you'd be heading westward, and sent forces to intercept you. By the time they realized you had disappeared, the alarm had gone out to the observatory, and they immediately quadrupled the guard, but you'd already been and gone. That would have been the convoy arriving just as you were leaving. They obviously didn't know you'd already been there and whether they searched for explosives, we'll never know, but they obviously didn't find them in time. When all that went up, the shit really did hit the fan, but you were already on your flight to Warsaw. Our Ambassador in Moscow was called in to explain, but he just pleaded total ignorance. We believe some senior heads are going to roll as a result because it was a massive clusterfuck on their side, and Kalygin isn't one to forgive and forget. But as to some of the other data so far recovered, that's becoming a little treasure trove. It refers to payments made to someone here in Washington with the codename 'Blackbird'. We haven't identified the owner yet, but it looks to fit Ingram to a T. The other thing it does is supply confirmation of payments made to Kalygin. As Powolski said at our previous meeting, Kalygin is totally corrupt. What with that and the information you uncovered about Ice Station Hap, I think the President has enough to run a series of exposés against Kalygin at the UN, should he wish.'

32

Later that week, Deacon received another request to attend the Pentagon to meet with the Admiral. In the meantime, he'd been working hard on some new Phylax contracts and been chasing the local Police, especially Detective Rissolini, on progress about Garry Moore's murder but to no avail. No suspects had been found, and what few leads there were had dried up. Without some new information or evidence, it was likely to become a cold case.

Garry's funeral had been the previous day and had been a somber affair. Cindy had been there with her mother, Hazel, along with Garry's parents and friends. Deacon had attended with Gina in support of Cindy, and everything had gone smoothly but unhappily. Detective Rissolini had also turned up but left when unable to answer questions as to the status of the investigation. With Ingram at the FBI under suspicion, there had been no movement from their investigation either.

The Pentagon meeting was with just Mitch and the Admiral. Although now a civilian, Admiral Carter still referred to Deacon by his rank.

'Lieutenant, another problem has arisen. Charles Ingram is now on indefinite suspension, pending further investigation and possible charges. The phone we've been searching for has been found in his safe and a private bank account in his name containing almost two million dollars has been found. He's pleading total deniability and claims he's being set-up, but that's to be expected.

He's now under guarded house arrest with all external communication ceased.

'To make matters worse, two days ago, another long-time CIA agent, Chris Bennett, was exposed and captured in the Ukraine province of Crimea, which is currently under Russian control since they occupied Crimea in 2014. He was captured by Russian rebels, not the main Russian Army, and is being held hostage for US$3M. These rebels are basically just crime syndicate gangsters. Most are ex-Army and their only allegiance is to money. Allegedly, Bennett was caught spying and taking pictures. But it's becoming a big diplomatic problem. So far, State has managed to keep the lid on it, and the only news media that know are CNN, who is whom the rebels contacted for the ransom. They've agreed to hold the story for a couple more days, but when it does hit the street, it will embarrass both the CIA and the President.

'As you know, if you've been keeping abreast of the news, Russia seized three Ukrainian ships and crew off the Crimean coast a while ago. There has been a big rise in tensions in the area. State, on behalf of the President, along with Britain and a number of other European countries have demanded Russia release the ships. But so far, Russia is ignoring calls for action, saying the ships were in Russian waters.

'So where normally we would send in a SEAL team to support the Ukrainian authorities and rescue our agent, especially as we believe he's only being held by a small group of rebel forces; because the Crimea is under Russian occupation, we can't. The President feels the repercussions, if discovered, would be too high. Moscow would consider it an invasion by our military forces into Russian territory, and it could likely start a US-Russia shooting war.'

'It's that serious?'

'At the moment, yes. Russia knows they are in the wrong occupying Crimea but are fighting world opinion. They have repeatedly stated any incursion by western forces to remove them would be considered an act of war. We can't risk that in an area of already heightened tensions.'

'So it's my team again, is it?'

'Unfortunately, Lieutenant, it is. The President has authorized the use of the US Navy as far as possible as long as the Navy stays clearly in international waters. Assuming you agree to go, the destroyer USS Carney is already patrolling within the Black Sea. She is only the second U.S. warship to enter the Black Sea in the last three years. She will close the Crimean coastline to a minimum of twenty-five miles where you and your men can motor in off fast RIBs. We believe Bennett is being held in a disused farmhouse.'

Just then, the phone on Mitch's desk rang. Mitch answered and nodded to the Admiral.

'Mrs. Kingman has just arrived. She will provide more details,' Admiral Carter said.

Lisa Kingman walked in and sat down.

'Lieutenant, this looks to be a reasonably easy mission. We have carried out satellite passes over the region, and the rebels are holding Bennett in a remote disused farmhouse about two miles from the coast. We've been keeping watch, and there are only six rebels.'

Raising a hand to halt the expected interruption, she continued, 'Yes, we believe our intel to be accurate. These six rebels appear only lightly armed with handguns and automatic rifles. There are always four at the farmhouse, and a maximum of two leave at any time. They have two vehicles, an old Mercedes car, and an open-back truck. As the Admiral may have already discussed, you will fly into Incirlik and helicopter out to the USS Carney to be dropped off offshore. A fast twin-engine RIB will be available for you and your team. The section of beach shown on the map is pretty remote and is coarse sand and rocks,' she said, showing a blown-up photo and map of the beach area.

Continuing and showing more photos, she said, 'The farmhouse is one and a half miles as the crow flies, but around another half mile by following this track. The farmhouse, as you can see, is one main building with a large barn next to it. We believe the rebels are holding Bennett in a cellar within the house. Satellite heat camera imagery show a faint, non-moving source that we believe to be Bennett. You and your team go in, rescue our man and then fast RIB back out to the Carney that will be on a reciprocal course ninety minutes after dropping you off. The entire operation should take less than two hours. The helicopter will be waiting to take you back to Incirlik, and you'll be heading home the same day. This folder has GPS coordinates and call signs. How many of you are going?'

'We'll be a team of six,' Deacon said. 'Why twenty-five-miles? Can we not chopper in and fast rope down, sir?'

'No, unfortunately not. Since the Russians invaded this area, they have upgraded their radar coverage of the entire coastline, and have introduced a twenty-five-mile economic exclusion zone around the coast which they patrol regularly. Any ship entering the exclusion zone is challenged. Any helicopter flying in would be detected, even possibly a Comanche, and would risk being shot down or starting an international incident. Unfortunately, this needs to be a stealth rescue,' the Admiral said.

Slapping Deacon on the back, she said, 'We have every faith in you, Lieutenant. Go get 'em, cowboy.'

Turkey

Forty-eight hours later, Deacon, Martock, Roberts, Canetti, Stockwell, and Maričić felt the wheels of the Boeing C-17 Globemaster gently touch the concrete at Incirlik Air Base in Turkey after a twenty-two-hour journey from Joint Base Andrews via Ramstein, Germany. Moments later, the four giant Pratt & Whitney turbofan engines were put into reverse thrust, and the heavy aircraft rapidly slowed.

After taxiing to its required parking spot, Deacon and his men quickly disembarked each carrying canvas bags full of equipment.

A Sikorsky SH-60 Seahawk helicopter was parked just yards away and was already slowly spinning up its motors. With flight clearance granted, Deacon and the team were airborne and on their way again within five minutes of arriving in Turkey.

With a cruising speed of 170 mph, this part of the journey was slower and totally uneventful. The distance to the current position of the USS Carney was 490 miles, and with the Seahawk having a flying range of 520 miles, or less than ten minutes extra flying time, the two pilots finally smiled with relief as the gray deck of the Carney eventually came into view almost three hours later.

With a whine of increased torque, the Seahawk gently flared, and the landing gear kissed the deck of the Carney so gently they hardly knew they'd landed. As the turbines spun down, Deacon shook the hands of both pilots and thanked them. They would wait while their helicopter was refueled and checked, while Deacon and his team rescued the hostage before heading everyone back to their base in Turkey.

The ship's captain ordered the Carney, an Arleigh Burke-class destroyer, to head north and slowly close to within twenty-six miles of the shoreline of Crimea. This would still be in international waters and far enough offshore ideally not to raise any suspicions. However, a Russian *Rubin*-class patrol boat was keeping pace three miles inside the exclusion zone as an escort.

After relaxing over a meal, Deacon and his men checked and double-checked their equipment before readying themselves for that night's operation. Only Martock knew the full tie-up between Deacon, Phylax and the Pentagon, and that this operation was for the government, but whatever the others suspected, no one bothered to ask. They knew they were rescuing an American held hostage, and that was good enough for them.

At 23:30, they boarded a fifteen-foot black RIB with twin Mercury outboards. Everything was painted matte black to minimize reflections, and the engine covers had a fine copper wire mesh covering them to absorb radar pulses to make them as stealthy as possible. Extreme silencers were fitted to the engines that reduced the exhaust noise to such a low level they became almost silent at a hundred yards distance.

The weather was raining and the wind was blowing Force 5, making a slower than wanted approach through the choppy sea, but the rain helped by reducing visibility, should anyone happen to be looking. After being lowered off the port side of the USS Carney, away from the prying eyes of the Russian patrol boat, everyone kept low in the RIB to avoid radar detection. Five minutes later, it was clear the ruse had worked. The Carney had sailed on, undisturbed, and the Russian patrol boat had kept pace with her. Relieved the low profile and detection countermeasures of the RIB had worked, coupled with the rough sea and heavy rain reducing the effectiveness of the enemy radar, they remained just floating in the RIB for another ten minutes.

Finally, starting the engines and keeping the speed well below the maximum the craft could easily make, they had a relatively quick run ashore in almost pitch-black darkness, stopping a little under a mile offshore and scanning the area with night vision binoculars.

With the entire coastline looking deserted, they kept their approach slow and headed towards the deserted rocky beach on the southwestern corner on the south side of Crimea.

As the fiberglass bow of the black RIB grounded against the coarse sand, Martock jumped into the surf, grabbed the bowlines, and tried to hold the craft stern first towards the incoming waves. The wind had risen in the past fifteen minutes and if the RIB turned sideways the waves would likely overturn it.

Just as Deacon and Canetti climbed over the side, a freak wave lifted the stern, and the RIB started to turn. Staggering back under the extra weight, Martock's left leg became trapped between two sharp rocks, and he fell sideways as the RIB rode up over him. Pulled under and trapped by his leg, he swallowed large amounts of seawater before his colleagues could move the craft and try to pull him free.

As his head broke the surface, he immediately vomited the saltwater, but his leg was still trapped and now bent sideways at an angle. His blood in the water didn't show in their NVGs, but the expression on his face said it all.

He'd suffered severe lacerations to the calf muscle, and two large flaps of skin were hanging off, completely exposing his shin bone. His calf muscle was also badly torn and bruised, and his knee had been wrenched. Dragging him up the beach far enough out of the water, Maričić and Roberts quickly pulled first-aid kits from their backpacks and started dressing the wound.

It was evident that Roberts couldn't walk far and Deacon, remembering the famous statement from the nineteenth-century Prussian military commander Helmuth van Moltke, who wrote 'No plan survives first contact with the enemy', immediately changed theirs.

Instead of hiding the RIB and leaving it, Martock would now stay on the beach, and the remaining five of them would storm the farmhouse and rescue Bennett.

After checking comms, they headed across the windswept beach and climbed the dirt path. The cliffs were quite high, and the terrain was hilly and rough, but they made good progress, and the farmhouse was in sight less than twenty minutes later. As shown in the aerial photos, the farmhouse was remote and looked somewhat rundown through their NVGs. Two rooms had lights on, but they could see no movement.

Approaching quietly to approximately three-hundred yards, Stockwell moved over towards a lone dying tree and took up a sniper position with a clear view towards the buildings. The other four spread out slightly and advanced.

Whether one of them tripped an undetected circuit was unknown, but suddenly, less than fifty yards from the building, and with little cover available, four disguised searchlights suddenly came on, and sixteen rebel weapons opened up at them.

Diving for what little cover there was, Goran Maričić was hit in the thigh and also lost his pinky finger to a salvo of rounds.

Yanking off their NVG's, they all immediately returned fire. From his higher angle, Stockwell opened fire and killed four in quick succession, before one of the rebels fired an RPG in his direction. Seeing the smoke trail as it was fired, Stockwell tried to leap clear and had managed to get almost ten feet away from the blast when it detonated but was severely hit in the upper back, shoulder, and arm by shrapnel.

Deacon, Roberts, Canetti, and Maričić returned fire from behind what limited cover they had, but there was no easy way to escape. Five more rebels went down to their concentrated aiming, but Deacon knew it was bad. Stockwell wasn't moving, but they could see his back and arm was wet with blood. Maričić wasn't as severely injured and was struggling to get a bandage around his leg.

Deacon knew they were on their own. The Navy couldn't help with air support as the entire area was squarely in Russian controlled and occupied Ukraine.

He was just radioing Martock and the USS Carney to state the mission was blown and got the message through when the rebels stopped firing. Two of them dragged a semi-conscious Stockwell, hands tied behind his back and face covered in blood, out into the clearing.

Just as Roberts and Canetti were about to waste the two holding Stockwell, another three, one of which seemed to be the leader, moved into place behind Stockwell and aimed their weapons at him.

'Stop firing and surrender, or he dies,' one of the gunmen shouted.

Barely awake, Stockwell managed to kneel as the barrel of an AK-15 was jabbed into the bloody mess of his back.

The rebel waited until Stockwell's scream died down before repeating, 'Stop firing and surrender or he dies.'

With no way out and no other option, the four of them threw down their weapons and raised their hands.

Canetti and Roberts helped Maričić stand, and they moved forward towards the approaching rebels.

A couple of them moved behind them and jabbed them forward with rifle barrels.

The leader waited until they were closer, then cocked his weapon and fired a three-round burst into Stockwell's back and head.

With a roar, the four of them shouted and rushed forward, before collapsing under the concentrated blows of rifle butts.

With a final violent strike to his head, Deacon slipped gratefully into unconsciousness.

33

The Farmhouse, Crimea

Slowly his eyes opened, and he could make out shapes and light through his blood crusted eyelids. His mouth was dry, and he ached all over. As the sensations in his body slowly returned, he could tell his hands and feet were tied. He could also tell he was cold. Really cold.

As the feelings fully returned, so did the pain. Someone had beaten him while he was unconscious. His lips were split, his eyes were crusty with dried blood and his stomach and back was throbbing. He was hanging from something by his wrists, and he was naked except for his boxers. Careful not to make a sound, he very slowly managed to open both eyes and blink them until his vision cleared enough in one eye for him to make out where he was.

His hands were tied with thick rope, and he was hanging from a hook embedded in a solid-looking beam in what appeared to be the barn. Blinking more rapidly, he managed to clear enough dried blood from both eyes to be able to focus adequately.

Carefully glancing around, he expected to see his men in similar positions to him, but he seemed alone. Every time he moved his head or neck, even slightly, massive pains shot up his into his skull before gradually subsiding.

Hanging there, he had no idea how long he'd been unconscious, but after another ten or fifteen minutes, the side door opened, and the four who'd held Stockwell as well as the person who'd murdered him walked in.

Swinging widely about Deacon shouted, 'You fucking murdering bastard. I'll fucking kill yo--' as a massive fist slammed into his kidneys, followed by a second and a third.

Hanging there, gasping in pain for breath, he heard the leader say in weak English, 'Your man was dying. Well, he dead now. And so you be soon. My name is Dimitri Vodolski, and you are US Navy SEAL Lieutenant John Patrick Deacon. You come to rescue prisoner. Problem for you.'

Not wanting to give anything away, Deacon merely stared him in the eye.

'Prisoner executed two days ago. We don't like Yankee spies. We don't like Yankees.'

'Where are my colleagues?'

'Close. Maybe you see them if you answer questions. Where is other man?'

'What the fuck are you on about?'

'You came from American warship. Six of you. Now only you and three other. And dead body outside make five. Where other man?'

Deacon kept silent which earned him another punch to his kidneys.

'I said where other man?' Vodolski shouted.

'Fucking your momma,' Deacon said, which earned him yet another two hard punches to his kidneys.

'OK, tough guy. We tough as well,' Vodolski said, turning and walking back outside with his men.

Five minutes later, the five of them returned with four of them wrestling a struggling Maričić in through the door and down onto his knees in front of Deacon.

Vodolski walked up behind Maričić, pulled out his weapon, and shot Maričić in the back of the head, execution-style.

Kicking and struggling and with tears running down his face, he could only watch as his friend and colleague collapsed onto the filthy barn floor.

'So, Mister Tough Guy. Try again before you run out of men, or I run out of bullets. Yes? Where is other man and where is boat?'

Inwardly swearing that he would kill this fucker in revenge for Stockwell and Maričić, he finally answered, 'Gone back to the warship. I need to radio him to come in again for our pickup.'

'OK tough guy, maybe you tell truth,' Vodolski said before turning and speaking to his colleagues in Russian.

Deacon didn't let on he could understand and just kept still, listening, as Vodolski was discussing with his men how two teams of two had gone to either end of the beach and searched but were unable to find anything. He'd then sent them further afield east and west to check the next cove, but they hadn't returned yet.

Two of the five rebels then dragged Maričić's body outside, leaving a visceral streak of blood and gray brain matter behind.

From listening to what had been said and to how many voices were heard in total, Deacon guessed there were now just eight rebels plus Vodolski himself.

There was a sound outside, and Vodolski sent two of his men to check.

With a nod towards one of the two remaining rebels behind Deacon's back, the beatings started again. After a couple of loosening up punches to his lower back and kidneys, Vodolski moved right up close to Deacon, almost nose to nose.

Breathing stale, smoke-laden breath into Deacons face, Vodolski sneered, 'You lucky man, Mister Lieutenant John Patrick Deacon. Your two men go sold to ISIS. They love to get hands on Yankees. Maybe film heads coming off on video. Yes? Send to Facebook, yes? You lucky. You too expensive for ISIS. You $10 million for your head. And hands. That all they want – head and hands, cowboy.'

All the time Vodolski had been talking, Deacon had been very slowly moving his head back away from the stale breath. Now, with a vicious forward thrust as hard as he could, he slammed his forehead down onto the bridge of Vodolski's nose immediately mashing and breaking it and splitting the skin into two.

With a shriek, Vodolski fell backward, blood and snot exploding across his face.

Staggering back, his hands to his injured face, he pulled out his handgun and aimed it at Deacon.

Deacon tensed, waiting for the flash and then blackness. But Vodolski hesitated. Walking over, blood and snot still running from his broken nose, he slammed the pistol once, hard, across Deacon's face. Deacon felt the skin split and his mouth filled with blood. At least one tooth was loosened, but his nose didn't break. It was smashed and bleeding, but somehow the cartilage had absorbed the impact. The force of the blow pushed him to the edge of consciousness and he just hung there, head lolling, waiting for the next blow.

Vodolski spat at him then turned and walked out.

Turning to one of the two guards, he said, 'I'll be back in a couple of hours. Keep yourselves busy with him.' With an angry look on his face, Vodolski walked towards the rear of the barn before crashing out through a small doorway. Moments later, Deacon heard a motorcycle start and wheel spin away.

The two guards began a concerted effort of sharp jab-like punches to Deacon's kidneys. Each one was agony and within minutes, Deacon was again on the verge of unconsciousness, when all three of them heard two soft plops outside followed by silence.

The senior of the two ordered the other outside to investigate. Half a second after walking out through the door, there was another two plops, and the rebel guard crashed back through the still-open door, with half of his head missing.

With a panicked look on his face, the last remaining guard grabbed his rifle from against the wall and rushed towards the door, passing close to Deacon hanging there.

Looking up, Deacon managed to get his hands around the hook supporting him and swung his legs up forward, managing to get his ankles around the guard's neck. With a rapid twist, first one way and then the other, the guard's neck snapped like a dried twig.

Dropping the body, Deacon swung his legs up and hooked them over the beam as he wrestled the rope around his wrists off the hook. Free, he grabbed the beam and swung back down, dropping to the floor just as the barn door burst open and the barrel of a weapon poked in.

34

Sean Martock stayed by the RIB while keeping watch. The wind had finally died down a little, and he spent the time looking along the beach and out to sea to check they hadn't been observed.

They all observed radio silence when on a mission, only using it when needed, but his position at the bottom of the cliff made reception intermittent. Although his colleagues were all using suppressed weapons, the rebels weren't; and their rhythmic chatter when they opened up on Deacon and the others carried faintly in the night air.

A normal person might have passed it off as distant thunder or even a noisy truck, but Martock knew better. The sound of the RPG exploding confirmed his worst fears.

Minutes later, Deacon's radio message confirmed what had happened. Martock immediately called up the Captain of the Carney and told them to stay local.

Heading up the steep path, he stopped and observed through his NVG binoculars. Almost half an hour after the initial gunfire, he saw four men nearly a mile distant heading towards the beach. From their movements and gait, he knew it wasn't his team. Hightailing it back down the path as quickly as his damaged leg would allow, he got back to the RIB with about ten minutes to spare.

Struggling with the pain in his leg, he managed to push the craft back out into deeper water, leaped on board, and started the engines, putting them in slow reverse.

The spinning propellers bit deep, and the boat crept astern into the dark night, quickly being lost to view.

With the engines making no more than a quiet murmur, he kept hidden low down behind the inflated tubes, watching the shoreline from three-hundred yards offshore. His NVGs and the light of their torches showed the men split into teams of two, as they split up and walked to either end of the beach. After ten minutes looking around to no avail, the four men headed off back up the cliff.

Martock watched them go. To make sure they had left, he gave it another ten minutes before quietly motoring in and beaching the RIB again.

From one of the crafts lockers, he grabbed a roll of heavy-duty duct tape along with two aluminum oars. Holding them in place, he quickly wrapped the black tape around them until they were strong enough to act as a simple crutch. Grabbing his suppressed Colt M4A1 automatic rifle, he climbed over the side of the RIB, donned his NVGs, and followed the men's tracks as quickly as he could.

It took longer than he wanted because he had to stop and redress his leg due to bleeding, but he was at the site where Stockwell had been hit by the RPG fifty minutes later.

Hiding down behind what little cover there was, he could see the dead bodies had been piled up near the barn ready to being loaded onto the truck. Creeping closer, he recognized the clothing on one body left in the dirt. It was Stockwell, and his injuries looked severe.

The faint sounds of voices approaching from behind alerted him. Then the sounds of shoes scuffling through the dirt and the faint chink of metal on metal.

Swiveling around and laying low behind a hawthorn bush, he could see through his goggles the two pairs of men from the beach walking up the path behind him. He hadn't realized he was ahead of them and now trapped between them and the farmhouse. They were obviously also unaware of his presence due to the noise they were making. They had their weapons cradled loose in their arms and were walking in a group of three with the last man on his own.

Quickly sighting, his silenced first shot hit the one on the left straight in his forehead. He went down without a sound. The one in the middle thought he'd stumbled and bent to help as the one on the right flipped backward, half his head spraying out wildly. As the one in the middle realized what was happening and turned back towards Martock, two quick rounds caught him in the throat and directly through his left eye socket. The guy at the back had been walking along, half asleep. First, he heard one colleague stumble, then felt half of a face slap him in the chest before more blood sprayed into his face as his third colleague collapsed. Just as his tired brain was realizing what was happening and he began automatically to bring his rifle up to defend himself, two more rounds hit him. The first was two inches below his throat. The second, half a second later, entered just under his nostrils taking most of his medulla oblongata or brainstem with it. He was brain dead before his body even began falling backward.

Resuming his previous position, Martock reverted to watching the barn again.

Suddenly, the farmhouse door opened, bathing the area in weak yellow light. Martock's goggles flared with the sudden brightness, temporarily blinding him, and he quickly yanked them away from his eyes. By the time his vision had returned, the door had closed again, and all he could see was the shapes of five men walking towards the barn.

248

He heard Deacon shout, '*You fucking murdering bastard. I'll fucking kill yo--*' before Deacon's voice was suddenly cut off and there was a sound of a punching bag being hit.

Their voices were lower now, so he couldn't hear what was being said. After a few minutes, a voice was raised, but not clear enough to distinguish whose it was or what was being said. Then the door to the barn opened again, and the five men headed back out to the farmhouse, returning minutes later with a struggling Maričić between them.

As the barn door opened briefly, Martock could see Deacon hanging there and Maričić being forcibly manhandled to the floor. Seconds later, there was a gunshot, and the bile rose in his throat as he guessed what had just taken place.

The door opened again, and he could see two of the rebels dragging the lifeless body of Maričić out before dumping him like trash in the dirt. As they stepped back into the barn, Martock picked up a rock and tossed it, landing close to the barn wall with an audible thump.

Something inside was said and the two turned around and headed back out to investigate. Both men used torches and started looking around, but Martock just waited and smiled.

The rounds from his rifle were powerful and were likely to travel straight through their targets. Problem was Deacon. Hanging like a side of beef in an abattoir, he would be directly in line for any through-and-through shots. Martock heard a shout from inside and another commotion, but he still couldn't get a clean shot at either of the guards. A few minutes later he heard a motorcycle start and drive away before, even from that distance, the sounds of body blows, just as the two guards with torches came back into view.

Not waiting any longer, he aimed and fired twice less than a second apart. At that range, the powerful rifle did its work brilliantly. Smiling grimly and partly in revenge, he watched his two well-aimed shots exploding their heads and heard their bodies fall with just a faint thump.

In the barn, a few words were shouted in Russian before another rebel came out through the doorway. Two quick shots later, one hitting the guy in the chest while the second took most of his face away, catapulted the body back through the doorway.

Rushing over, weapon at the ready, he kicked the door open again and walked in just as Deacon dropped down and landed on his feet next to a body on the floor.

'Hello, boss. How's your day going?'

'Sean. Boy, am I glad to see you.

He rushed over and quickly cut Deacon's hands and feet free, saying, 'Are you injured?'

'Just bruises, I think. Have you seen the others?'

'Only the bodies of Goran and Andy. The bastards have left them outside like trash.'

Walking over to the wall, Deacon found most of his clothes and boots. He quickly got dressed before Martock handed him a pistol, and the two of them headed to the door. There could have been some men left hiding in the farmhouse, so they skirted around carefully checking, but apart from the escaped Vodolski, the rebels were now all accounted for.

Kicking open the farmhouse door, they found Canetti and Roberts. Both were tied hand and feet but were alive. They had dried blood on their faces, and Canetti's nose was bent at a strange angle. After cutting them free, both grimaced in pain as they were helped to their feet.

'We heard shots just now. Where's Maričić?' Canetti wheezed.

Deacon just shook his head. They had all liked both Stockwell and Maričić, but Canetti and Maričić had become firm friends and Deacon knew he'd take it worse than the rest of them.

'Broken ribs?' Deacon asked.

'Yeah, they beat us pretty bad. Lots of kicking. I've got at least three bust ribs; I reckon Jose the same, plus his nose. Couple of bust fingers as well,' Roberts answered.

Martock walked back into the room, carrying some of their weapons. 'They are all here, boss,' he said, handing a rifle over.

Finding all their equipment, they moved towards the door.

'Check the dead for phones then sanitize the area. Leave all their stuff, but make sure all ours is gone.'

In one of the rebels phones Canetti found a number for Vodolski.

Deacon immediately powered up his Iridium satellite and dialed.

Fifteen seconds later, Mitch answered.

'Mitch, mission gone to shit. I need an immediate position on a local phone. Can you get the NSA to track it?' he said after reading off the number.

Mitch had been just about to leave his desk when his phone had rung. He'd already heard the mission had been blown and had reported it to the Admiral. Hearing Deacon's voice gave him new hope his friend would be ok. He hit speed dial on his handset and a moment later was talking to a senior officer at the National Security Agency in Fort Meade, known as 'Crypto City'.

Back at the farmhouse, Martock had been looking around for any transport back to the beach when he found four more bodies in a small lockup. Three of the bodies were of an old man and woman, possibly his wife, and a younger woman in her late teens. All had been murdered with a single shot to the back of their heads. They could very well be the grandparents and granddaughter. Or maybe the young woman was helping the older couple running the farm. Or maybe the young woman was an employee. Either way, it hadn't stopped Vodolski murdering them all in cold blood. The young women's clothes were mostly missing, and her body was covered in scratches and bite marks. Human bite marks. It looked like she had been violently assaulted and most likely repeatedly raped before being murdered.

The fourth body was of the CIA agent they'd been sent to rescue. He'd also been killed execution-style.

Deacon and Roberts were now the fittest of the four of them, so Deacon lifted the body of Stockwell across his shoulders while Roberts did the same with Maričić's before heading back along the track towards the beach. Martock and Canetti walked point protecting them, Martock doing the best to keep up with his damaged leg.

As they were climbing down the final part of the path onto the beach, Deacon's satellite phone rang.

'John, the phone you're tracking. It's stopped at a location about six miles north and one mile east of the farmhouse. Been there a while now and not moving. It seems to be a local bar. Sending you the co-ordinates.'

Quickly reading the location, he powered down the phone to conserve battery life as an idea came to him. Helping the others put the bodies of Stockwell and Maričić in the RIB, Deacon ordered the three of them back to the Carney.

'I'll come with you, boss,' Canetti said.

'No, guys. This is personal. This bastard murdered two of my men in cold blood. You're all injured. I'll do this alone. You take Andy and Goran back to the Carney and get yourselves checked over by the docs. However, if one of you would care to come back here at exactly midnight later tonight to pick me up . . .'

After getting reluctant nods of agreement, he continued, 'It'll be light here soon, so watch for my signal tonight. It'll be 'J D' in Morse. If I'm not here, go. If need be, I'll find my own way out of here. Good luck, guys.'

He pushed the bow of the RIB out into deeper water while Martock started the engines, and then picked up his assault rifle.

As he walked back across the beach, the gentle purr of the two outboards faded as the RIB disappeared out into the gloom.

35

The soft purr of the twin-silenced outboards foretold an uneventful journey back to the USS Carney for Martock and his colleagues.

Nothing, however, could have been further from the truth. The weather had slowly worsened as the night had moved on, and the winds had increased, but the rain had lessened. Radioing the Carney, Canetti was informed due to the change of plans earlier in the evening, that the Carney was now not in the correct position to pick them up. The original course of the Carney was NW when the team had been dropped off. An hour later she was to reverse course and intercept them ninety minutes after dropping them off. That plan had been canceled after Deacon and his team were ambushed. Staying on the same NW course had meant she came within range and interest to the massive Russian naval base in Sevastopol. Assuming she was on a spying mission, even though clearly in international waters, the Russian Fleet had sent another patrol ship to join in the chase, as well as sending fighter jets to 'buzz' the Carney.

Apart from the fighter jets, Russian naval scouting helicopters were watching from a distance. The Carney was now being shadowed by one ship just inside the exclusion zone while the other held position just outside, effectively stopping her making any deviation from her course. To be picked up, their RIB would need to be directly on the Carney's course at least a mile ahead, but without being detected by the Russians.

Typically, to make a fast passage in larger waves, the answer was to power up the RIB until it leaped from one wave crest to the next. However, the effervescent trail this produced would be easily seen by both waterborne and airborne craft. Traveling at higher speed the RIB was also more likely to be detected on radar. Because they had twenty-five miles of enemy water to transit through, and detection would likely result in total destruction by enemy fire; the only answer was extreme stealth.

The Executive Officer onboard the Carney radioed them an exact lat-long coordinate to be at in precisely two hours and eight minutes for pickup. Making a final course change, the captain on the Carney radioed the Russian chase ships and bade them a fond farewell. The captain then ordered increased speed on an exact time intercept course.

As the propellers of the USS Carney increased revolutions and the bow wave surged, Canetti was quickly trying to plot a course to intercept. Completed, he instructed Martock, and the RIB began an uncomfortable slow back-and-forth plowing motion east through the turbulent waves. Being all dressed entirely in black, with black fabric also covering the RIB, and proceeding slowly so as not to produce a wake, detection by the enemy was unlikely.

Although once overflown by a low-flying helicopter, they made slow but eventful progress to the pick-up point. Arriving five minutes ahead of schedule, Martock aligned the craft in the direction the Carney was following and held her steady on minimum throttle. In the distance, the navigation lights and white bow waves of the approaching Carney and her two escorts could be seen.

As the Carney came closer, at the last moment she changed course slightly, offering her port side to Martock.

Momentarily hidden from view from the Russian escorts, Martock expertly powered up the RIB's engines to match the Carney's speed while laying less than a yard off her port beam. Two crane davits were swung out over the port side of the Carney, and two snap hooks were quickly lowered. Canetti and Roberts took less than a second to clip the hooks over the support strops before shouting to Martock, who blipped his radio.

High-speed motors lifted the RIB and its passengers up to deck height within two seconds, outboard engines still screaming in protest. Three seconds later, two ensigns were tying down the RIB onto the deck with strops as the three survivors just sat there in relief.

After taking the bodies of Stockwell and Maričić to the sickbay to be prepared for the upcoming flight home, the three of them headed to the bridge. The captain shook hands with each of them and said Admiral Carter was waiting with a live video link for Martock to discuss what had happened.

As Martock was taken to the captain's cabin for privacy, Roberts and Canetti headed back to the sickbay for a check-up and for their injuries to be treated before heading to the mess for food.

'Chief, tell me exactly what happened,' Admiral Carter demanded, his voice gruff and with a look of extreme displeasure on his face. Over the next twenty minutes ex-Chief, PO Sean Martock explained in as much detail as he could who had done what and when.

Before finishing the call, the Admiral explained the Carney couldn't hang around any longer as he'd already received a formal complaint from his counterpart in the Russian Navy demanding the U.S. ship leave Russian waters and any failure to comply could result in hostile action being taken. Besides, further Russian naval vessels were being dispatched from Sevastopol to keep the U.S. away.

Seething with anger at not being able to tell his Russian equal to 'go soak his head', or worse, the Admiral realized any further provocation would only escalate matters, so in this instance, he backed down. However, Deacon would now have to find a different escape route, and he instructed Martock to call him to inform him.

With their hand-held radios only having a short-range, Martock went up on deck and hit the speed dial on his encrypted satellite phone, again and again, trying to connect.

But all he received was the 'connection unavailable' tone.

36

Arriving back at the barn, Deacon quickly searched it again. He found a laptop, but it was password protected. Searching the bodies of the rebels more thoroughly, he found a set of keys. Walking around to the old Mercedes, he tried them, but they didn't fit. However, they did fit the truck and its engine started on the sixth turn. It wasn't the smoothest ride he'd ever experienced as the the engine ran rough, and the steering kept pulling to the right, but hey, third-class driving is always better than first-class walking, he thought.

Following the directions sent by Mitch and the NSA, it only took less than ten minutes to drive the seven miles to get close to the bar. Stopping on the side of the small road, he extinguished the headlights, grabbed his rifle, and approached on foot.

The building was small and dirty. There were no lights showing outside, but as Deacon got nearer, he could see chinks of light escaping around some ill-fitting curtains. There was a motorcycle propped against the wall. Making sure there were no obstacles or gravel likely to make a noise, he quietly moved closer and placed his hand on the engine. It was still warm. Not hot, indicating only just driven, but warm; meaning it had been used maybe an hour ago.

Feeling more confident he had the correct place, he moved forward slightly and peered through a gap in the filthy curtains.

The room was dense with tobacco smoke, but he could see the shapes of four men sitting there playing cards.

Suddenly, one of the shapes stood and moved towards the window. Not sure if he'd been discovered, Deacon darted back out of sight while at the same time raising his rifle, ready to fire.

With a click of the latch, the person inside opened the window to let some of the smoke out, before returning to the card game. Now Deacon could hear them talking and the chink of glasses as they drank. Looking again through the gap, Deacon could just make out the features of the farthest person sitting at the table. As that person leaned forward to drop a card on the table, his face caught the lamplight, and Deacon could clearly see it was Dimitri Vodolski, face and nose covered in a bandage.

All he could do was wait. Moving off into dense shadows, he settled down to watch from where he could keep an eye on the doorway, as the sky began to lighten slowly in the East.

Thirty or so minutes later, the voices around the table became louder, and he heard chairs being pushed back. Two men walked out and climbed into a car before driving off. A minute or so after, Vodolski appeared and walked towards the motorcycle.

As he went to pull the crash helmet over his head, Deacon hit him once, hard, on the back of his neck with the rifle butt. Vodolski collapsed without a sound.

Vodolski came to slowly. His entire head and shoulders ached with the slightest movement, and his arms felt to be on fire. As his senses returned, he realized he was hanging from his thumbs, and the pain was intense. Unlike Deacon earlier, Vodolski was still dressed, but his feet and thumbs were tightly tied, and the cord around his thumbs was over the same hook that had suspended Deacon. His feet were also secured to another lower beam, making movement virtually impossible.

Lifting his chin and looking around, he saw Deacon sitting on an upturned barrel, watching him, while gently stroking the ten-inch blade of an evil looking knife.

'My, my, my. How the tide has changed. Perhaps you might care to answer my questions now,' Deacon said.

Vodolski spat towards Deacon and said, 'Ty che, suka, o'khuel blya? Ya tebya ub'yu!'

Leaning forward, Deacon seemed hardly to move his hands at all, but next moment Vodolski's foot was racked in pain and he cried out.

'English, my friend. English,' Deacon said, holding up Vodolski's newly removed small toe.

Through gritted teeth, Vodolski said, 'You are so fucking dead,' before finishing with more Russian curse words.

Ignoring him, Deacon asked, 'Why kill Bennett the CIA agent? Surely he was worth money to you?'

When Vodolski didn't answer, Deacon stood and moved closer. Reaching up, he gripped Vodolski's broken nose through the bandages and twisted it firmly, feeling the cartilages snap again.

Sitting back down while Vodolski let loose another series of swear words in Russian, Deacon waited until he'd finished then tried again. 'I asked you a question. Why kill Bennett? He must have been worth money to you?'

Spitting at Deacon again, Vodolski replied, 'You worth more.'

'How much more?'

'He was $3M. You $10M.'

'And my men?'

'$3M each.'

'Who was paying?'

At that, Vodolski decided to keep quiet. It took the removal of his other small toe and the threat of an ear before he finally answered.

'Fuck you, bitch. No name.'

'You know a name. Tell me, you fucker, before I cut your balls off.'

'Fuck you.'

Leaning forward again, Deacon slit Vodolski's belt and started pulling his pants down.

'Okay, okay. I sell your men to ISIS,' he shouted.

'And me? Was I destined for ISIS as well?'

When Vodolski didn't answer, Deacon swept the blade up toward his face. With blood now running into his mouth as his septum was sliced in two, Vodolski finally muttered, 'Your friends.'

Hardly believing his ears, Deacon asked once more. 'You're lying.'

'Truth, American. Mighty US want you dead. Who is bitch now, huh?'

Moving away for a few moments, deep in thought, Deacon walked back to Vodolski and said, 'Why the old couple and the girl? What harm were they to you?'

'They in way. Girl was good. She was shlyukha. Slut. We enjoy her. Old woman cry watching.'

Deacon had already seen a couple of photographs in the farmhouse of the old couple along with the girl. They'd been taken in happier times, and it was apparent they had known the girl as she'd grown up so they were likely her grandparents. These 'animals' had killed them without a thought after using the girl for their own sick pleasure. Worse, they'd made the grandparents watch.

Looking Vodolski in the eye, Deacon said, 'My men were willing to die to protect others. You murdered them in cold blood. They were my friends. This is for them, Bennett, and the old couple and their granddaughter, and all the others you've ever murdered. Rot in hell.'

And with that, he pulled his pistol from its holster and shot Vodolski twice straight through the forehead.

Walking back to the farmhouse, he grabbed some bread and cold meat from the fridge, two bottles of water, and left.

He wanted to bury the old couple and their granddaughter and show them some dignity, but he also knew all the bodies would be investigated. It was best to leave it assumed to be an internal fight or robbery gone wrong. He didn't know when someone might arrive, so he decided to move on as quickly as possible.

Heading back down towards the beach to find somewhere to lie low until the evening, he switched on his encrypted satellite phone.

It rang almost immediately.

37

'Boss, I've been trying to reach you for ages. Where the fuck are you?'

'Just been tidying up loose ends. What's up?'

'The Carney's out of here. Too much Russian heat. There's no way I can come get you tonight. You'll need to find another way.'

'Fuck! Okay, let me think,' Deacon said before considering his options.

After a minute's silence, he finally came up with an idea. 'This is just between you and me. Don't inform Washington. In fact, don't inform anyone. Leave it as you couldn't contact me. I'll make m--'

'But boss, how will you get out? You're in Russian-controlled territory?'

'No buts, Sean. Just do as I say. Don't inform anybody. The official answer you give is you couldn't reach me. I'll make my way north close to the border with Ukraine and find a way across. You and the guy's head on back to Washington. OK? Don't forget, you haven't reached me! I'm counting on you, Sean,' he finished, before disconnecting the phone.

Half-jogging, Deacon quickly headed back to the farm and outbuildings, stopping near the tree Stockwell had been wounded at. Staying behind cover, he waited a few minutes to check whether anybody had turned up, but found no evidence of disturbance.

In the farmhouse, he quickly searched the bedrooms for suitably sized clothes he could wear -- he was currently wearing black battle fatigues -- and luckily found a threadbare and worn greatcoat at least four sizes too large. He also found various sets of pants and shirts, but most were too small for him. Deciding on the greatcoat, he also found an old used backpack full of plastic bags and western porn magazines. Emptying it on the floor, he put the food and water he'd taken earlier into it, leaving space for his equipment. Grabbing a couple of plastic bags, he wrapped his NVG's, radio, phone, and the laptop up before also placing them in the backpack before wearing the greatcoat on top.

Heading back out, he removed the bike keys from the dead body of Dimitri Vodolski before climbing back into the truck and heading back to the bar.

The motorcycle was an old model. The logo was faded, but Deacon could see it was manufactured by Dnepr -- one of Ukraine's oldest motorcycle manufacturers. Although old, it still seemed to run okay. It started on the third kick, and after blowing a large plume of black smoke out its exhaust, it settled down to tick-over sweetly. Deacon had been tempted to stick with the truck, but the steering was shot, and it was slow. At least on the bike, he would have a chance at outrunning someone, if necessary.

Fitting the crash helmet, he mounted the bike and set off.

He joined the T0177 and headed north, away from Yalta -- made famous in February 1945 during World War II due to the conference between British Prime Minister Churchill, U.S. President Roosevelt, and Soviet Premier Stalin; now a popular holiday resort, and headed towards Tankove. An hour later, he was about to change onto the HD6 towards Simferopol, but as he rounded a corner, he could see his first roadblock two hundred yards ahead.

Since Russia occupied the Ukrainian peninsula in February 2014, Russian armed forces regularly checked the identities of locals traveling throughout the area. Deacon knew he couldn't pass muster at such an inspection, so turning quickly, he headed along some back lanes and across a farmyard, before rejoining the T0177 three miles further along.

Thirty miles later, he entered the outskirts of Simferopol, the second-largest city on the Crimean Peninsula and the capital of the Republic of Crimea. With a population close to 400,000, and many roads and back-roads, roadblocks were few and far between. However, by keeping to the back roads, he avoided any security checks that might have been in place.

Twenty minutes later, he was cruising north on the H05 towards the peninsula border with Ukraine. As he cleared Simferopol, he found a dirt track leading to a group of trees. Pulling in behind them, he stopped for lunch. He needed to keep his energy up and hadn't eaten for over twenty-four hours. He also didn't know when he might eat again.

Four more hours of steady riding saw him closing on the town of Krasnoperekopsk when his luck ran out. Rising up over the brow of a hill, he saw the road was blocked by two army trucks stopped at forty-five-degree angles three hundred yards ahead. There was nowhere to turn. His only option was to try and brazen it out.

As he got closer, he could see the trucks were offset, allowing traffic to chicane through slowly.

Two guards were stopping traffic in both directions and checking paperwork. There were at least a dozen guards just standing around. All were carrying weapons, but none were expecting trouble as all their weapons were either holstered or shouldered.

Four vehicles in front . . .

Three vehicles in front . . .

Two vehicles in front. There was an issue with something. This vehicle was ordered to pull over, and three other guards approached it and started shouting at the driver. Perhaps they would be so busy he could go straight on, he thought.

One vehicle in front . . .

Then it was his turn.

'Dokumenty!' *(Papers)* the guard ordered.

'Srochnyy biznes. Dayte mne proyti!' *(Urgent business. Let me pass!)* Deacon replied.

'Bumagi, mudak. V nastoyashcheye vremya!' *(Papers, asshole. Now!)* the guard shouted.

With that, Deacon kicked him in the balls while slipping the Dnepr into gear, releasing the clutch, and revving the engine.

As he pulled rapidly away, two guards moved in front to try and stop him while also trying to unshoulder their weapons. One was struck by the end of the handlebars in the chest while the other went down to Deacon's raised foot. As he twisted and turned the accelerating bike past the second truck, the shouts went up and a couple of soldiers, quicker off the mark than their colleagues, opened fire, their bullets going wild and striking the trucks.

As he pulled away, he glanced over his shoulder and could see at least four soldiers raising their weapons in his direction. Rapidly accelerating past the last vehicle to have cleared the roadblock in front of him, he bent low over the handlebars and twisted the throttle for all it was worth.

A fusillade of shots struck the rear windshield of the vehicle behind him, killing both occupants instantly. The dead driver's foot jammed against the gas pedal, making the car immediately accelerate straight across the traffic lane before crashing into the line of vehicles coming from the other direction, one of which was a gas tanker. The soldiers continued firing, their rounds hitting a number of the vehicles in line, including the tanker. A ricochet caused a spark, and with a whoosh, the leaking fuel from the tanker ignited and began to burn fiercely.

More rounds hit the tanker, allowing more fuel to escape before catching alight. Before Deacon had gone a half-mile, four other vehicles had caught fire, burning their occupants to death.

Out of range of the gunfire, the sudden boom of the tanker exploding caught Deacon by surprise, and the shock wave almost made him fall. Dropping his speed from extreme to merely excessive, Deacon continued racing north towards Krasnoperekopsk and possible freedom.

As he roared through the town, his heart sunk as he heard a siren start-up. He saw the glow of red and blue flashing lights of a police car reflected in the glass windows of the houses he was passing.

Cursing, he knew there was no easy escape, so he again twisted the throttle as far as it would go, ducked his head even further down, and started to pull away from them.

His pursuers also increased speed and must have called for support because suddenly another two police vehicles joined in the chase. They had also radioed ahead because as Deacon roared along the main road through Krasnoperekopsk, weaving and dodging past slower vehicles, he could see an army truck partly blocking the way ahead in a hastily set up roadblock.

Five soldiers were manning the roadblock and were aiming rifles at him. They wouldn't be caught a second time.

Swerving, he turned a sharp right and sped along a narrow side road, the police cars following him. A half-mile further on the road turned left towards housing, but there was a large open grassland area immediately in front of him. With long grass and coarse bushes covering most of the area, Deacon made rapid progress along the winding dirt tracks, quickly leaving his pursuers struggling behind.

Exiting onto the canal path, he turned north again and accelerated. The police cars were now far behind him, lights flashing and sirens still wailing, but again he increased the distance between them before slewing left through a group of low-lying fields and speeding across the main E97 Ukraine to Crimea road.

The Russian imposed border was only eight miles away, but he knew the border would now be closed and impossible to cross. Already, police and army vehicles were heading his way to intercept him. Accelerating again, he headed left onto narrow tracks west of the E97 towards the coast. Here the land was flat and marshy. Some parts had been sectioned off and dried, with crops growing, but the remainder were sunken and wet. The tracks followed the outlines of the fields and what few crops were growing offered little protection. Soon the zing of bullets flying close to him made him hunker lower over the handlebars as stray bullets chipped small stones off the track. With his hands aching from the pressure on the throttle, he slewed left and right to upset their aim as he squeezed and coaxed every last ounce of power from the old, but reliable, engine.

Finally, his options ran out, and he jumped off the bike before it had even stopped, leaving the engine sputtering and chinking as it slowly cooled. The sea was a mere fifty feet the other side of the fence, and he flung the greatcoat over the barbed wire for protection. Leaping over, he ran as fast as he could down the sloping beach, while bullets peppered the sand and waterline around him. At least two hit his backpack, but neither penetrated to injure him. Jumping through the numbingly cold waves, he dove under as soon as the water was a deep enough depth to cover himself.

As he dove down, something red hot slammed into his left shoulder, and the sudden pain made him gasp and choke. Surfacing once briefly, he gagged in a mouthful of seawater and air and quickly ducked down again as more soldiers opened fire at him.

His movement slowed, and a dull red mist swam across his vision. As he began to sink, he could feel all his pain ebb away as all he could hear was the roaring in his ears getting louder and louder.

38

It took a few seconds before the shock of the icy cold sea brought Deacon back to his senses. The red mist in front of his eyes was his own blood escaping from his shoulder wound, and the roaring in his ears was the waves breaking on the pebbles and sand. His pain ebbing away was likely the chill numbing his external senses.

Swimming gently underwater into the direction of the waves slowly took him into deeper water, and after a minute, he risked slowly putting his face to the surface to breathe. Only his nose and mouth was clear of the water, and although the waves broke over his face making him gag, the troughs between waves hid him from his pursuers on the shore. Taking another deep breath, he ducked below the surface again before heading further out to sea until he was out of range from his pursuers.

There was still sporadic firing coming from the shore, but with no target to aim for, nothing came close.

The new international border between Russian-occupied Crimea and Ukraine was in the middle of the Perekops'ka gulf, with the gulf being only six miles wide here. Regularly patrolled by Russian inshore craft, and alerted to someone trying to escape capture, the Russians were on full alert and would happily exceed their orders and head into Ukrainian waters to carry them out.

As the sky darkened, the patrolling craft switched on searchlights, machine-gunning any splash or wave movement they didn't like. Their sweeping beams of intense light made it easy for Deacon to keep clear, and as the sky darkened further, he became almost invisible amongst the many waves. However, the cold of the water was severely hampering him, and by now, his shoulder was almost immovable. One benefit of the water temperature was the bleeding had appeared to slow, but the pain was returning, and every movement of his shoulder was making him gasp.

A healthy person could stand up to forty minutes in water of that temperature before beginning to suffer badly from hypothermia.

Deacon had been swimming over an hour and wasn't even yet halfway. He had kicked off his heavy boots, but they had slipped out of his grasp and he'd lost them.

His thick clothing was slowing him down but he knew he had to keep going. Relentlessly, right arm, left arm, gasp; right arm, left arm, gasp. Minute after minute, stroke after stroke. The patrolling craft had lost contact and given up by now, but Deacon never would. Continuing on, digging deeper and deeper into his very being for the next stroke, already he couldn't feel his hands or feet. Even his arms and legs had gone numb with the cold. Only the burning pain in his left shoulder kept his mind focused. Right arm, left arm, gasp; right arm, left arm, gasp.

With his vision dimming and with his energy almost totally spent, he suddenly heard a new sound. A new sound that urged him to swim just a little more. A new sound that revitalized his exhausted body. It was the sound of waves breaking against the shoreline. The Ukrainian shoreline.

His feet touched the seabed, and he staggered the last few feet before sinking to his knees in the rough sand. But he knew he couldn't rest. The effort of the swim and the cold of the water had sapped his strength dangerously low. If he didn't find shelter soon, it would have all been worthless. He knew he was already suffering a severe level of hypothermia. Unless he could find shelter, and find it quickly, he would surely die.

His original plan had been to get as close to the border as possible before commandeering a dinghy or powerboat to cross the gulf to Ukraine. His ideal landing place had been Oleksandrivka, a small fishing town on the Ukrainian coastline. Unfortunately, outside influences had forced a plan change, and his urgent swim had resulted in him landing on the empty beach of the Mala Kosa peninsula.

Staggering along the beach barefoot, he slowly climbed the grasslands beyond. The only lights visible were from Oleksandrivka over a dozen miles away. The chill wind was making his wet clothes stick to his body, further wicking away what little heat his body was trying to produce.

An outline of a small building showed against the gray of the sky. Shivering uncontrollably, Deacon realized it was an old small animal shed. Pushing what remained of the old wooden door open, he half-walked half-fell inside, grateful to be out of the wind at last. Most of the roof had collapsed, and the ground inside was littered with rubbish. Slipping his backpack off his numb arms, he fumbled with the zipper and eventually pulled out his NVG's and looked around.

Either someone had used this place recently, or more likely, some young people had used it as a semi-romantic meeting place. There was a pile of filthy straw in the corner, but it had been crushed by the weight of one or more bodies. There was at least a half-dozen used condoms discarded, and some empty bottles of cheap gut-rot vodka. On the positive side, there were two dirty blankets covered in stains that defied identification, a few candle stubs, and some discarded food wrappers.

Murmuring to himself, he said, 'Like Patrick said. How romantic?'

Pulling the straw apart close to where the candles were, he found a few dropped unused matches.

'Not exactly the Hilton,' he thought, 'but it'll do.'

Using a broken piece of the door, he cleared an area in the corner of the barn. Placing some of the straw with the discarded food wrappers, he added small pieces of the broken door to make a fire, all made more difficult due to his numb fingers. Two of the matches he had found were too damp, and their heads just crumbled, but he rubbed the third one through his hair for a few minutes before holding it in his hands and blowing gently across it. The salt near his scalp absorbed the damp, plus his warm breath dried the match slightly, and it lit on the second attempt.

Lighting one of the candle stubs first, he then used the candle to light another before igniting the paper and straw. It took a few minutes, but finally, the straw caught, and the flames increased. He quickly added more straw and bigger pieces of the broken door until the wood also caught. At least being in the barn and out of the wind had reduced some of his shivering. His clothes were still wet, and his hands and fingers were blue, but the feeling began to return as he flexed his hands in the growing heat of the small fire.

Stripping off his sodden clothes, he hung them over part of the broken doorway. With a look of distaste, he pulled the two filthy blankets over himself, reasoning he didn't know what or where the stains had come from, but it couldn't be any worse than what he'd experienced today. His clothes would take a while to dry, but as the warmth increased in the small barn, Deacon gradually felt better and finally stopped shivering.

Next on the agenda was food and drink. He pulled everything from the backpack and was disappointed to find the damage from the bullet holes. Two had hit the laptop but had passed through the plastic bags protecting some of the other items. The seawater had done the rest of the damage. The bread he'd brought was ruined, but luckily some of the meat was still edible, and one bottle of water was salvageable.

He downed half the water in one go. He was badly dehydrated from the swim, but also from swallowing varying amounts of saltwater. Although most of the roof of the barn had collapsed long ago, and the sky was exposed above, the warmth of the fire reflected off the walls, and he settled down in reasonable comfort as he ate, just hoping it wouldn't rain.

Then it was time to look at his wound. It had stopped bleeding while he was swimming, and he'd already found it was a through-and-through. He'd left it until now as food and warmth were more important initially. Luckily, both the entry and exit wounds were small. Both had tightened up as the body automatically tried to begin healing itself. He knew they were not caused by an actual bullet. The entry was small enough to have been from a 5.45mm standard Russian military, but not the exit. He'd seen plenty of exit wounds. Most were the diameter of a cup. Some as large as a bowl or dinner plate. No, if this had been a standard full-metal-jacket round he'd be able to put his fist in the exit hole and he'd likely be dead by now.

Likely this was a fragment of pebble thrown up from a wayward round. But it had still gone completely through his shoulder, entering just above his shoulder blade and exiting through the muscle and out the front.

Miraculously, it hadn't hit bone. Ideally, it needed stitches and a shot or two of antibiotics, but he had nothing available. The salt in the seawater would have helped clean the wound, and he hoped it would just heal.

What he didn't know because he had no way of examining inside the entry wound, was some of the material of his shirt and jacket was lodged deep inside his body. What he also didn't know was his white blood cells were working overtime, trying to expel the foreign invader within their domain.

He sat there for almost two hours in the direct warmth of the fire until his clothes had dried enough. Dressing, he stocked the fire up a little before settling down on the straw. Finally, exhaustion overcame him, and he lapsed into a deep sleep. All the while, his white blood cell count continued to grow.

39

Ukraine

By five am, he was feeling ill. His body temperature was 103F, but he had no way of checking. All he knew was he was unwell. His shoulder was throbbing more now than when swimming. The wound had been weeping, and his shirt was stuck to both the front and back of his shoulder. Gently peeling back the material brought tears to his eyes. There was still a reasonable red glow of the fire but not enough light to see properly. Had he had a working torch, he would have seen the exit point of the wound had now reopened almost four times as large and was oozing small speckles of pus along with a clear liquid.

The entry wound on his back was even worse. Here, larger amounts of pus were being expelled from the opening, and the skin around it had turned a deep red. He was suffering from early stages of septicemia and in urgent need of hospital treatment and antibiotics.

A dog barked.

Deacon froze.

Grabbing his pistol, he raised himself and looked out an opening in the crumbling brickwork. He could make out the shape of a person approaching, carrying a torch. He was coming directly to the barn. He was accompanied by a dog. A large one. The depth of the bark made it possibly a German Shepherd or a Doberman. The figure came closer and closer until he was a mere twenty feet away. Deacon could see the dog was a German Shepherd. He could also see the figure was carrying a shotgun.

Suddenly the figure stopped.

'Hey, you! You in the barn. Identify yourself. I have a gun. Come out with your hands up,' the figure shouted in stilted Russian.

Deacon waited.

'You! You in the barn. Come out with your hands up, I said. I have a gun. Come out,' it repeated.

Again, Deacon waited.

Finally, the figure tried once more. 'I will send my dog in if you don't come out!'

'You do, old man, and your dog will die. Who are you?' Deacon shouted.

'I am Oleg Soroka!' the man replied, with a sound of surprise in his voice. 'I own the barn you have been sleeping in. I own all this land,' he said, sweeping his arms around.

'Leave your dog and weapon outside and come in. Don't try anything heroic,' Deacon shouted.

Commanding his dog to sit, the man laid his shotgun on the ground, stood up, and straightened his clothes before walking straight into the barn.

Deacon was standing the far side of the barn, mostly in shadow aiming his pistol at the intruder.

'That's close enough,' Deacon said.

Oleg stood still and looked Deacon up and down. 'You don't look Russian, and you're not from around here. Where are you from?' he said.

When Deacon didn't answer, Oleg continued, this time in fluent English, 'Look, you escaped across the gulf last night. You don't look Russian, but you are western. I'd guess you're American. From your clothes, you are obviously a soldier of some sort. You're being hunted by the Russians, and by the looks of you, you're wounded. In fact, you look close to collapse.'

'What's it to do with you?' Deacon replied.

'Look, my friend. I and most of Oleksandrivka heard of your escape last night. Heavy machine-gun fire travels easily across the water and watching their fast boats trying to find you was better than watching TV. Half the town is out looking to find you and hand you over to the Russians. I saw the fire in the barn last night. Why do you think I am here alone instead of bringing half the Russian Army to get you.'

'How do I know I can trust you?'

'You don't. But I'm here alone, and if you kill me, my wife won't be very happy, and the other half of the town will track you down. Now may I suggest you sit down before you collapse. In case you haven't noticed, your pistol is pointing at the floor, and you are looking very pale.'

With that, the room began to swim, and Deacon felt himself sink to the floor. The pistol dropped from his fingers, and as everything started to close in on him and go dark, the last thing he saw was the man rush forward to try and break his fall.

As his eyes slowly opened and objects came into focus, the first things he saw were the patterns on the ceiling. There were lines and squiggles, and it took a few moments to realize they were cracks in the plaster. Trying not to move anything apart from his eyes, he looked left, right, up, and down.

He was in a large bed, lying on his back. Daylight was coming in through a window. The room he was in contained the bed itself, a chest of drawers, and a chair. His shoulder was bandaged, and he was just wearing his boxers. His clothes were missing, but his backpack was on the floor by the side of the bed. He was alone.

Spending a few minutes lying there carefully looking around, he tried to remember how he'd gotten there. He had dim memories of being half-carried across the fields, but that was all.

Pushing back the covers, he swung his legs over the side and tried to stand up, just as the bedroom door opened, and a woman in her late fifties walked in.

'Slowly, slowly,' she said in English, rushing towards him to help.

'I don't think we've been introduced,' Deacon replied, rapidly sitting down again as his head spun.

'I am Kateryna Soroka. You've already met my husband. He brought you here,' she replied.

'And here is where?'

'Our farm, of course. Now, if you want to try to stand, let me help you,' she said, offering an outstretched steadying arm.

'Has your husband gone to round up the remaining villagers of Oleksandrivka?'

'Hmmm, he said you didn't trust him. Do you want coffee? What about something to eat. Oleg will be back soon. I'll go down and make you a coffee. You come down when you're ready and if you are able. Here are some spare clothes about your size you can wear while yours dry,' she said, heading towards the doorway.

Sitting on the edge of the bed, Deacon looked a little stunned. Quite how he'd gotten there and how long he'd been there were unknown, but he was glad he had. He slowly dressed, slow enough not to cause dizziness, before very gradually standing and moving cautiously toward the door. Heading out onto the landing, he carefully headed downstairs.

As he reached the bottom stair, Oleg walked in.

'Ahh! The secret American soldier. Or are you a secret CIA agent? You know, the Russians are still searching for you. According to them, you are Superman. They've even offered a reward. Five thousand Rouble. About seventy-five U.S. dollars.'

'So are you going to turn me in?'

'What? Five thousand Rouble for Superman? I don't think so. Come, let us have a vodka,' Oleg said, taking his good arm and directing him towards the kitchen.

'How long have I been here?'

'Just under six hours. You were unconscious or sleeping all that time. I am sure you know, but you have been shot. Your wound is badly infected. Kateryna has cleaned it and bandaged it as much as possible, but you need medical help. Urgently.'

'Can we not call a doctor? I have money. I can pay. We are in Ukraine, after all.'

'No, my friend, not here. This area close to the new Russian border is very pro-Russian. Russia pays well for information about subversives. You are lucky I found you. Most people here would have turned you over to the border guards you escaped from. It is all over the local news about an enemy of the people escaping. It seems you are a murderer, a rapist, and a thief. You also raped two little boys. Everyone around here, including at the hospital, wants you captured and sent back for trial and execution,' Oleg said.

'But not you or Kateryna? You don't feel that way?'

'You may be all the bad things they say about you, but I don't think so. I think you are a soldier, an American soldier, but I don't think you are a bad one. We prefer to help.'

'Both of you speak very good English. Did you learn it here?' Deacon asked.

'We are both Ukrainian, but we met at Iowa State University. We didn't know each other before. Kateryna was raised north of Kiev. This farm has been in my family for seven generations. When we came back here, this was the obvious place to settle. Kateryna's younger brother ended up taking over her family's farm up north. Our son, Stefan, is currently studying at Iowa State. We have much love of America and Americans,' Oleg continued. 'But for now, we have a problem. You need to get medical help, but there are roadblocks and checks around here. If you travel, even with us, I think you will be captured. Can you get someone from your embassy in Kiev to come to help you?' Oleg asked.

'Can I stay here for a day or two?'

'Of course. You are safe here. Just don't show yourself if anyone visits.'

'Actually, Oleg. Where is here, exactly?' Deacon said while rummaging through his backpack for the satellite phone. Pressing the power button, he silently prayed it would work and still have enough power in the battery. With a playful tune the phone powered up, the screen lit up, and it began its search for a satellite link.

Checking the display, it showed less than fifteen percent power remaining. Silently cursing, Deacon knew he had no way to recharge it. Recalling a number from memory, Deacon punched in the numbers carefully. After a twenty-second delay, he received a busy tone. Waiting a few minutes, he tried again, with the same result. Five minutes later, with the display now showing twelve percent power, he tried again for the third time. After waiting for what seemed hours, but in reality, only thirty or so seconds, the highly encrypted phone finally managed to connect.

Before the person receiving the call could speak fully, Deacon interrupted him, blurting out, 'Shane, Deacon. I'm in the town of Oleksandrivka in Ukraine, close to the Crimea border. Been shot. Not life-threatening yet, but I urgently need antibiotics and assistance. No passport.

Can't involve Langley. In fact, keep this totally unofficial. Can you authorize someone to assist?'

After listening to Shane for a minute or two and giving over the address of the farm, he eventually ended the call.

Turning to the Soroka's, he thanked them profusely before explaining a colleague would be arriving the day after tomorrow.

Feeling exhausted after even such little effort used, he managed to down a meal of hot meat stew and bread before Kateryna ordered him back to bed. The pain in his shoulder had continued worsening. She had only cleaned the area two hours before, so after carefully removing the bandage, she was dismayed to see the swelling had deteriorated, and the skin had turned black directly around the points of entry and exit. As she pulled the bandage off, a lump of green pus had oozed from the rear wound, and smaller amounts of pus escaping from the front. The skin itself was hot and severely inflamed.

Giving Deacon a rolled-up towel to bite down on, she told him to lie on his front and brace himself. She gently squeezed around the area to expel as much pus as she could, before placing an ice-cold compress on it to try and relieve the swelling. The only painkillers she had were standard ibuprofen and aspirin, which Deacon dosed himself on, but they were too weak to really make much difference.

40

By midnight the fever had returned and worsened. With a temperature close to 106F, he was barely conscious but totally unaware of where he was or even who he was. Shouting and ranting, he was delirious and convulsing. When he began vomiting and kicking wildly, they decided he needed to be tied down.

Forcing him onto his front, Oleg tied a cord around his wrists and ankles and secured him firmly to the bed. At least in that position, Kateryna could continue to treat him without injuring herself. With the bandages removed, the smell of the pus from his wound was overpowering, but she continued gently squeezing and wiping.

Suddenly she saw something amongst the yellowy green secretions.

'Oleg, quickly bring scissors,' she cried.

With Oleg putting all his weight on Deacons back to force him still, Kateryna gently probed the tips of the scissors in through the entry wound. It took her four attempts, but finally, she managed to snag the black object she had seen deep inside him. Gently pulling it out, something hard and small also came with it. Placing them in a bowl, she could see it was a piece of material less than an inch long, along with what looked to be a fragment of stone or similar. These were what Deacon's body had been fighting against. These items, alien to his body, were causing a massive infection, and, in turn, had caused his white blood cells to go into total overdrive to try to overcome.

Over the next hour, more yellow and green matter was expelled from his body, but the amount was less. Kateryna continued cleaning the area, but his temperature failed to drop and was still dangerously high at 107F.

Even bathing him with a towel soaked in cold water and placing an electric fan to blow over him was not lowering his fever. Having looked on the internet, Kateryna knew if she couldn't get his temperature down soon, he was likely to suffer severe and permanent brain damage if, in fact, he hadn't already done so.

They only had one option left. Filling the bathtub with cold water, they manhandled a now unconscious Deacon and submerged him in it up to his neck. Over the next hour, they gradually added ice from the freezer to slowly cool his body, and took it in turns to stay with him to ensure he didn't move or slip under the water completely.

Finally, with a cry of relief, Kateryna monitored his temperature and found it was back down to 104F. Still not good, but at least heading in the right direction. Placing him back on the bed, they kept the fan blowing over him until the cold water had dried on his body, further reducing his temperature another degree. For the rest of the evening, they again took it in turns to keep an eye on him, although he was still unconscious and would remain that way for another day.

Oleg looked up when he heard a car approaching the farm. He was in the barn attending the cows so stepped quickly out into the yard.

'Yes, can I help you?' he said in Ukrainian.

'Do you speak Russian?' the tall, attractive woman replied.

'And other languages. What can I do for you?'

'I am looking for a friend. A friend who is not well,' she said.

Aware some of the local townsfolk were still looking for the escaped Russian felon, Oleg was reluctant to admit anything until he was sure.

'I think you have come to the wrong place. There is no one here.'

'Are you sure? Shane sent me,' she said.

'What does he look like, this person you are seeking?'

'He's six-two, dark-haired and has a bullet hole in his back. You must be Oleg?' she said.

Slightly startled she knew his name; he just stood there open-mouthed.

'I'm from Kiev. I flew in earlier this morning. You are Oleg Pavlov Sokorov. Your wife is Kateryna Maria Sokolov. You married in 1991. You own this farm. You have a son, Stefan, currently studying advanced agriculture techniques at Iowa State University. Need I continue?' she said.

'I?. . . how do you? . . . I mean . . . ?'

'It's OK, Oleg. I am from the U.S. Embassy. We do our homework before coming out to site. So, where is the patient, and how is he?'

Guiding her towards the farm, he gave her a quick summary of what had happened. Introducing her to Kateryna, he realized he didn't know her name.

'This is Kateryna, my wife. And you are . . .?'

'Just call me Linda.'

<><><>

An hour later, Linda began to relax. She'd received a call, in private, from Shane soon after he and Deacon had spoken. Aware of the sensitivity, she had spoken with the Station Chief and requested an immediate leave of absence for one week. She then booked a one-way flight from Moscow to Odessa. Arriving early this morning, she booked a car and drove the remainder. Although embassy staff, she didn't have diplomatic status, so wasn't provided any special privileges.

She had inspected Deacon and was pleased with the treatment Kateryna had provided. The removal of foreign material from the wound had been essential. Otherwise, by now Deacon would very likely have died. Linda wasn't a nurse, but all U.S. Embassy employees were trained in basic first-aid, especially with the risk of terrorism. She had administered a massive double-dose shot of antibiotics as well as cleaning the wound again and packing the entry and exit points with an antiseptic healing gel. The skin around the wounds wasn't as red and swollen as before according to Kateryna, but the blackened skin still worried her. Deacon had remained unconscious, but his temperature was down to nearer 100F, and it looked like the worst was over.

The following morning Deacon finally awoke. His temperature was back to almost normal. Looking around, the first face he saw was Linda's.

'Time for my first lesson?' he asked.

'Yes. Don't get shot. It hurts you and worries others,' she said.

'You were worried?'

'I never said that,' she said, smiling. 'I said it worries others.'

'So you mean you weren't worried even a little?'

Smiling again, and going a little red, she said, 'Well, maybe a little, but only a little. Anyway, how do you feel?'

'Pretty shit. Mouth's as dry as a kangaroo's crotch, and I have an amazing headache. As to my shoulder, don't go there.'

'Well, Mister. You owe Kateryna and Oleg a big thank you. You were close to death a number of times. Had they not cooled your body down, you'd be brain dead now. The same had she left the pus insde you. Luckily whatever was in you causing the problem seems to have come out. There may be more fragments, but unlikely. Anyway, only an X-ray or scan will show that.'

Together they looked at the contents of the dish, amazed at such a small piece of material and fragment of rock or pebble could cause everything he went through.

Although unsteady on his feet, he managed to shower slowly – the first he'd had for days. Feeling exhausted after his efforts but at least now clean, Linda redressed the wound yet again. The red swelling had reduced drastically, and even the blackened skin was looking better. The area of black had reduced in size, and overall the skin looked far less inflamed. The one thing Deacon really felt better after was brushing his teeth. Oleg had purchased a new toothbrush in town yesterday for him.

Deacon rested two more days until he felt well enough to travel. On the third day, they drove to Odessa Airport after many hugs and 'thank yous' as they departed. Deacon knew he'd never see them again, and he owed them his life. He promised to look up their son, Stefan, and make sure he was OK in Iowa. In the airport, he ordered and paid delivery for a crate of Khortytsa Platinum premium vodka, considered by many to be the best in the world, certainly the best in Ukraine. Adding a card, it read, *My life was literally in your hands. Thank you!*

Linda had brought clothes, shoes, and a replacement passport for him with her. It used one of the photos she had taken of him when in Moscow recently. It was a genuine U.S. passport and would pass close inspection. Shane had authorized it.

The flight to Warsaw was quick and uneventful.

Sat in business class, Deacon said, 'So didn't your husband object to you making this trip?'

'What husband? I'm divorced.'

'But when I asked for your number in Moscow, you said your husband wouldn't approve?'

'That's right. He wouldn't. But I didn't say I was still married, and I didn't say I'd listen to him anyway,' she said, with a mischievous glint in her eye.

Turning to him and smiling, she said, 'At least your dress sense has improved. Maybe you should ask again?'

That night they spent an enjoyable evening dining together in the Victoria Lounge at the Sofitel in Warsaw, overlooking Pilsudski Square and the Vistula River, the longest river in Poland. The next two days were spent on vacation doing touristy things, before Linda had to return to Moscow, after promising to meet up again on her next return to Washington.

Deacon stayed one more day making arrangements, before flying home.

41

Washington
Arriving back in Washington, Deacon had to help arrange funerals. Maričić wasn't married, but Stockwell was and had two young sons. Their families would be well looked after from a monetary perspective - that was an agreement Deacon had with the President before setting up Phylax and agreeing to work for him, but no amount of money could console Stockwell's wife and boys. The funerals were low-key and respectful, with Deacon and the Admiral making speeches at both. Many of their former colleagues turned up, and a number of their wives promised Stockwell's family would be well looked after.

After attending both gatherings, he said he had something to do.

Lisa Kingman parked her car, walked to the door of her two-story detached house and unlocked it. Closing it behind her, she walked into the lounge and froze. There was a man leaning against the far wall facing her with a glass of whiskey in his hand.

'Hello Lisa, surprised to see me?'

'W . . . what . . . Oh, Lieutenant, it's you. What are you doing here?'

'You lied.'

'What do you mean?' she said, slowly gaining back her composure.

'You said there were only six kidnappers. You lied. There were almost twenty.'

'Well, I might have been wrong, Lieutenant, but it was an honest mistake,' she said, her voice getting stronger as her confidence grew.

'Was it? Your mistake caused the death of two of my men.'

'Well, I'm sorry, but you all know the risks,' she said.

'Why did you do it?'

'Do what?'

'Don't fuck with me . . . You're a spy, and you're feeding the Kremlin information.'

'What? You're mad. I'm calling security,' she said, moving towards her desk.

'One more step and I'll come over there and fucking kill you.'

Stopping abruptly, she turned to Deacon and said, 'Whatever you're thinking, you're wrong. And what the fuck do you think you're doing breaking into my house? I'll have you arrested. You'll never work for the government again.'

'Me arrested? You're the traitor. You've got blood on your hands, and you're the one going to jail.'

Leaning back against the wall she faced him and said, 'I don't know where you got your ludicrous idea from, but you couldn't be more wrong. I'm sorry the intel we supplied was inaccurate, but it's not my fault alone. We base our estimates on data supplied. Everything I and my department prepare is checked by Charles and he approves it. If it caused you a problem then I'm sorry, but you need to blame Ingram. He's the spy, not me!'

'Ingram? The head of the CIA? You're out of your mind!'

'But it's true. Charles Ingram has been arrested. They suspected him, and he was under house arrest being investigated. They have since found large sums of unexplained money in a private bank account, and they also found an unlisted burner phone in his personal safe. He's now been arrested for treason by the FBI. I told you, he's the traitor, not me.'

'Ingram arrested? Where is he being held?'

'I don't know. The FBI took him away somewhere.'

'No, that can't be right. The evidence points to you.'

'It's true. I've told you what's happened, you can check with anyone. He's been under strain heading towards his retirement and I noticed a while back his work was getting slack. But I never imagined he'd sell his country out. I couldn't believe it either when I was told.'

Slowly swilling his drink around, Deacon began to relax and apologized. He moved to the couch and sat down, saying, 'But I was convinced the evidence pointed to you. How could I have been so wrong?'

'What evidence? Tell me, what convinced you I was a spy,' she said, before adding with a little laugh, 'Hah, me a spy. How funny?'

'I wrote it all down. I have it here,' Deacon said, patting his jacket pocket.

Moving over to her bureau, Lisa said, 'Just a simple misunderstanding. Anyway, I've got something here you might be interested in,' as she slid open a drawer.

Glancing up, Deacon was startled to see the black ring of the barrel of a nine-millimeter pointing at his face.

'So it was you. You are the traitor,' he gasped.

'Take your gun out VERY slowly. Fingertips only with your left hand. Drop it on the floor and kick it away. Try anything, and at this range, you're dead. And you should know . . . I'm a damn good shot,' she said, keeping the barrel pointing directly at his head.

Realizing she had the total drop on him, he did as commanded, carefully extracting his handgun and placing it on the floor. He kicked it hard, and it skittered away.

'Now slide yourself right back on the couch and don't try anything,' she said.

As he settled back he found himself at an obvious disadvantage to move quickly. A couch is comfortable but not easy to move off of speedily. She also made sure she was far enough away to be out of his reach, should he try.

'What made you suspect me?' she said.

'You bitch. You're directly responsible for the death of countless agents including a number at the CIA, the collapse of numerous operations, and the death of two of my work friends. And on top of all that, the lives of a whole lot of innocent people including a close friend of mine and of an innocent twenty-year-old.'

'What twenty-year-old? What are you on about?'

'The boy, Garry Moore. You had him killed, thinking it was me.'

'No! I admit to the agents and your work colleagues. The lady in your apartment was unfortunate, but I know nothing about this boy Garry Moore.'

Strangely enough, although Deacon wouldn't trust her an inch, he believed her about Garry. Her body language showed surprise when he'd mentioned his name, and anyway, the three bullets in the head had always seemed overkill.

'So how did it all start, Lisa? What made you turn traitor?'

Feeling a bit more confident now, she moved to the refrigerator and took out a bottle of wine. Removing the screw top, she smiled and poured herself a glass, never once letting the barrel of her gun waiver from his face.

'I might as well tell you. My secret will die with you. When I first joined the agency, I was office-based. When I finally got promoted to fieldwork, my first assignment was a six-month drafting to Stockholm. I worked in the Embassy. I was young and attractive, and it was my first real experience away from America. Stockholm was, and still is, a vibrant city for the young and single. I used to go out most evenings. At a club one night I met a nice man. Or he seemed to be. We had a few drinks and arranged to meet again. Soon it developed, and we became lovers. I didn't mind. I was single, away in an exciting city and loving life. He asked for something simple at first. Something like the internal phone list - I can't remember exactly. I didn't see it as important, so copied one and gave it to him. Then he wanted more, and I said 'No'. Then he showed me photos of us in bed together. Me doing . . . things. He threatened to show them to the Ambassador. I knew I'd be sent home would likely be fired, so I got him the next bit of information he wanted. By then I was completely caught up in it. Up to then I thought I loved him. He was good looking, with a beautiful strong body. He was good in bed. More experienced than me, and I fell for him. He even had a nickname for me. He called me his 'Blackbird'. But once I'd become fully involved, he dumped me. I knew I was stupid, but it was too late. Much later I found out his real name was Viktor Kalygin. At the time he was an officer at the KGB. Then the Berlin wall came down, and the KGB was pretty much disbanded, and I lost all contact with him. I thought I was safe. I forgot about him and hoped he'd forgotten me. I was moved to other embassies a few more times before finally being posted back to Langley. By that time Kalygin was senior at the FSB, and then he was finally made Russian President. I didn't hear from him for years. I met my future husband Bill, and we got married, and we both had good careers. His was in teaching. I gradually got promoted until I finally became Deputy Director of Operations.

'Then eighteen months ago, Bill became ill. Took doctors a long time to discover he had a growth - a brain tumor. By the time they found it, it was too large to operate. Then I saw a medical report from Russia. They claimed a new method, experimental, but they'd had success with it. But we couldn't go. State Department weren't happy for me to go with Bill. Said it was too high a security risk, but left the final decision to Ingram. He fully supported State. I was too important to risk, he claimed. I knew too much about operations and the workings of the CIA. Wouldn't even consider it. State refused to issue me a temporary diplomatic pass claiming I wasn't a diplomat. Ingram then imposed a travel ban on me. Eventually Bill travelled there on his own. He died on the operating table, and I got his body back a fortnight later,' she said, slurping wine.

Topping up her glass, she offered one to Deacon again, but he refused. The aim of her pistol hadn't altered.

'I hate that bastard, Ingram. Swore I'd seek revenge. Then I got a call out of the blue,' she continued. 'It suggested I come to Stockholm again for a holiday, so I did. Viktor was there waiting, and we had a wonderful few days together. It was like time had stood still. Then when he asked me to help I thought 'Why the hell not'. I didn't want to get paid as I felt that would be cheating on my country, but what had my country done for me? Where were they when I needed help? The one time I needed help that bastard had stopped me going. So we came to another arrangement. I passed information to Viktor, and suddenly a number of CIA missions were compromised. It was fun to get back at my own. Even better, I could put all the blame on good 'ol Charles Ingram, and he suddenly wasn't as popular anymore. How the mighty quickly fall.'

'You really are a callous bitch,' Deacon said.

Lisa didn't seem to hear or care, and continued, 'In the meantime, Viktor had become incredibly rich by skimming a little off a lot of various projects. He had just started a new one. His researchers had discovered a diamond field just under the surface in the Arctic. Russia needed the diamonds for some new plan of something, and Viktor offered me a cut of them in exchange for information. So that, Lieutenant high and mighty Deacon, is how it started.'

By now, her eyes were slightly unfocused.

'So how did you get the phone into Ingram's safe? What about the hidden bank account? And why try to get me killed?'

'That was easy. I've been in Ingram's office many times. I often saw him open his safe. A digit here, a digit there . . . It took a while until I knew his complete combination and he never bothered to change it. Once I knew it, it was child's play. I just waited for him to be out and I stashed it right at the back where it was unlikely to be seen. The bank account was easy too. Viktor got someone over there to set that up. And as for getting you killed, you were delving into the Arctic scheme. I wanted you to stop. You might have found out about me. And about Viktor. I tried with your rescue in Venezuela. Made sure I under-estimated the bad guys, but you pulled it off anyway. And you kept digging. So I tried again in Vorkuta, but didn't count on a greedy Police Chief.'

'Why my apartment?'

'It seemed easier to kill you here. I put you on a terrorist blacklist and said you were planning an attack. Our wet team did the rest. It would have worked too if that stupid bitch hadn't helped you at the door.'

'And the last attempt?

'Well I informed Viktor about you going to Amderma, but they already guessed from the aircraft exchange. And you were too damn good. Not only destroyed Amderma, but blew up his little laser project. That hadn't been in your briefing so I hadn't said you were heading there. It really pissed him off. Then he was angry at me, so I had to come up with something else. Bennett never was very good at what he did, so exposing him to a group of rebels was easy. I made sure they got the message that one of the rescuers, you, would be worth $10M. They fell for it.'

'I should have killed you just now when I had the chance.'

'Should have, would have. Missed your chance! But I don't mind telling you because you won't be leaving here alive. But something you can tell me. What did I do wrong? How come you suspected me?' she asked.

'I didn't with Venezuela. I just thought you were poor at your job. Then Garry Moore was killed here in Washington --'

'I told you before, that wasn't me.'

'Okay, okay. Then in Vorkuta, I saw the fax the Police Chief received. It had our fake names, Wintergreen and Fortescue, on it. That had to come from someone inside. Someone who had access to our details.'

'That doesn't mean anything. A whole range of staff worked on those names,' Kingman said.

'True. But then the bomb at my apartment. Obviously meant for me, and yet another innocent gets killed. Still didn't tie it to you, though. But in Amderma, General Yermilov had our real names, not our fakes ones in our documents. The way the CIA is departmentalized, those working on our legends wouldn't have had details of our real names. I checked with General Dreiberg . . .'

'Yeah, that was sloppy of me. Anything else?' she asked.

'The final coup de grâce was when Dimitri Vodolski said something to me. He said, '*That all they want – head and hands, cowboy'*. Cowboy -- such an unusual word. Last time someone called me that, was you. Time before that was also you. Could have been a coincidence, but I don't trust coincidences. Things began to click, and you seemed the right candidate. Confirmed it now and for that you're going to pay,' Deacon said.

'So how, Lieutenant high and mighty Deacon, do you propose that? I have the weapon, and I will shoot you and claim self-defense.'

'And you think that will be believed?'

'The word of a trusted CIA deputy director against that of a deranged ex-SEAL. One who has been attacked and injured in the line of duty. I think maybe a few clothes ripped and saying you threatened to rape me and I had to defend myself would do the trick. Don't you think?'

'I prefer to think of you rotting in jail for the next thirty years, you traitorous bitch. What if I've made a recording of our conversation?'

'I will pluck it from your dead fingers,' she said.

At that, Deacon pulled the recorder from his pocket and showed her, before raising himself off the couch and moving towards his discarded pistol as Kingman pulled the trigger.

The hammer fell on an empty chamber. Racking the automatic system, she fired again. Nothing.

Deacon picked up his pistol and aimed it at her, while at the same time pulling a handful of nine-millimeter rounds out of his pocket and tossing them towards her.

'Do you think I wouldn't have found your gun before you came home? Lisa, really?'

She hurled the empty weapon at him, but he just sidestepped, and it flew by, hitting the wall behind him.

'You can kill me, but I won't be going to jail. Washington won't want a court case. Too embarrassing for them. I know far too much that the powers-that-be won't want made public. I'll cut a deal and tell all. I know lots of Viktor's secrets as well. I'll just retire early with a nice payoff. I don't think Viktor will be too happy –but he knows I'd never tell everything I know about him. I think a nice little house by the sea with my golden handshake is far more likely. You'll be caught. So shoot away, Mr. Cowboy, and spend the rest of your life in jail,' she said, smiling.

A mole or spy in the agency wasn't a new idea. Hatred, jealousy, a martyr complex, some Dudley Do-Right who only saw black and white and the letter of the law; there was always someone willing to trade their soul. Deacon knew some clever lawyer would get her off. Minimal, if any, jail time. And the government would want it kept quiet. All that rubbish about dirty washing in public. No, he knew he couldn't let that happen.

'You are one cold-blooded bitch. I'm not letting you get away with it,' Deacon said, his finger going white as he gently took first pressure on the trigger.

42

Two days later, Lisa Kingman left her house to drive the twelve miles to work as she'd done most days for the past number of years in her Toyota Prius. As she stopped in the line of cars at the red lights ahead, she didn't notice a motorcyclist dressed all in black slowly meander his bike down between the traffic lines. The license plate was obscured, and there were no manufacturer markings on the polished black of the bike.

As it pulled level with the gap behind, the rider reached into his leather tunic and pulled something looking like a four-inch-tall cone out. Twisting the top, he gently accelerated his bike until he was directly next to the driver's door. Just as the lights turned green, he placed the cone on the vehicle roof, directly above the happy and smiling Lisa, and pressed the small button on top. The built-in magnet would keep it in place however violently the vehicle should move before the six-second counter reached zero.

With a twist of his wrist on the throttle, he sped away quickly disappearing into the traffic.

Exactly six seconds later, just as Lisa, accelerated over the crossing, a two-ounce shaped C4 charge exploded downward through the roof. Had the roof been made of three inches of hardened steel, the force might not have penetrated. Being made of 1/32 painted steel was as if it didn't exist. The force of the blast blew Lisa's head, shoulders, and chest cavity down below the seat level.

Microseconds later, the car exploded into a mighty fireball, igniting cars on either side of her as well as behind her.

One day after Deacon had met with Lisa at her home, Shane Walker, CIA Captain at the US Embassy in Baghdad, enjoyed a thirty-minute break from his regular duties and ventured to a local hookah cafe selling coffee. It just happened to be the regular haunt of his equal from the Russian Embassy of Iraq, Colonel Maksim Leskov. Sitting down at Leskov's table, Shane pulled out a recorder and pressed play. They were together for no more than fifteen minutes before Leskov hurried back to his embassy and began making urgent phone calls.

President Viktor Kalygin didn't like loose ends either.

Three weeks later, Mitch received an urgent email from his friend at the NSA. Picking up the phone, he called Deacon.

'John, my colleague at the NSA has been surfing the dark web. You know where bad things happen, and weapons etc. are sold?'

'Yeah, Yeah, I know what the dark web is.'

'Well bad news, pal. There's a hit out on you.'

'Is it from our friend Lisa at the CIA?'

'No, no, it's not.'

'The Russians?'

'No, no, that's why it's worrying.'

'Well then, who's it from?'

'John, it's from . . . .'

Fact File

- With the receding of the Arctic ice sheets, Russia has flexed its military might. In the past few years a newly aggressive Kremlin has been building a swath of new (and reactivating many old) military bases along its Arctic frontier, something that has not gone unnoticed by the Pentagon.

- In March 2019, Russia formally announced they would sink foreign ships using the Arctic sea route that links the Atlantic to the Pacific unless it is given 45 days' notice of voyages and vessels take a Russian pilot on board. The statement continued: "The notice must indicate the names of military ships and vessels, their goals, routes, and duration of the voyage. It also must indicate main ship parameters, such as the displacement, the length, the width, the draft, and characteristics of the power unit. It is also necessary to report the military rank and name of the captain. The ships will be compelled to take Russian pilots aboard. Russian icebreakers will lead foreign ships through the ices if necessary."

- In February 2019, a U.S. Defense Intelligence Agency report stated China and Russia are developing lasers and a host of other anti-satellite weapons. The report also estimated that China would deploy a terrestrial laser that can shoot down satellites in low Earth orbit by 2020 and may be able to hit targets in geostationary orbit "by the mid-2020s."

  The report concluded, "Russia has begun delivering a laser weapon system to the Aerospace Forces that likely is intended for an anti-satellite mission."

About the Author

I am the author of the John Deacon series of action adventure novels. I make my online home at www.mikeboshier.com. You can connect with me on Twitter at Twitter, on Facebook at Facebook and you can send me an email at mike@mikeboshier.com if the mood strikes you.

I love hearing from my readers so please drop me an email. I try to reply to every one.

The books I enjoy reading are from great authors such as Andy McNab, David Baldacci, Brad Thor, Vince Flynn, Chris Ryan, etc. to name just a few. I've tried to write my books in a similar style. If you like adventure/thriller novels, and you like the same authors as I do, then I hope you find mine do them justice.

If you liked reading this book, please leave feedback.

www.mikeboshier.com

Books & Further Details

High Seas Hijack - Short Story

Follow newly promoted US Navy SEAL John Deacon as he leads his team on preventing pirates attacking and seizing ships in and around the Horn of Africa in 2010. When a tanker carrying explosive gases is hijacked even Deacon and his team are pushed to the limit.

The Jaws of Revenge

The fate of America lies in the hands of one team of US SEALs. The US mainland is under threat as never before. Osama bin Laden is dead, and the world can relax. Or can they? Remaining leaders of Al-Qaeda want revenge, and they want it against the USA. When good fortune smiles on them and the opportunity presents itself to use stolen weapons of mass destruction, it's Game On!

Al-Qaeda leaders devise a plan so audacious if it succeeds it will destroy the USA for good. With help from Iran and from a US Navy traitor, it can't fail.

One team of US SEALs stand in their way. One team of US SEALs can save America and the West. However, time is running out. **Will they be too late?**

Terror of the Innocent

As the Iraqi Forces build up for the liberation of Mosul, ISIS wants revenge.

The UK and USA are in their sights ...

In a daring rescue mission to release aid workers held hostage by ISIS, US Navy SEAL John Deacon stumbles across an ISIS revenge plot using deadly weapons stolen from Saddam's regime.

Masterminded by Deacon's old adversary, Saif the Palestinian, and too late to save the UK, Deacon and the world can only watch in horror as thousands suffer a terrible fate.

Determined to stop the same outcome in the US, it's a race against time.

Using all the resources he can muster including his friends in the Pentagon, Deacon must find and stop Saif before the lives of hundreds of thousands of Americans are ruined forever.

Crossing a Line

Once a respected US Navy SEAL, now shunned by friends and colleagues and wanted by the police, John Deacon has gone rogue ...

Recruited by a fanatical religious cult intent on returning the USA to the ways of God, and headed by a man known as The General, Deacon's weapons skills and combat knowledge are put to treacherous use ...

Deacon has crossed a line ... But has he gone too far? Can he ever cross back?

The Price of Deceit

In a world violated by terror, the once black and white terms of engagement have become gray.

One man is determined to stop World War Three.

Now a civilian, to the public ex-US Navy SEAL John Deacon is a businessman running his own security company offering personal protection to VIPs and dignitaries.

Only a few very senior people under the President know the truth ...

Funded with 'black' money from secret funds, Deacon is the guy the President calls on when certain dilemmas or complications need resolving. Dilemmas and complications the President can later deny.

From helping rescue hostages taken by Boko Haram to the delicate discussions with a would-be defector - the daughter of a senior Chinese official - Deacon handles it all.

But when an enemy submarine starts attacking shipping and China plans to impose passage taxes in the South China Sea, and the US and China move closer and closer to all-out war, Deacon takes on his biggest and most dangerous mission yet.

Deep behind enemy lines and with the odds stacked heavily against him, capture will mean certain death.

Success or failure is a mere hairsbreadth apart ...

Check out my web page http://www.mikeboshier.com for details of latest books, offers and free stuff.

VIP Reader's Mailing List

To join our VIP Readers Mailing List and receive updates about new books and freebies, please go to my web page and join my mailing list.

<u>www.mikeboshier.com</u>

I value your trust. Your email address will stay safe and you will never receive spam from me. You can unsubscribe at any time.
Thank you.

Printed in Great Britain
by Amazon